NICOLA LINDSAY

POOLBEG

Published 2003
Poolbeg Press Ltd.
123 Grange Hill, Baldoyle,
Dublin 13, Ireland
Email: poolbeg@poolbeg.com

13 5 7 9 10 8 6 4 2

A catalogue record for this book is available from the British Library.

ISBN 1-84223-101-4

Typeset by Patricia Hope in Goudy 11/15
Printed by
Nørhaven A/S, Viborg, Denmark

www.poolbeg.com

About the Author

Eden Fading is Nicola Lindsay's third novel. Born in London, she has lived in Ireland for the past thirty years. A latecomer to writing, she is enormously encouraged by the fact that people seem to enjoy reading her work. She just hopes she won't wake up one morning to discover that she's run out of steam or ideas! She has three adult daughters, and a pair of plastic fish in the fishpond to confuse the local heron.

Also by Nicola Lindsay

Diving Through Clouds
A Place for Unicorns

Acknowledgements

My thanks to all at Poolbeg for their help – in different ways and at different times. And especial thanks to Gaye Shortland without whose patient promptings, syntax and sense would quite often come to grief!

For my daughter, Alexandra,
who – like Rachel – just keeps on getting braver.

Chapter One

Rachel reread the five scrawled lines on the back of the postcard. There was no mistake. She was being offered a house in Tuscany for a whole month in return for feeding two cats, watering a couple of horses and generally letting the local village know that she was 'in residence'.

Perhaps life was going to improve after all. Perhaps all the traumas of the past year could be, if not forgotten, at least pushed to the back of her mind for a little while. Perhaps she could even learn to be happy again. She considered that possibility, turning it over in her mind tentatively.

Since Simon's death six months earlier, it had been a struggle just to drag herself out of bed each morning. It had taken six weeks before she'd been able to face sleeping in their bed; three more before she had summoned up the courage to sort through his things.

Just looking at the Italian shoes from Brown Thomas brought back the memory of a sunny October day a year ago. They'd gone into Dublin with no particular plan in mind. Rachel had seen them first in the shop window.

"Look at those shoes, Simon. They're beautiful! You *do* need some new ones."

"They are very beautiful but, at that price, I think I can manage without them!"

"Ah, just try them on. Go on!" she pleaded.

They were a perfect fit, the soft leather light and supple.

"You'll have to buy them," she insisted. "They look so good on you!"

Laughingly, he'd given in and bought them.

"Now I'll have to lug them around with me for the rest of the day," he joked as they left the shop.

Arm in arm, they had wandered through the arcades, sampling olives and goats' cheese, laughing at the outrageous designer-labelled clothes in Powerscourt Townhouse. Simon bought her a cloche hat in pale grey and wine that caught her eye. They stood, hip to hip, arms linked, watching the jugglers and accordion players in Grafton Street. Later, taking a breather, they'd demolished fresh salmon sandwiches and creamy pints of Guinness in their favourite pub near Stephen's Green. In the afternoon they'd gone to see a steamy French film, stopping for drinks afterwards in one of the smart cafés in Temple Bar. Then they hurried home to make love.

When she knew she couldn't put off the task of sorting through her dead husband's clothes any longer, Rachel had opened the wardrobe door and stared bleakly at the jackets and trousers hanging in a tidy row. Suddenly, she buried her face in the sleeve of his favourite corduroy jacket, the one he used to wear for going to art exhibitions and book launches with her.

"Casual but elegantly bohemian, don't you agree?" he'd asked her, grinning, the first time they'd gone out together, to what he called "one of your arty do's!".

She'd had to dissuade him from wearing a large, spotted bow tie with his corduroy jacket.

"Are you sure? I don't want to let the side down! As you know, we solicitors are renowned for our boringly conservative sense of dress – as well as our inflated idea of what an articulate and dignified lot we all are!"

"Lose the bow tie! It looks like a pregnant butterfly. Don't worry, Simon! You'll look quite arty enough without it – *especially* in that jacket," she'd said, dying for him to get a move on so that she could show him off to her colleagues.

He was by far and away the most gorgeous man she'd ever gone out with: the thick mass of blond hair that smelled faintly of the coconut shampoo he liked, the blue eyes that so often turned in her direction, the natural way he had of talking and moving. Simon was the only man who'd asked her out who was completely himself – self-confident and yet not self-satisfied. When she looked at him on that first real date together, she felt an overwhelming desire to see him without his corduroy jacket, or silk shirt – or any clothes at all.

No trace of him lingered in the jacket. Rachel had pulled

jerseys and ties out of drawers, desperately hunting for some slight scent, a hint of his favourite Armani cologne or after-shave lotion.

She'd ended up standing in the middle of a twisted heap of silk ties and shirts, looking down at a pair of small silver and ebony cufflinks in the palm of her hand, while tears rolled down her cheeks.

Early next day, she'd hurriedly dumped the plastic dustbin bags of clothes outside the Oxfam shop, feeling that what she was doing was further diminishing her husband's memory. Another part of him had gone. She knew it made sense to get rid of them. It would be unbearable to go on seeing his clothes hanging in the wardrobe. But a sense of guilt stayed with her all that morning.

Rachel knew the women who ran the shop. By going there before they arrived to open up, she avoided the pitying looks, the well-meant enquiries into how she was coping, the kind reminders that she was to let them know if they could help in any way at all. She knew that she was being ungracious. But her whole being felt too raw and fragile to allow herself to be exposed to their eagle-eyed attentions or to pretend that she was managing all right. That was far from the truth.

Death had charged out of a clear blue sky in the shape of an articulated lorry jack-knifing on an icy road, its driver vainly fighting to keep control as it ground its way remorselessly towards the dark green Jaguar. Simon was already white and cold by the time firemen cut him from the wreckage of his crushed car, while the police waved on the stream of slowed traffic, with the craning, half-shocked, half-curious faces. They said he'd died immediately on impact – that he hadn't suffered.

As she lay awake, night after night during those first weeks, Rachel wondered for how many seconds before oblivion had Simon known that no power on earth would stop the sliding monster bearing down on him. What thoughts had flashed through his mind before he died? Did he have time to be afraid?

It wasn't just his dying that had knocked her off her feet. What had dealt her the body blow, when she was already reeling, had been the small spray of flowers she'd found on Simon's grave the day after his funeral. A simple arrangement of white roses with a note attached in angular, strong handwriting:

For my brother – from his sister, D.

Simon's parents had died in a boating accident several years before he and Rachel had married. He was an only son, with no living relatives. That's what he'd said. She'd never had the slightest reason to disbelieve him. Now there were these flowers and a message from a sister to her brother.

What did the D stand for? she'd wondered. Deirdre? Dorothy? Delilah? Perhaps something even more exotic, like Desirée?

At first, Rachel refused to believe that her husband had lied to her for the six short years of their marriage. It was easier to think that some jealous woman, who was part of his past, wanted to make some sort of a claim on him. But during the sleepless nights when her mind refused to stop churning, she found herself thinking, *What if he does have a sister?* After all, how well does anyone really know the person with whom they live? She'd read about that sort of thing in the papers often enough – people who seemed to be living ordinary, decent lives and who suddenly turned out to have second families or who were discovered to be serial adulterers. What if . . .

She turned the card over. The colour photograph was of rolling hills with rectangles of gold, dotted evenly with olive trees, which looked like a children's giant board game. Here and there, dark cypresses, slim and graceful, pointed to a ridiculously blue sky. Rachel sighed. It would mean chucking in her job at the publishers. She knew they would replace her without any trouble. Her boss had never liked her.

Walking over to the window, she stared out at the rain-sodden April garden. It would be lovely to get away from the Irish weather and Simon had left her well off. They'd never discussed making a Will and Rachel, if she'd thought about it, had relegated the dismal task to some time in the distant future. People in their thirties had plenty of time for doing that sort of thing later on. There was no rush, she'd told herself happily.

Unknown to her, Simon had insured his life more than adequately. Now, his thoughtful generosity reminded her of how much she missed him. A feeling, as if a hand had reached inside her, caught hold of her guts and twisted them hard, making her catch her breath and wince. But then, at the back of her mind, there always lurked the same niggling thought that perhaps her husband's generosity was the result of a guilty conscience.

As the ache receded, Rachel leaned her forehead against the cold glass and slowly opened her eyes, trying to focus on the church spire at the other side of the line of houses that bordered the end of their small garden. How ugly, she thought, as she always did when she looked at it.

It was a typical example of 1960's Irish Catholic church architecture – all weird angles and unlovely spiky bits – as though the architect, lacking in inspiration, had resorted to shock tactics to get his creation noticed.

It too was a reminder of Simon. The funeral service had taken place there, even though he could hardly have been counted as one of its frequent visitors. He had gone there at Christmas and Easter and, very occasionally, when he wanted to be alone and quiet. He'd sit in a corner, hunched up with his head in his hands. She'd seen him like that on a couple of occasions but had slipped away, not wanting to intrude but feeling a little left out.

Had he been thinking of a woman when he sat there like that? A sister perhaps? she wondered, as she absent-mindedly wiped away the small patch of condensation her breath had made on the windowpane. A pang of guilt, mixed with grief, shot through her; then anger. Why should *she* be the one feeling guilty?

Rachel turned away from the dreary view. She'd drive herself mad if she continued down that road. The best thing to do would be to get away from everything that reminded her of Simon or thoughts of his non-existent sister. She'd ring Caroline and Guy and tell them she would be delighted to accept their offer of a month in the sun – and to hell with her job. If the worst came to the worst, she could manage quite comfortably until she found some other work. Come to think of it, with no brothers and sisters of her own, there wasn't all that much to keep her in Ireland. What was to stop her moving to Italy for good if she found that she liked it there?

Moving quickly to the phone, Rachel thumbed through a battered telephone book. Without pausing, she started to dial – as though afraid that, if she hesitated, the sensible side of her nature might make her change her mind.

The unaccustomed Continental ringing tone almost made her hang up until she remembered that it wasn't an engaged signal.

A click and a languid female voice, *"Pronto?"*

"Caroline. It's Rachel in Dublin."

"Good Lord! Rachel! How are you?"

"Well, thanks. I got your card."

There was a slight pause during which she could hear Caroline muttering, *sotto voce*, to her husband that it was Rachel on the phone.

"Good! Can you come? It would be really marvellous if you could. We're a bit stuck. Our usual house-sitter let us down."

"Yes! I'd love to – if you're quite sure you'd be happy to leave me in charge of things."

A pause, followed by a slight chuckle on the other end of the line.

"My dear! I can't think of anyone more perfect for the job!"

Fleetingly, Rachel wondered why she always felt slightly uncomfortable when Caroline paid her a compliment. Probably because Caroline only paid compliments when she wanted a favour and most of the favours were never quite as straightforward as they first appeared.

"It *is* just looking after the horses and cats, isn't it?" she asked, seeking reassurance.

Caroline sounded amused.

"Of course! The girl will be in each morning to tidy up and do any shopping for food in the local market. You don't speak Italian, do you?" Her tone was condescending, as if it were quite understandable that poor Rachel couldn't be expected to have mastered a language other than her own.

"Well, a few words. But I'm sure I'll improve when I have to make the effort. When do you want me to come?"

She could hear what sounded like the other woman hunting through a pile of papers.

"Hang on a sec. I've lost the flight details . . . Oh, God! Where has the bloody thing got to? . . . I know it was here the other day. *Finalmente!* Here we are! We fly out at five on Saturday the third of June. So could you be here by the Thursday? Then we'll have time to show you where everything is and Percy and Rollo can get used to you before we abandon them to your tender mercies."

"Percy and Rollo? Are they the cats or the horses?" asked Rachel.

The voice at the other end of the line sounded suddenly impatient, "Don't worry about all that now. I'll fill you in

9

when you're here. Your best plan is to fly to Pisa and then get the Rome express as far as Grosseto. We'll meet you there. Just let us know your arrival time. I must dash. We've got to go out. Give me a ring or e-mail me when you've booked. *Ciao, bella!"*

It struck Rachel that Italian didn't suit Caroline's affected drawl. Feeling she had been taking up too much of the other's valuable time, she said a hasty goodbye into an already dead line and put down the receiver.

She stood looking down at the silent instrument, wondering if, after all, she had made the right decision in agreeing to look after the Haywoods' house and animals.

I've got to start living again, she reminded herself. I've got to get away from this place and the feeling of being in limbo. It's only for a month, after all. Caroline won't be around to make me feel patronised and clumsy. It's just what I need – all that sun and beautiful scenery. Rachel pushed back her brown hair from her brown eyes, remembering how she'd once heard Caroline refer to her auburn looks as 'mud-coloured' to a mutual friend at a party. But then, that was the sort of thing that Caroline said, even about her supposedly close friends. It was silly to get upset over her little bursts of spitefulness. Still, there was an underlying tone to the recent conversation that made Rachel doubt that the other was any kinder or gentler now that the woman was in her early forties.

Perhaps there would always be a slight tension between them. At thirty-two, Rachel was a good ten years younger than Caroline, and Guy never bothered to hide the fact from his five-foot-two wife that he found Rachel's tall, slim figure attractive. It was not a feeling she reciprocated. She'd never taken to sandy-haired men with pale eyelashes, wiry beards and clammy hands – although she found him amusing company, in an offbeat sort of way.

Rachel liked the fact that he didn't seem to care what he wore – Hawaiian shirts in garish colours under a pinstripe suit or a bright purple tracksuit and silver trainers – it didn't matter. She'd often wondered what he got up to in his business dealings. Guy always seemed to be involved in risky property adventures with shady characters, who were too disreputable to be invited to the Haywoods' frequent parties – even though some of the invited people she'd met at their house, before Guy and Caroline moved to Italy, had seemed to Rachel to be rather strange: inhabitants from the world of film and stage. No one terribly famous but they had a trait common to them all: a bitter frustration that their talents hadn't been recognised on a grand enough scale and a terrible, gnawing hunger for success and all the trappings of success.

Once or twice, Simon had wondered aloud quite why it was that Caroline bothered to invite them. Rachel had come to the conclusion that the other woman found Simon not unattractive and that Guy harboured affectionate feelings for Rachel. If he fancied Rachel's company, then Caroline probably reasoned that he should be humoured. A contented husband was easier to manipulate and was less likely to interfere in his wife's life. It had annoyed Rachel a little that Simon had always rather liked Caroline.

"But why?" Rachel had asked him after a particularly wild Hallowe'en party at the Haywoods'.

"Probably because she's very much a man's woman. She's such enormous fun," he replied, peering at her through matted strands of a warlock's wig. "She makes me laugh. She always comes straight to the point – no beating about the bush," he said, grinning. "What's more, she's a wicked lady and she thoroughly enjoys being wicked."

Rachel tried to sound nonchalant, "She's dangerous, I do know that. I'm surprised she hasn't made a pass at you. I know she fancies you."

Simon grabbed her round the waist and kissed her.

"Not half as much as I fancy you, my darling. Come to bed, you sexy witch you! All this dressing up has made me as randy as hell."

He had propelled her up the stairs in front of him, sliding one hand in under her skimpy top and the other through the slit in her skirt, cupping one buttock cheek in his hand.

"I love it when you climb stairs. It does marvellous things to your glutinous maximums or whatever they're called," he whispered, as he nibbled the back of her neck.

By the time they reached the bedroom, Rachel was clad only in black stockings and a witch's hat that had developed a severe list to starboard.

He turned her round to face him and then lowered her onto the bed. Immediately, he entered her, supporting her head gently with both hands, while staring down into her face. It seemed to her that his eyes looked almost navy blue in the half-light from the landing.

"I hope you realise you are my most favourite of all witches?" he said.

"Mm," she replied, wrapping her legs more tightly around him.

The next morning, before getting ready for work, hungover and slightly disorientated from lack of sleep, Rachel staggered around the house, bending over gingerly to pick up the trail of black garments. She'd half-heartedly attempted to hoover up glitter that clung to the carpet on the stairs and landing.

Now, during the never-ending nights, as she lay, arms crossed over her chest, holding herself tightly, eyes open in the dark, Rachel tried not to think too much about their lovemaking. But images kept creeping into her mind – how Simon had insisted they christen each room in the house when they first moved in.

"There are eight rooms, so we have to make love in eight different ways – to suit each room. A room a day and twice on Sunday!"

"How do you make love to suit a room?" she'd asked, laughing.

"Dear me! Haven't you read your *Kama Sutra* and *Perfumed Garden*? You just have to use your imagination. I'll show you. It's easy."

Although Rachel had been intimate with other men, she felt very much a novice in her relationship with her husband. When he suggested that it might be fun to try lovemaking on the dining-room table, she said it would be too uncomfortable and anyway, someone might look in the window and see them.

"So what?" he demanded. "It's our house, our dining-room table and we are married. We can bonk in the garden if we want. If anyone sees us and disapproves, then that's their problem."

However, in deference to her modesty, Simon pulled the curtains before persuading her to try.

"I'll get rid of the candlesticks and salt and pepper – you don't want spices in funny places. Then we'll just scatter a few napkins around. You'll see, it's a splendid way to polish the table!"

When it came to it, they'd had to abandon the idea because they were laughing so much.

By the end of their first week in their new home, Rachel was dazzled by his inventiveness and energy and rather abashed by her own unadventurousness.

She wondered now if, secretly, he hadn't found her approach to the physical side of their marriage unexciting – even prudish. He'd never said anything the slightest bit critical.

When she once questioned him about whether he minded the fact that she found it difficult to be the initiator of sexual romps, he'd laughed, then pulled her close to him.

"You are the perfect woman, Rachel. Don't try to play the whore for me. I assure you, I much prefer making love to a lady!"

Up until the time of Simon's death, Rachel believed that she made him happy. But ever since the discovery of the flowers, with their attached message, she found she'd begun to wonder if she hadn't been deluding herself; that perhaps, a sister did exist. And what was more, if Simon had kept the existence of this woman hidden, then what else hadn't he told her?

Determined to try and stop thinking about it, she started organising herself for her Tuscan trip.

She chucked out the wilting pot plants on the kitchen and bathroom windowsills with their coating of sticky aphids. Remembering that she'd lost Simon's door keys, Rachel had another set made so that the woman next door could drop in occasionally and make sure all was well while she was away. The small garden was weeded and the clutter of garden tools that had been left to rust beside the broken flowerpots was cleaned and stored neatly in the shed. Never terribly tidy, Rachel did her best to bring some order into the house in which, at unexpected moments, she felt her husband's presence filling the too empty rooms.

Chapter Two

After some thought, Rachel decided to buy a one-way ticket to Pisa. After all, she reasoned, that way, I don't *have* to come back by a certain date. The decision seemed quite daring to someone who had in the past, always left buying tickets and organising itineraries to Simon. Before he'd entered her life, she'd usually travelled abroad with a group of friends from work, booked by the office, and before that by the school or her parents. It really is time I grew up, she thought, irritated at herself.

Feeling in limbo, wanting to leave and yet, at the same time, nervous of beginning a new chapter in her life, she cleared out old scrapbooks, postcards and a cardboard box of mementos from an unromantic weekend in Paris, a stormridden visit to the Aran Islands, a miserably cold cruise in the Norwegian fjords when she'd developed gastroenteritis. She'd spent most of the week firmly below deck, wishing she could quietly die and be buried at sea.

16

When she'd finished, it surprised her when she saw how much room was left in the cupboards. Room for what? she wondered. All the beautiful things she was going to bring back from Italy. That's what, she told herself firmly.

It gave Rachel a certain amount of satisfaction to tell her boss that she was giving a month's notice. Phyllis Dillon looked genuinely shocked.

"Do you mind me asking if you are moving to another publishing house?"

"Not for the moment," said Rachel, with a demure smile.

"You mean, you haven't got a job lined up when you leave here?"

"No, I don't actually."

"So, what are you planning to do?"

"I'm going to spend a month in Italy and then I'll see what I feel like after that," said Rachel, smugly.

It was good to be in a position of not having to watch her words for once. Phyllis Dillon had always seemed to go out of her way to make life unpleasant for the other females in Greene and Rowntree. However, she was always sweetness and light in her dealings with Marcus Rowntree or Eugene Greene, who believed that she could do no wrong.

Rachel sensed the other's unease at this unheard-of situation. No one ever resigned from working in Greene and Rowntree – unless they had a very good reason – and now, if she were to be believed, Rachel was leaving – to go on holiday.

She must be mad, Phyllis Dillon decided. Either mad or she wasn't telling the truth. Perhaps she *had* been poached by one of the other publishing houses. She glared at

Rachel over the top of her gold-rimmed, half-moon glasses, longing for more information but damned if she'd beg for it. When she next spoke, Ms Dillon fairly spat her words out at the woman sitting opposite. She despised, and yet a part of her longed for, the attractive, well-cut, simple clothes the other wore so easily, the glossy hair that framed Rachel's face in soft waves, the dark brown eyes that looked larger than usual because her face was pale. She was aware of the other's loss but found it difficult to feel truly sorry for her. Why should she, when the girl had been given so much and so early on in her life? Whereas Phyllis had never had any luck – in looks, in men . . .

"Of course, you realise that nowadays readers are two a penny?"

Rachel looked at the other woman's painted narrow mouth and wondered if a man had ever been moved to kiss those thin lips. Was it remotely possible that the bitter woman sitting opposite her had ever used her mouth to give pleasure – rather than just as an instrument of sarcasm or sour criticism? She thought probably not.

Getting no response, Phyllis Dillon, unaware that she had sprayed the pile of letters in front of her with a light coating of spittle, continued, "I suppose you'll be wanting a reference?"

Rachel gave her a broad smile and said quietly, "If you think you could manage to give me one, it would be very nice." She got up and made for the door. Another breach of protocol in Phyllis Dillon's book. "Anytime over the next month will be fine. Thank you."

Rachel gently shut the door behind her, reminded again of

just how much she hated people who bullied or manipulated others. Well, Phyllis Dillon could go and play power games with some other poor sod, not with her any more, thank you! She found herself trying not to laugh out loud at the expression on the woman's bony face. She had looked as if she'd nearly swallowed an unripe lemon, and couldn't decide whether to finish the job or cough it back up.

Telling her parents that she had handed in her resignation was more difficult for Rachel. Jean and Patrick Kerrigan were elderly. They'd both been well into their thirties by the time they married in 1950. They belonged to a generation that expected anyone lucky enough to have been given a job to be grateful, loyal and to remain there until retirement, death – or pregnancy in their daughter's case – ended the contract between employer and employee.

When Rachel first introduced Simon to them, Jean Kerrigan found him charming. However, her husband was deeply suspicious of that charm, telling his wife, after the young couple had left, that the man was too polite, too agreeable, too worldly to be trustworthy.

" . . . and he's got an expensive taste in clothes. He's not the type I want my daughter to be going out with. I hope Rachel won't get serious about him," he muttered, as he searched for the paper to finish off the day's crossword puzzle.

"Rachel likes expensive clothes too, don't forget. He's a solicitor so I expect he can afford to buy beautiful suits. I thought he was rather nice," said his wife, in her gentle way.

"You never were a good judge of character."

"Was that why I married you, dear?" she asked, with a

sudden, untypical flash of annoyance that surprised them both.

It had been a cause of incomprehension and sorrow to them that Simon and Rachel had not produced children.

"There's plenty of time for all that, Mum," Rachel had said after her mother had been going on about how they weren't getting any younger and how lovely it would be to have at least *one* grandchild.

"Rachel, you have to remember that you're getting older too, dear. Time doesn't stand still, you know. I had you when I was thirty-five and it was rather a struggle – even at that relatively young age. Things would have been much easier if . . . well, if we hadn't left it quite so late."

"My fault again, no doubt," remarked her husband from behind the *Irish Times*.

Her daughter tried to be pleasantly reasonable, when what she really wanted to do was tell her mother to stop interfering; to leave them to organise their lives in the way they wanted.

"We're very happy as we are. Simon agrees with me that there's no hurry."

In fact, Simon had told Rachel that he'd prefer not to have any children.

"The world's too full of people as it is, darling. When you think of all the unplanned pregnancies . . . Why spoil things when it's so good with just the two of us?" he said.

But Rachel hadn't repeated that to her mother. It would have been too unkind.

Then Simon's death put paid to Mrs Kerrigan's hopes. At least for a while.

"I know it's hard to believe now but, one day, someone will come along. You wait and see," she said, with an encouraging smile, as she dusted and re-arranged the silver photograph frames along the top of the upright piano. Its wooden sides shone from hours of repeated polishing.

Rachel was outraged. "I don't *want* anyone to come along! Someone coming along is the last thing I need right now! I'm sorry if that means you're denied grandchildren, Mum, but I can't help how I feel."

"There's no need to shout at your mother," her father said.

"She's upset," said his wife soothingly, as though she knew it would all soon blow over and everything would be normal again. "Give her time. She'll be all right."

No, I won't, thought Rachel, angrily. I won't be all right. Nothing will ever be all right again. How could it be? Why didn't they see that Simon couldn't be replaced like a family pet? They had simply no idea how angry she felt – how confused and miserable. They didn't know that she'd believed she and Simon had had no secrets from each other and that now there were things about his life she didn't understand. She couldn't begin to tell them how much she missed him and yet, at the same time, how horribly let down she felt.

Rachel was beginning to realise that she wouldn't be able to lay Simon's ghost until she'd unravelled the mystery of his so-called sister. The spray of white roses remained a malignant memory long after they'd shrivelled and been thrown away on the compost heap by the sexton.

21

She had never felt so far apart from her parents. It saddened her but she couldn't see how she could do anything to remedy things. Because of their age, they were more like puzzled grandparents than a mother and father in whom she could confide. She knew they loved her but they seemed incapable of offering the support and understanding she needed.

When she told them that she was leaving Greene and Rowntree, they were appalled. When she told them she was spending a month, maybe longer, in Italy, they thought their daughter was in the throes of some sort of a mental breakdown.

"But you can't just chuck your job in like that," her father said.

"I'm sorry, Dad, but I've already handed in my notice and it's been accepted."

Her mother looked at her anxiously with faded blue eyes that seemed to water all the time these days.

"I know that Simon left you well provided for but you have to have work of some kind, Rachel. You can't just disappear off to Italy without even having a job to come back to, surely?"

Rachel heard the tremor in her mother's voice. She'd guessed long ago that her father had probably vetoed any suggestion of his wife ever having a career of her own outside the home. As gently and patiently as she could, she explained how she had to get away; that she badly needed a holiday and a change of scene.

At the end of a frustrating hour, Rachel knew that she was no nearer persuading them that what she was doing was the right thing for her at the moment. Her father's frown seemed more deeply etched and the shake in her mother's hands more pronounced.

Feeling frustrated at her inability to close the ever-widening gap between them, she left, promising to go and have Sunday lunch with them the following weekend.

Somehow, the next few weeks were lived through, the farewell party at work survived and the sorting and packing completed.

Her friends at Greene and Rowntree seemed genuinely sorry that she was leaving. Rachel was surprised and touched when they gave her a Good Luck card, enrolment in *The Folio Society* and a generous cheque that was more than enough to cover the cost of buying at least half a dozen beautifully bound books.

"We will miss you. You were the only female in the place who ever had the guts to stand up to that Dillon wagon," said Jessica Boylan, with a grin.

She was the youngest of the readers. Rachel had shown her the ropes when she'd first arrived. She'd also covered up for her on a few occasions when 'the Dillon wagon' had been on the warpath.

On the evening before leaving, Rachel went to say goodbye to her parents. After an awkward meal, during which everyone seemed to find it difficult to make conversation, she excused herself as soon as she'd swallowed her cup of decaffeinated coffee.

"I've got an early start," she said apologetically, "and you know how hard I find it to get up in the mornings."

Her mother had kissed her and said understandingly, "Yes, of course, dear. You go and get a good night's rest."

Guilty at her feelings of relief to be on her way, she deliberately slowed her step as she walked along the path, trying not to look as if she were hurrying away from them. As she turned to wave from the gate, she thought how small they looked – as though they had shrunk into themselves – as they stood, side by side in the doorway, her mother giving little, nervous waves of her hand, her father stiffly unsmiling and reproachful.

I'll make it up to them when I get back, she promised herself as she got into her car.

Rachel had one more thing to do before the day ended.

The grave was at the far side of the cemetery, near the dry-stone wall, close to the foot of a giant yew. A blackbird was singing, hidden in its dark branches. The sound was full and lovely, echoing through the cool, evening air. Some of the tension of the past hours left her neck and shoulders and she began to feel less edgy. Sounds of distant traffic hummed faintly in the valley below. Her feet crunched on the gravel as she walked, sounding loud in the stillness of the place.

Rachel approached the simple headstone with its black lettering standing out against the grainy, mica-flecked granite. She could see a large mound of flowers at its base. They looked fresh, still beaded with tiny drops of water, as if they'd only just been sprayed and placed there. All the flowers were white: carnations, roses, freesias and lilies. They looked expensive. Bending down to place her small bunch of apricot roses on the grave, Rachel slipped out the card from the elegant white floral display. She tilted it towards what little daylight remained and caught her breath.

The writing was the same as it had been on the card belonging to the first spray of white roses. Only the message was different.

You won't be alone for long. D.

Suddenly light-headed, she crumpled into a kneeling position on the damp grass at the graveside. What the hell was going on? *'You won't be alone for long.'*

The hair on the back of her neck prickled. Her mouth felt suddenly dry. Perhaps whoever was responsible for this was ill – disturbed in some way? It wasn't the sort of thing a normal person would write. She tried to stop her hand from shaking. This time, there was no mention on the card of the writer being a sister.

With a sudden percussive beating of wings and a warning call, the blackbird flew away. Darkness gathered under the trees and along the wall. Rachel experienced an uncomfortable sensation of not being on her own. She glanced furtively around her, almost expecting to see a retreating figure moving silently among the gravestones that glimmered palely in the surrounding twilight.

Chapter Three

As she walked down the steps from the aircraft, a blanket of warm air enveloped Rachel. After the unseasonable, damp chill of Dublin, it felt wonderful. Thankful to be off the plane, she breathed in the smell of fuel and hot metal as she followed the untidy crocodile of her fellow travellers making their way over to the airport building. The Alitalia pilot had landed rather too fast – and with several bounces that she'd found rather unnerving. As the plane had roared to the end of the runway, Rachel reminded herself that Italian pilots probably flew aircraft the same way that she heard they drove their cars – with the emphasis on flamboyant style rather than safety.

Once inside the terminal, waiting for her luggage, she watched the seething mass of people around her. A group of Italian teenagers, whom she'd noticed on the Dublin flight, seemed to be swopping experiences of their holiday. They draped themselves over their trolleys and any available seats as they too waited on the other side of the carousel. She caught the word *Dublino* and some imaginative attempts at pronouncing place names like Glendalough. She thought they all looked remarkably cheerful, in spite of the dreadful weather they must have experienced in Ireland. It amused her the way they used their hands all the time and she liked their animation and energy. How much more attractive they were, with their olive skin and dark, shiny hair, than the average Irish teenager. She noticed how beautiful their eyes were: large, deep brown and black-lashed.

Rachel was so taken with the noisy youngsters that she suddenly realised that her case was disappearing around the far end of the carousel. She caught hold of it on its next circuit and hauled it onto her trolley.

The man in the ticket office was plainly bored. He waited, expressionless, while she carefully articulated her well-rehearsed request for a single ticket, via Pisa central station to Grosseto. Without looking at her, he rattled off what sounded like a demand for extra payment if she wanted to take the Express. Hoping she had guessed correctly, she handed over what seemed to her an obscene amount of money, which he took, unsmilingly, shoving some coins and notes, decorated with only a few zeros, into the metal tray with a contemptuous sigh. The *Grazie tanto* died on her lips and she retreated. Wow! Perfect example of the wrong man in the wrong job, she thought as she hunted for signs indicating the whereabouts of the train for *Pisa Centrale*.

Two and a half hours later, Rachel arrived in Grosseto,

feeling tired and limp after the stuffy rail journey. The elderly woman sitting opposite her had refused to let her open the window. Rachel's first attempt was greeted by a barrage of words and much headshaking. From the grimaces and repeated references to *artrite*, she guessed the woman was a martyr to her arthritis. With limited Italian and diminishing energy levels, Rachel had smiled and given in gracefully. Closing her eyes and feeling rather like a poached egg, she tried to doze, occasionally rallying to look at the view through the window.

Most of the journey appeared to follow the coast. She caught a glimpse of coloured beach umbrellas and a stretch of inviting blue sea as they flew through the station at Livorno. Further south, the scenery had become dramatically rocky – cliffs and gorges and steep outcrops with pines clinging to them. Then the land had flattened out again and she began to see large rice fields, which surprised her, followed by olives and vineyards, laced with cypresses around their edges. With pleasure, she saw that the countryside had taken on the golden hue of Caroline's postcard.

Guy was waiting on the platform as the Express pulled in. He was wearing a bright pink shirt, decorated with what looked like small lizards, and a pair of crumpled blue trousers. His feet were encased in denim clogs. On his head sat a battered straw hat with what seemed to be the remains of an old school tie loosely knotted around the crown.

His face lit up when he saw her as she tried to negotiate the steep step down from the train with her heavy case, handbag and shoulder bag, which kept slipping down her arm. He hurried over.

"Here, let me do that!" Setting the case down on the platform, he looked her up and down admiringly without hiding the fact. "Well! You're a sight for sore eyes! Give us a kiss! It's been far too long since I saw my most favourite publishing person."

He'd grabbed her around the waist before Rachel could take evasive action and planted a moist kiss on each of her cheeks. His beard rasped against her skin. She'd forgotten how his pale blue eyes had a tendency to bulge. His breath smelled strongly of garlic and he was perspiring heavily. Stepping back from his grasp, she put a hand up to brush back a lock of her hair that he'd dislodged in his enthusiastic lunge. Inadvertently, her elbow knocked his hat, which fell to the ground. Guy, slightly off balance, promptly trod on it.

"Oh, your hat! I'm sorry!" she said. "You caught me by surprise. I'd forgotten that everyone here kisses each other all the time."

"That's quite all right! Caroline insists I've gone completely native. But it's great fun – you'll have to try it!" He looked at her, eyes narrowed. "You've lost quite a bit of weight since I last saw you at . . ." He stopped, discomfited.

"Since you came to Simon's funeral," Rachel said, quietly.

"Sorry! Stupid of me. Always been a problem of mine – engaging tongue before brain was in gear. Anyway, you look particularly slim and ravishing, if I may say so."

Rachel gave him a minimal smile.

"If you have to. Just don't say that sort of thing in front of your wife, Guy. You know how it annoys her."

"Oh, Caro doesn't mind what I say. She's used to me putting my foot in it. As long as the money keeps rolling in, she's not going to get fussy over my manners – or lack of them." He picked up his dented hat, punching it roughly back into shape and slapped it back on his head. "Come on! Let's get you home for a long, cool drink. You look as if you could do with one."

He *has* gone native, thought Rachel, gripping the edge of her seat. He's driving just like a lunatic Italian. She tried hard not to jam on imaginary brakes every time they roared around a corner, only to be met by another vehicle coming straight at them and overtaking in the middle of the road.

"Do they always wait until a dangerous bend before they pass each other?" she asked.

"Usually! It's all a matter of split-second timing. It's safer than it looks!"

"I find that rather hard to believe," said Rachel, uncomfortably aware that a bright red sports car was sitting about two inches from their back bumper.

She glanced at the dials on the dashboard. The speedometer was registering 140. She tried comforting herself with the thought that at least that wasn't miles per hour.

Guy waved a plump hand at the vast fields of sunflowers.

"Mussolini did a few good things in his day. Not only did he get the trains to run on time, he had all the area around here drained. Apparently it was mostly swamp and seething with mosquitoes. It's called the *Maremma*. They even have a special breed of horse here. They can survive without shade, even in the hottest part of the day if they have to. Which is just as well when you consider how badly most Italians treat their animals."

Not for the first time, Rachel was struck by the way he so often played the bumbling fool and yet he was interesting and knowledgeable on a wide range of topics. She knew perfectly well that Guy had a remarkably quick mind and that he was devastatingly astute in his summing up of people and situations. She'd seen him in action often enough at the parties he and his wife gave. Someone had once remarked that it paid to keep on the good side of Guy Haywood when it came to business. She wondered why he felt it necessary to hide behind a façade of clumsy jocularity. It had the effect of making her even less ready to relax in his company than if he'd been prepared to show himself to the world as he really was. In the past, there'd always been the protection of being married to Simon. She'd have to be careful during the next couple of days, she thought. But at least he and Caroline would be gone by Saturday.

After forty minutes' high-speed dicing with death, Guy had to slow down, stuck behind a tractor with a large trailer, loaded with hay. He impatiently tapped one hand on the Alfa Romeo's steering wheel in between swerving in and out, craning to see if the road ahead was clear. There always seemed to be traffic coming in the other direction. Rachel realised that every muscle in her body was tensed. Again, Guy made a foray over the centre line, revving the engine hard.

"Jesus! When we used to come here on holiday ten years ago, there was hardly anyone on the road at two o'clock in the afternoon. The place has gone to pot! What's happened to their bloody siesta?"

Rachel tried concentrating on the scenery. The land had become undulating with numerous small hills scattered around. Several of them were topped by buildings. In the middle of each town, the spire or tower of a church stood out among the cluster of pink roofs below it. She noticed that most of the towns had a tall water tower sticking up against the skyline like an old tooth. The fields of cereal and sunflowers had been left behind. Now they drove past miles of olive groves and vineyards. Wild broom, smothered in fragrant yellow flowers, grew everywhere. It reminded her of the gorse that covered the sloping sides of the Wicklow hills where her parents lived.

"How pretty!" she exclaimed suddenly, pointing to abundantly flowering rose-bushes, planted at the ends of tidy lines of vines.

"They're not planted to be pretty." Guy's increasing frustration at the slow-moving tractor was obvious. "Why can't the bugger pull in?" He gave a prolonged blast on the horn. The tractor driver kept chugging along.

"Guy, you're making me nervous. We don't *have* to be there by a set time, do we?"

He immediately smiled over at her, putting a hand on her arm. "Sorry! I shouldn't get so annoyed. I should be used to the damn tractors by now. You were saying how nice the roses looked in the vineyards. In fact, they're not for show. They plant them there because they show signs of mildew early on and then they can spray the vines before they become infected as well. Quite clever really! The best solutions are usually the simple ones."

To Rachel's relief, he removed his hand as the tractor turned off down a dusty side road. Guy put his foot down and the yellow car surged forward so powerfully she wished she felt strong enough to walk the last few kilometres. It was rather like riding an out-of-control hornet, she thought.

They started to climb. The road seemed to snake round in almost complete circles so that it was difficult to tell in which direction they were travelling. A monastery Guy had pointed out to her a few minutes earlier on their right, disappeared, only to materialise in front and to the left of them.

"How on earth do you know which way is north on a cloudy day?" she asked him, laughing.

"I've given up trying to work it out. I just follow the signs and hope for the best. We're nearly there!"

Five minutes later, he swerved onto a side road that led steeply downwards through graceful iron gates and along an avenue lined with chestnut trees. Coming to an abrupt stop in a cloud of dust, Guy switched off the engine.

"Well, here we are. I bet you thought we weren't going to make it!"

Rachel looked up at the house, towering above them on a large outcrop of rock. Its walls were creamy, faded and peeling in the blazing sun, reminding her of similar idyllic houses, decorating postcards sent by friends on holiday through the years. Roses and jasmine bloomed in the shadier corners and a white honeysuckle covered nearly the entire front of the building. Dark green shutters were closed over most of the windows. The sound of cicadas was almost deafening. It was as if all the air around them was humming, vibrating with insect sound. Rachel could feel trickles of sweat beginning to run down her back.

"Come on!" Guy said to her. "You take the small bag and I'll carry the case. Let's go and see where Caro has got to."

Obediently, she collected her belongings and set off behind him up the steep path. As she walked, Rachel hungrily took in her surroundings. The house was set in the middle of lawns that were brown rather than green. Giant fig-trees shaded a small building a few yards from the main house. Below and all around them, a sea of oak and chestnut leaves rippled in the slight breeze. She could see that the precipitous slopes above the house were also thickly wooded with chestnut. Rachel glimpsed a few jumbled roofs, belonging to the local village, peeping over the crown of the hill; and above them, the ubiquitous church spire and water tower.

With an exaggerated sigh, like air suddenly being let out of a tyre, Guy dropped her case onto a wide step outside heavy double doors that looked as though they dated back to when the house was first built. He took out a red spotted handkerchief and dabbed ineffectually at his face. Beads of sweat rolled down his cheeks and off the end of his nose. His face had become even more suffused after the two-minute climb, clashing with the red of his handkerchief. Rachel wondered if he suffered from high blood pressure or was the man just generally unfit for forty?

Just then, shutters were suddenly thrown open so that they bounced with a clatter against the wall. A cool, pale face appeared at one of the upstairs windows. Eyes the colour of jade looked down at them.

"*There* you are! I was beginning to think you'd absconded with her. Whatever took you so long?" Without waiting for an answer, Caroline threw Rachel a quick smile that didn't extend as far as her eyes. "Hello, Rachel. Come on up."

She'd disappeared before Rachel could return the greeting.

Pushing open one of the doors, they proceeded to climb steep stairs with marble treads and whitewashed fronts. At the top, a Siamese cat watched them unblinkingly through sky-blue eyes.

A door opened and Caroline reappeared, wearing a dress of pale yellow silk. She looked very petite and unsweaty. She kissed Rachel on each cheek, ignoring her husband.

"Was the journey bloody? You look as if you could do with a drink. Let's go and find one." She turned to lead the way. "Guy, put Rachel's things in her room, would you?"

It sounded like an order rather than a request, the younger woman thought.

Rachel followed her through darkened rooms and into a spacious bright kitchen with a high, wooden-beamed ceiling. Terracotta tiles covered the floor and the uneven walls were painted white. Old wooden cupboards and shelving lined one wall. A beautiful antique dresser, laden with blue and white china, stood at one side. Flowers dropped their petals onto the large oak table standing in the middle of the room. A smaller table and two comfortable-looking chairs with brightly coloured cushions had been placed in front of the domed window at the far end of the room. It struck Rachel that the view from the window was like looking at an oil painting. It was all there: cypresses, olive trees, distant vineyards, golden rolling hills, the blue, blue sky. It felt as though she were a million miles from rain-soaked, dirty old Dublin.

When Caroline had made two large gin and tonics, they carried them, ice tinkling gently, through the French doors and into the garden. Sunlight streamed down through the leaves of a large olive tree. Its trunk was so contorted it looked to Rachel as though it were woven around itself. They walked through its speckled shade and out into the full glare of the sun. Ahead lay a blue-tiled swimming pool with a mosaic dolphin cavorting on its floor. Bougainvillea, hibiscus and palms in large urns and pots surrounded the clear, sparkling water. The reflected light from it was so intense she had to put a hand up to shade her eyes. Roses and white and pink geraniums cascaded over the edges of raised beds bordering the paving. A small green lizard darted from under the shade of one of the pots. For a few seconds, it stayed unmoving, its black eyes seeming to watch her as it baked itself on the hot ground before suddenly vanishing behind a clump of bright yellow daisies.

Caroline led her to a table that was shaded by a smart rectangular umbrella and picked up some sunglasses. Slipping them on, she slid languidly into a chair and waved a hand lazily in Rachel's direction.

"Take a pew. When you've had your drink, you can change and have a swim if you'd like." Rachel could feel the other's eyes scanning her hot face, taking in her hair, clothes, style – or lack of it. "I've seen you look better. How are you coping now that Simon's not around to look after you?"

Typical Caroline! Wading straight in, always asking the sort of questions that others would not ask or at least would leave until a more opportune moment. Rachel took a sip from her drink, breathing in its combined perfume of lemon and juniper, before answering.

She was saved from having to reply by the arrival of Guy. He had shed his clothes and was dressed in bright orange swimming-shorts that nearly reached his knees. A solid-looking spare tyre half hid the waistband. Putting a tall glass filled with ice floating in a pink liquid down on the edge of the pool, he dived untidily into the water with a large smacking sound. He proceeded to splash his way towards the far end of the pool. The two women watched him, Rachel amused by the chaotic, unstylish crawl. Caroline's face showed irritation, verging on boredom.

Before she could start quizzing her again, Rachel said, "I saw one of your cats on the stairs. He's very beautiful."

"Chocolate and cream or pale grey?"

"Chocolate and cream."

"That's Percy. The pale grey is Rollo, who's not nearly as aristocratic as Percy. In fact, he's a bit of a fool really. Reminds me of my husband – always expending large amounts of energy chasing birds and inevitably looking rather ridiculous in the process."

"That's a bit hard, Caro!"

Caroline stared ahead into the pool, made choppy by Guy's inexpert back crawl.

"If you had to live with him, I fancy you'd find it difficult to stay sweetly tolerant." She turned towards Rachel, eyes masked by her sunglasses. "Men are such unreliable sods. *All* of them, in one way or another."

Rachel felt her stomach muscles suddenly knot. What was the other woman implying? Did that mean she thought Simon came into that category too? Could it be that Caroline knew about Simon's sister – or whatever the woman was? Trying to keep in mind that Guy's wife was a stirrer and troublemaker, she made an effort to control her sense of panic, forcing herself to sound as casual as possible.

"What do you mean, Caroline? Simon wasn't a sod."

Caroline switched her attention back to the pool.

"Oh, they all have their little secrets. Don't pretend that you believe Simon told you everything about himself. No one could be that naïve!"

Rachel was on the point of admitting that no, she had no idea what the other meant. But if she did that, she would look a complete fool. She decided not to say anything that would give herself away.

"Simon and I were very happy together. I don't really want to talk about him if you don't mind. It still makes me feel miserable when I'm reminded that he's *not* around any more."

She suspected that Caroline would only be honest with her if and when it suited her. Rachel would never understand how her mind worked. Perhaps the only way she could find out what the other was hinting at was to tackle Guy. At least he wouldn't go out of his way to spin yarns in order to upset her.

Suddenly, Rachel wanted the clock put back – to be in Ireland with her husband again. Most of all, she wanted to be away from the woman sitting beside her in her expensive silk dress with her pale legs stretched out in front of her and her black bob with the fringe that half hid the cool, green eyes under the dark glasses.

Chapter Four

They'd finally left. Rachel was on her own and none the wiser. It had proved impossible to question Guy.

He disappeared after dinner on her first evening, saying that he had some last-minute things to do in the neighbouring town of Castel del Piano. Caroline, having almost completely ignored her during dinner, suggested after their coffee that they have an early night.

"I'll show you the ropes in the morning. It's too late to start now," she said, before vanishing into her bedroom. Her head reappeared briefly around the door. "You needn't close your windows but don't for God's sake open the shutters or you'll have a room full of bats."

Rachel had seen Guy coming out of a separate bedroom before the evening meal. Things were obviously not all that cosy at the Haywoods'. In case he decided on a little midnight rambling, she made sure her bedroom door was locked.

Lying awake on that first night, tired and yet not sleepy,

Rachel thought of her dead husband. A nightingale sang in the oak tree outside her window. She'd only heard recordings of them before. It really was beautiful – the effortless trills and small silences, followed by bursts of cascading sound. It was the sort of thing you should share with the man you loved. How Simon would have adored this place, she thought sadly. No sooner had the thought entered her mind than the doubts stubbornly elbowed their way in. Trying to relax her body and unclench her hands, she remembered a sentence she'd once read. *A mind too active is no mind at all.* It didn't seem to matter how much she attempted to lie quietly, to think pleasant thoughts, the doubt and confusion refused to budge.

Wreaths and bouquets of white flowers filled her dreams that night. Simon's grave seemed to be sinking under the weight of petals, the earth caving in, suddenly crumbling at her feet. There in the black hole lay an open coffin. It was empty. Only a slight indentation in the white satin lining showed where a body had been lying. She woke with a jump, staring around her, disorientated. Seeing slivers of moonlight piercing the shutters and silvering the worn tiled floor by the open window, she remembered where she was.

On her first day on her own, Rachel decided to familiarise herself with the place. Caroline had been less than helpful. Pulling garments out of drawers as last-minute additions were added to her already bulging cases, she replied to a query about rubbish collections with an irritable, "Thursdays! You'll soon work it all out. There's nothing to fuss about, Rachel. You've met one of the cats. Rollo will appear at some point – he sometimes goes missing for days at a time. Angelica will be in on Monday and she'll do any washing or shopping you need. The horses' drinking trough will need topping up every day. Francesco, the chap who looks after them and does the odd bit of gardening, will drop in every so often. You can always ask him about anything you don't know. There's plenty of cat food in the cupboard. Really, that's all there is to it." Then she added, "You may find the odd person calls in, possibly the Digby-White woman. Don't let her put you out. Just mix her a drink, smile sweetly and send her on her merry way. People are just curious when there's a new arrival on the scene, that's all."

The telephone rang before Rachel had time to ask what were the names of these curious people, apart from 'the Digby-White woman'. Were they friends? Neighbours? Were they likely to be Italian, English-speaking, or what?

She heard Caroline say '*Pronto,*' and then was aware of the door being quietly closed. Presumably so that the ensuing conversation would not be overheard. Was Caroline filling one of her friends in on the latest 'arrival on the scene'? After hanging around for several minutes, Rachel gave up and went in search of Percy – last seen waiting patiently for a lizard to reappear from under one of the downstairs doors.

It had been such a rush at the end that it was only after they'd gone she remembered some of the questions she had meant to ask them. Guy had handed her a piece of paper, just before leaving.

"You know our London number, but here's my new mobile number, in case of emergencies."

"What sort of emergencies could there possibly be? Unless the visitors get out of hand," said Caroline from inside the taxi, with a small laugh.

Rachel was uncomfortable at the intensity of the other's regard. Could it be that Caroline's feelings towards her were thoroughly negative, rather than just ambivalent?

She'd manage to dodge Guy's farewell kisses by standing well back from the car, clutching an unwilling Percy to her. It was surprising what a dead weight he could be when he didn't want to be picked up or cuddled.

Rachel decided to explore downstairs first. The entire basement area under the main house had once been used to stable animals. Guy had told her that it had been common practice to do this with all the farmhouses in the area. As the property was fairly high up, it became very cold in the winter with a fair amount of snow and so it was a good way of ensuring the wellbeing of the animals. It had now been turned into storerooms full of garden equipment and shelves overflowing with bottled fruit and jars of olive oil. Enormous curved glass containers of wine lined a wall in one of the outer rooms. Another housed a washing machine and a large chest freezer. There was a section for airing clothes or bed-linen in the winter months. The walls and floors were made of stone. Rachel ran her hand over a wall, admiring the craftsmanship of the domed ceilings and the way the floors sloped gently and evenly towards a central channel. She could imagine the dung and dirty straw being sluiced out, flowing under the thick chestnut doors into the open, to lie, steaming in the winter cold. One room led into another; the outer ones lit by small arched, unglazed windows, the inner, full of shadowy corners and sizeable spiders' webs.

Cautiously making her way past some rusting farm tools, she peered through an archway. In the gloom, it was possible to just make out the shapes of an assortment of containers, buckets, woven baskets and an old bed, upended against a wall. Higher up, a collection of broken chairs, leather straps and pieces of metal hung from large hooks. It felt dusty and airless down there, though not nearly as hot as outside. As she turned to go, a sudden movement near a pile of flowerpots caught her attention. A large black scorpion scuttled past her, not two feet from where she was standing. All at once, the afternoon heat outside seemed infinitely preferable to sharing accommodation with a scorpion. How many more of them were there, lurking in the shadows? What other nasties would she find if she hung around?

Caroline hadn't warned her about them, although Guy had told her not to go into the nearby building that looked like a small, windowless house.

"It's where they used to roast the chestnuts but it's been unused for some time and the snakes love it in there. They slide down the chimney."

Rachel had smiled.

"I don't mind snakes. I remember there was a viper that lived at the bottom of the garden belonging to an old aunt of mine in England. It was the high point of the holiday when I was a child, crouching in the undergrowth for hours, stalking the snake!"

"I'm not sure quite how poisonous these ones are but they'd put the fear of God into you, some of them," he replied, wagging a pudgy finger at her. "They can be four or five feet long and they're a very vivid green. The locals go crazy when they see them. Everyone charges around shouting '*Serpente!*' and falling over each other while the snake quietly buggers off until the fuss dies down."

She'd agreed not to go into the chestnut-roasting house.

Once outside, she almost tripped over Percy, lying on his back in the shade of one of the many olive trees that dotted the garden. Rachel bent to stroke his soft, cream underbelly. The blue eyes closed and curved claws sheathed and unsheathed from chocolate paws.

There was a sudden scuffling sound from above them, which made both cat and woman look up. A pair of yellow eyes stared out from the silvery green leaves. Then more rustles and scuffles and a small, grey cat landed with a slight thud at the foot of the tree. Rachel held out a hand, which was briefly sniffed. Rollo then turned his attention to the still spread-eagled Percy. Crouching and springing in one fluid action, he landed on top of the other cat. Before Percy had time to respond, Rollo cantered away, tail erect, and vanished into a clump of lilies. He had a sort of devil-may-care attitude about him that made Rachel smile.

Following the path that wound through a vegetable garden, she made her way down to the fence, where the horses' drinking trough stood under a massive cherry-tree.

Rachel carefully climbed in between the two strands of electric wire. Ripe cherries littered the ground. They were dark red – almost black. Rachel tried one. A small explosion of sweet juice burst in her mouth, staining her lips and tongue with its wine-coloured richness. The fruit tasted delicious. It was like sampling the essence of summer, she thought. She picked up several more, eating them one after the other without a pause, spitting the pips out into the long grass on the other side of the wire.

There was the sound of hooves, followed by a gentle whinny. A chestnut stallion, closely followed by a grey mare, was approaching through the trees. As the horses came nearer, she could see that they were in good condition, if a little thin. The chestnut eagerly nuzzled her outstretched hand, looking for food. When he didn't find any, he lowered his head into the trough and drank long and noiselessly. He must be Fortunato and the grey must be Allegria. Guy had told her that they were both friendly and that Fortunato was always on the look-out for any goodies that might be on offer.

"He's a tinker, that one! He'll try and get into your pockets if you let him. Caro and I used to ride fairly regularly but recently we've become rather lazy about it and the horses have had too easy a time. They'll soon have forgotten what it's like to be taken out for a canter. Francesco doesn't approve at all!"

Rachel wondered if that was another sign of how bad things had become between Guy and Caroline. Did they share any pursuits or interests these days? She had turned down the offer of riding, saying that she preferred just being around horses rather than on top of them. Attempting to jump a large gate as a child on a small and spirited pony had left bad memories of a nasty fall. The bruises had faded quickly but her terror at being dragged along by the bolting animal, one foot locked into a stirrup, had left a lasting impression. As far as she was concerned, horses were best admired from a standing position – from the front, a little to one side and at arm's length.

She stroked the velvet nose and chin of the chestnut, her mind wandering aimlessly. The sound of bees and a distant strimmer, combined with the heat, was soporific. All those books she'd brought with her to read, all the places she'd promised herself to visit; if she wasn't careful, she would spend her month here talking to the animals and snoozing in the shade.

Later that evening, as she sat at the kitchen table, a mushroom omelette and a glass of wine in front of her, something moved on the terrace outside. Thinking it must be one of the cats, she didn't take any notice. They'd been out there a little while earlier before it got dark. Percy had been driven into a corner by the agile Rollo. In the end, the exasperated older cat had boxed him soundly. Rollo had somersaulted out of the way, then casually wandered off to groom himself while Percy recovered his dignity.

Then a sound, as if a garden chair had been pushed a short distance along the uneven surface of the terrace made her get to her feet. That wasn't the sort of noise a couple of cats would make! Clicking on the outside light, Rachel stood by the open doors, eyes scanning the garden.

Nothing! Telling herself not to be a jumpy fool, she stepped over the threshold and went out onto the terrace.

It was still very hot. There was no sign of the cats – or of anything else. A chair stood tidily at each side of the garden table. It didn't look as though anything had been disturbed. The only sound now was the bell-like triple call of a hoopoe and the only things moving were the flickering lights of fireflies as they danced in and out of the trees. Hesitating a moment, she wondered if she should take a quick walk around the house to make sure there was no intruder. Somehow, the thought didn't appeal to her very much. It was probably something like a porcupine, reason told her. She'd picked up a long cream and brown spine from near the terrace that afternoon. Guy had mentioned that you hardly ever saw them – just the damage they did to the flowerbeds where they'd been rooting the night before.

Rachel moved back into the house, closing and locking the French doors behind her. It would be all right when she'd got accustomed to the place. Every house had its own collection of sounds. Those sounds always took on a greater significance when darkness fell. She'd just have to get used to all the different animal and insect noises.

In spite of three glasses of wine, Rachel found it difficult to get to sleep. She turned first one way then the other in the large double bed, the sheet tangling around her legs. She'd lain awake, hot and sweaty, gazing up at the thick chestnut beams above her. Ornate wooden carving, decorating the foot of the bed, was silhouetted against lines of moonlight coming through the shutters. Its curves were also reflected in the blotched antique glass on the enormous wardrobe standing near the bedroom door.

Before getting into bed, she'd opened a shutter to look out at the full moon, suspended over the stippled expanse of trees below the house. Rachel could make out the path leading down to the snake house, as she'd renamed the building at the edge of the front lawn. For a moment, she thought she saw something move near its end wall. A slight shimmer, a tiny disturbance of moonlight? She'd stared until her eyes ached but all that was visible was a fig-tree that cast a giant shadow over the parched grass, its large leaves stirring momentarily in the night air.

She didn't know what it was that woke her after she'd finally managed to drift off. She just knew that something had disturbed her sleep. She sat bolt upright in the bed, heart thumping. An owl called further down in the valley. The nightingales and hoopoes had given up their nocturnal serenading. Even the crickets had fallen silent. She stiffened; there was a sound – a kind of muffled bump from somewhere inside the house. It was definitely inside rather out. It seemed to come from the stairs that led down to the main door into the garden. Rachel was certain that she'd locked it before going to bed. She remembered, however, that she hadn't bolted the door to her own room. With Guy gone, there had been no need.

The moon had disappeared and the surrounding night seemed blacker than black. Nervously, she groped for the bedside light switch. With an over-loud click, light flooded the room, making her blink. As quietly as possible, she eased herself off the bed, wondering what she could use to threaten an unwanted visitor. The pretty vase of flowers, hairbrush or talcum powder on the dressing-table were hardly options. Leaning down, Rachel groped under the bed for a slipper. It wasn't much but it helped to have something in her hand. She could always lob it at the first thing that stirred on the stairs. Taking a deep breath, she flung open the bedroom door, erupting onto the landing, slipper clutched firmly in her right hand. Light from the bedroom behind her shone onto the stairs. She was just in time to see a startled Siamese cat stop in its tracks halfway up the stairs. Percy's blue eyes bulged with fright as he whirled round. He retreated hastily down the steps and disappeared with a thud through the cat-flap in the door at the bottom.

Leaning against the wall, Rachel laughed weakly. God! What an idiot she was! Spooks in every corner. If she weren't careful, she'd end up like her timorous mother, afraid to walk to the end of the garden once night came. This holiday was obviously well overdue! She slept soundly for what little remained of the night.

Chapter Five

It was Percy, scratching at her door that woke Rachel next morning. She reached for her watch, peering at it blearily. Half past nine! The cats would be wanting their breakfast. Yawning, she rolled out of bed, picked up a cotton wrapper that had fallen to the floor during the night and tied it loosely around her.

As soon as she opened the door, Percy threaded his way through her legs, rubbing against her and purring. His fright at her apocalyptic appearance during the night seemed to be forgotten or at least forgiven.

"Poor old Percy!" she said, bending down to stroke him. "Are you dying of starvation? Come on, let's go and find some food!"

He followed her into the kitchen where Rollo dozed in his basket beside a stuffed panda. As a tiny kitten, he had been found abandoned at the side of the road by Carlo, the postman, who offered him as a companion for Percy.

Rachel had learned from Guy that the man brought the panda up to the house the next day, in case the tiny kitten needed something to cuddle up against. The postman's children had outgrown the large black and white toy with its many bald patches and one missing ear.

"Most unusual for anyone around here to be so soft-hearted," Guy had commented to Rachel, with a laugh. "But he looked so pathetic, Carlo couldn't bring himself to just drive past. We were his next port of call, so we got landed with another cat – much to Percy's displeasure. He's still not quite sure if he likes Rollo even now!"

When the cats had been fed, Rachel unlocked the door and stepped out into the hot morning sunshine. The geraniums in the pots on the terrace were smothered in flowers and she could smell the lavender and roses in the nearby border. I'll bring my breakfast out here and drown in the view, she thought, turning back to the house.

As she did so, she saw that the chairs, so neatly set around the garden table the night before, were now arranged on the grass in a line facing the terrace. Rachel was struck by how it almost looked as though they had been placed there in readiness for a missing audience; and the terrace and house were part of the stage setting.

Somehow, in the bright daylight, it didn't worry her as much as it might have done if the discovery had been made at night. It must be some local children playing a prank, she thought. Still, it was strange that she'd heard nothing except the cat-flap bumping shut during the night. Anybody wanting to get into this part of the garden would have to pass directly under her bedroom window and walk around the end of the house.

She glanced towards the pool, glinting in the sunshine. The sun-chairs that had been at the far end the day before were nowhere to be seen.

"This is ridiculous," Rachel muttered out loud.

As she got near to the pool edge, she saw the four chairs, lying in the water at the shallow end, their attached cushions swaying gently around them.

A small cough made her turn quickly. A short, dark-haired man with skin the colour of oak was standing only a few feet away. He slowly looked her up and down, dark eyes taking in the tall, pale stranger with her hair piled untidily on top of her head. She felt suddenly underdressed, uncomfortably aware that she was wearing nothing but the thin cotton wrap. Crossing her arms in front of her, she attempted to gain a degree of control over the situation by standing as straight as possible. She gave him an enquiring look.

He smiled at her politely.

"*Buongiorno, signora Martin,*" he said, holding out a hand. "I am Francesco."

Rachel gave his hand a quick shake and let go. She looked at him blankly.

"Francesco?"

"*Sì!* Horses . . . garden . . ."

She heard the 'r' pronounced in the two words in a way that made both horses and garden sound suddenly exotic. He looked expectantly at her. Then Rachel remembered that Guy and Caroline had both mentioned to her that the man who looked after the horses and garden was called Francesco.

"Oh, yes! Of course! *Buongiorno, Francesco.*"

But he had turned his attention towards the pool, his face now wearing a puzzled expression. He looked at her and gestured at the submerged sun-chairs. It was obvious that he was struggling to find the right words.

"*La signora . . .*" he stopped and waved a hand in her direction and then back to the chairs.

Rachel realised that the man thought she must be responsible for the apparent idiocy. He must think I got blind drunk and chucked them in on my first night alone here, she thought, appalled.

"I didn't put them there," she said, quickly. He was still looking at her with a perplexed stare so she thought she'd better make things as simple as possible. Shaking her head vigorously, it was Rachel's turn to point at the chairs. "*Io, no!*" she said, with great emphasis.

She regretted the fact that she'd never got round to doing more work on her Italian exercises before coming to the Haywoods'.

"I understand what you say me, *signora,*" came the uncertain response. "*Dunque, chi l'ha fatto?*"

Guessing he'd asked who had done it, she shook her head again and made a helpless gesture with her hands.

"I don't know!"

The man called Francesco still didn't look very convinced. He stared at her for a few moments more. Rachel wasn't quite sure what to say next. Then he smiled suddenly, a broad, beguiling smile that lit up his serious face.

"*Va bene!* I will take the chairs from the water."

"Thank you very much. *Grazie*."

Rachel walked as nonchalantly as she could in the direction of the house, aware that he might be watching her. She couldn't wait to get on some proper clothes.

It was strange that as well as not hearing the night-time visitors, neither had she heard Francesco's approach. As she stepped into the kitchen, she wondered if everyone in that part of the world went around on tiptoe, regularly giving each other heart attacks.

When Francesco eventually left, still throwing the occasional searching look in her direction, Rachel sat down to a late breakfast on the terrace overlooking the valley. It had been built at one end of the house, over the top of a kind of giant vat that used to store water. When she moved a chair across the tiles, the sound echoed in the hollow space underneath. On the outer edge of the terrace, the drop below her to the path leading down to the cars must have been a good twenty feet. Rachel got up and went to look over the edge. The railing round the terrace felt very unsafe. It shook when she leaned on it. She also noticed that some of the bricks under the railing had worked loose.

Over a second cup of coffee, she admired the view. It really was just like the photo on the front of Caroline's postcard, inviting her to stay at Podere Vecchio. She'd looked up the name of the house before coming to Italy. *Podere* meant farm or holding and *vecchio*, she had already known, meant old. 'Old Farm'. Simple and accurate!

The slight haze, smudging the outline of the distant vineyards earlier that morning, had vanished. She could see the outer wall and roofs of two nearby towns, nestling on top of their respective hills. Sunday bells chimed from somewhere in the village above her. The hoopoes were calling again, this time much closer to the house. She'd never seen one. Perhaps she'd get a look at them today.

Pulling the map Caroline had left out for her closer, she tried to get her bearings. It seemed she was looking at Montegiovi and Monticello but she wasn't completely sure. Out loud, Rachel pronounced some of the place-names that were scattered in amongst the hectic thumbprints of land contours: Monte Amiata, Segiano, Santa Fiora, Monte Laterone and the village above Podere Vecchio, Santo Lorenzo. They seemed to roll off the tongue so easily, like glycerine off a spoon. She wondered if it were possible that they looked as perfect as they sounded.

Rachel decided to check the horses' water, have a swim and then take the car and do some exploring. The mystery of the moving chairs seemed insignificant as she sat there in the dappled light, chin resting in the palm of one hand, elbow propped on the pretty iron table. It was pleasantly warm here in the shade from the olive tree. The countryside beyond glowed, corn-coloured and inviting. Moving statues in Ireland – peripatetic chairs in Tuscany! So what? The world was full of unsolved mysteries and perhaps all the better for it!

Hair still damp from the pool, Rachel walked down to Caroline's car that was parked beside Guy's dust-sheeted

Alfa Romeo. The Audi looked very new and its dark blue paintwork, glossy.

When Caroline had given her the car keys, Rachel asked if the other was sure she didn't mind her using this beautiful, new machine.

"Don't you have something less spectacular for me to drive?"

"The only other car is Guy's and *no one* drives that except him," replied Caroline.

"What if I have an accident? The driving here is pretty dreadful."

"Then, I shall probably kill you."

It had been said with a slight smile.

Rachel was more than a little nervous as she climbed into the shiny vehicle and settled into the cream leather seat. Well, let's hope that all the lunatic drivers are safely at Mass, she thought, as she gingerly turned the key in the ignition.

At the gates, she paused. Left, up to the village or right, down into the valley? She decided to take the valley route. The road here was hardly a road at all – just a wide track full of potholes that had been patched up any old way with stones and what looked like odd chunks of builders' rubble. As she bumped along, dust rose in a creamy plume behind the car, making the trees invisible.

After a while, the track narrowed and Rachel noticed that long, trailing bramble shoots had started to creep over the edges and onto its surface. The going got steeper and more uneven. She started to think she'd made the wrong choice, coming this way. There appeared to be no entrances or gateways into which she could turn. It had become too narrow now to even think of trying to turn the car round and Rachel didn't much like the idea of backing for a couple of miles. Just as she was starting to feel really anxious, she came round a bend to find a small footbridge over a river. There was a flat area where the track petered out under some trees. Relieved, she pulled up in their shade and got out. The powerful heat was a shock after the air-conditioned comfort of the Audi.

Shade and the enticing gurgle of the river drew her to the low stone wall on the narrow bridge. Leaning on her hands, she looked down. Disappointment filled her. She'd been expecting to see clear water meandering along, reflecting the overhanging trees and patches of blue sky. Instead, the river was coffee-coloured and reflected nothing. Blobs of dirty foam were caught in between the boulders at its edge. A plastic Coke bottle floated slowly along. Even here! How could it happen, seemingly in the middle of nowhere? She wondered what had caused the pollution.

Rachel turned back to the car, dispirited. Why did life so rarely come up to one's expectations? Perhaps the reason was that you expected too much and so it was only natural that you were constantly disappointed. It was the same with people. It was difficult not to want your friends to behave in the way you'd like; for them to fulfil what you saw as their true potential. Why should they? For a moment, she remembered her parents, standing at their door the week before, with her mother, trying to pretend contentment, waving goodbye to her. Rachel knew perfectly well that she'd only succeeded in pleasing them on rare occasions.

She started the car and slowly began to make the bumpy ascent. When she reached the turn off to the gates of Podere Vecchio, she decided to go on to the village. That would *have* to be a better experience than the dirty river and the travelling curtain of dust that had accompanied her.

Almost immediately, the track improved and a couple of minutes later, it was tarred. It climbed steeply, joining another, slightly less narrow road. She turned at the junction and swung up towards the village. Half a dozen elderly men sat on plastic chairs in the shade outside a house. Their lined faces all wore the same leathery resignation that spoke of generations of toil and little expectation of joy from life. It made Rachel think of how few people one saw in Ireland these days with that same lingering look of hardship. They stared at her, expressionless, as she drove slowly past, feeling uncomfortable. On the spur of the moment, she gave a small wave and smiled in their direction. As far as she could make out, the response consisted of one man giving a minimal nod. Then she remembered that Guy had warned her that if she expected to see happy peasants decorating the landscape, San Lorenzo was not the place in which to find them.

The road ran around the hill in serpentine curves. The houses looked poor with peeling plaster, rusting grills on some of the lower windows and sun-bleached doors that had once been painted. Shutters were pulled over most of the windows in the fierce midday heat. She found herself wondering what it was like in August.

Since Caroline and Guy's departure, Rachel had left the shutters open at Podere Vecchio. The house was a lot hotter that way but she was sufficiently sun-starved not to mind. It was bliss to walk barefoot into a room and catch a glimpse of Tuscan hills through the windows. She loved the way light poured into every corner, filling the place with warmth and radiance, making the tiled floors glow a soft ruby colour. She especially liked the way the olive tree outside her window flashed its silvery grey leaves in a breeze – so that the reflected light was segmented and danced in a million tiny dots in front of her eyes. It made her think of the Impressionist paintings she had fallen in love with at the Musée d'Orsai – the one high point in the unromantic weekend with the unlovable lover in Paris. She had been incapable of reciprocating his passion and it had all ended on a sour note. At the time, it had seemed rather tragic. Remembering the experience now, faintly absurd. And it had all happened so long ago.

There was an empty-looking post office but apparently not a single shop in the place. She turned the last bend to find that the road ended in a small square opposite the church. She parked and went up the steps to the unadorned wooden doors. Rachel turned the handle only to find that it was locked. Mass was obviously over and everyone had disappeared back home for lunch. Smells of cooking and snatches of conversation wafted up from behind the shuttered houses lower down. Retracing her steps, she stood by the car in the glare of the day, hand over her eyes and looked around.

If the view from Podere Vecchio was spectacular, the

panoramic sweep of country that she saw now took her breath away. She thought it was like looking at a giant model for the most splendid train set ever made. Tiny lakes shone like silver puddles in the distance. Great tracts of trees covered the slopes of what she thought was probably Monte Amiata, and beyond. And everywhere, the crooked golden rectangles and squares with their tidy lines of olive trees. She could see acres of vines, battalions of them, curving over the hillsides, each one planted at a precise interval from its neighbour. They looked like miniature furze bushes from where she stood. What looked like a monastery that she hadn't seen from lower down showed up, white against the surrounding fields. The land adjoining it was fringed with dark green cypresses like feathery exclamation marks.

Rachel felt the sun baking her arms and the back of her neck, but the breeze up there made it pleasant. Thoughts of Simon flooded back and she wished with all her heart that he were there beside her. She wanted him to be there, not just to hold and be held, but so that he could explain to her the mystery of the unknown woman who claimed kinship with him. If she couldn't have her husband alive, at least she wanted the solace of knowing that she hadn't been wrong in trusting him so absolutely, that there was a perfectly satisfactory explanation. Above all, she wanted to know that he had not kept any secrets from her during their time together – that he was as honourable as she'd always believed him to be.

Rachel watched a pair of butterflies, following their erratic dipping and climbing. Their wings were bright blue, almost jewel-like against the backdrop below and beyond her. She suddenly realised that she'd not put any sun cream on. Her pale skin would probably feel cooked later in the day if she didn't retreat into some shade quickly. But there was no shade in the empty square. The breeze had dropped. The stones hurled back the glaring heat into her face so that she felt she was being cooked alive. She also had a strong sensation of being on show in this open space, like a beetle under the microscope in some laboratory. The atmosphere had become suddenly hostile. She was sure that there were eyes watching from behind those closed shutters. There were no sounds now, apart from the din of crickets, hidden in the trees further down the hillside. In the blazing sunlight, Rachel suddenly shivered.

Chapter Six

Rachel thought she'd never seen anyone quite as ugly as Angelica. The young woman's face was pockmarked – whether from a childhood disease or a bad attack of acne in her teenage years, she wasn't sure. There was no way of finding out either. Angelica seemed incapable of understanding a word of English. Caroline must have spoken to her in Italian. She gave the strong impression that Rachel's presence was unwanted, that it even made her angry.

Their first encounter was the day after Rachel's abortive attempt at exploring the neighbourhood. Sunday had left her feeling uneasy. The idea of Italy being full of happy, laughing people who sang snatches of operatic arias at the drop of a hat and who were friendly and made you feel welcome was starting to slip a little. She'd found it difficult to sleep that Sunday night, expecting to hear strange sounds outside; more garden furniture being shifted perhaps. Several times, she got up to quietly open the shutter and peer out to see if anything was moving in the moonlight. Twice she heard the sound of the cat-flap thumping shut as Percy or Rollo came and went.

On Monday morning, all seemed in its rightful place in the garden. In the house, however, things became far from tranquil. Angelica arrived when Rachel was in the middle of feeding the cats. The woman ignored the visitor's outstretched hand with a toss of her head and a muttered *"Buongiorno"*, accompanied by a scowl.

She laid into the previous evening's washing-up with such a clattering of cutlery and pans, the cats, ears back and tails twitching, left their breakfast half-eaten and escaped into the garden.

Trying to keep out of the other's way, Rachel prepared her own breakfast to take out to the terrace. While she waited for the coffee to percolate, she observed the woman, who stood at the sink with her back to her. She was short – not even as tall as Caroline. That must have been one of the reasons Caroline had employed her, Rachel guessed. It gave her the rare opportunity to talk down to someone shorter than herself. Angelica's legs were slightly bowed as though she'd just climbed off a horse and her wiry black hair was like a mop that had dried with all its ends sticking out from the centre. Her skin was the colour of old piano keys rather than the swarthy brown of Francesco's or the smooth coffee-coloured tan of the young girls Rachel had seen at the airport. Sweat stained her blue shirt under each arm. Rachel suspected the woman couldn't be much more than thirty but she'd noticed when the other had first entered the kitchen that already there was a fine black fuzz beginning to bloom on her upper lip. The smell of an insufficiently washed body, coupled with a strong tang of garlic, reached the corner of the room where Rachel stood. All in all, she decided, Angelica had been misnamed.

Just as Rachel turned to go out into the garden carrying the tray, Angelica paused in the middle of drying dishes and stared at her over her shoulder. Her thick, black eyebrows seemed to meet in a straight line over the bridge of her nose so it was difficult to tell if she wore a constant frown. Or was it only when she looked at Rachel? Determined not to be intimidated, Rachel gave her a friendly smile and retreated thankfully outside, registering the fact that the answering smile was very minimal indeed.

As she sat in the shade of the olive tree, she wondered what was the cause of Angelica's antipathy. Was it because she saw Rachel as belonging to the comfortable world inhabited by the Haywoods? A world to which she could never aspire? Perhaps she was offended that Guy and Caroline considered it necessary to ask someone to come and house-sit for them. Was it possible that the woman thought that she could have perfectly well been left in charge? Or was it that she just didn't like strangers in the house, making more work for her when she could have been taking things easy with the Haywoods away? Whatever the reason, it was obviously not going to be easy to get along with her. Rachel reached for her dictionary and began to look up some of the words she needed to learn. It might just help if she were able to speak a little more Italian to the woman other than just *buongiorno* and *arrivederci!*

Completing a shopping list took a little time. Caroline had said that Angelica would do any shopping Rachel needed but she'd forgotten to explain that the woman walked down from San Lorenzo and Rachel would have to drive her to Castel del Piano in order to shop. Having met the beetle-browed Angelica, Rachel decided that she would be quite happy to do any shopping on her own. She didn't mind if she made a fool of herself, asking for what she wanted. If she were really stuck, she could always point at items, smile and look hopeful. Perhaps she would even find a supermarket. Then all she would have to worry about would be finding out how much she owed. They might even take credit cards. She found the idea comforting.

The morning was spent avoiding Angelica. The woman attacked any job she did with such aggression that the house reverberated as though under bombardment in a war zone. Furniture was roughly dragged from one part of a room to another. There would be short silences, followed by bursts of energetic hoovering. Doors were slammed, shutters thrown back against the walls with such force Rachel thought they would come off their hinges. Empty wine bottles were chucked into a box with a crash. Rachel could hear the glass breaking from where she sat.

She noticed that Rollo had disappeared up a nearby olive tree and Percy was curled up on the tiles beside her, croissant-like in the shade, ears twitching at each detonation coming from the house.

It was twelve o'clock when Angelica finally departed, without so much as a glance in Rachel's direction. It was like getting rid of an angry, small cloud that had been hovering overhead, threatening tempest and lightning strikes. Rachel breathed a sigh of relief and wondered if it was going to be as bad every weekday.

She had been waiting to see if Angelica would do anything about the shopping but neither by word nor gesture had the subject come up. She reckoned that the woman was as unwilling to go shopping as Rachel was to take her. Good! But that meant she would have to do something about getting food in herself. There was plenty of stuff in the freezer but she wanted to sample some of the fresh local fruit and vegetables – and cheeses.

She checked the route, propping the map up on the steering wheel. It wouldn't be difficult to find – and anyway, there would be signposts. Remembering how dazzled she'd been the day before, Rachel had brought her sunglasses with her this time. It was nearly one o'clock. She must try to set off on these trips earlier in the day. For a moment, she wished she had Simon there to organise her, make choices, do all the things that he was so good at doing. She shook her head, remembering how she'd left so much in his capable hands. It struck her that, compared with Caroline, she was not at all a proactive sort of person. In fact, she reckoned that really, she was rather pathetically lazy. She was surprised that it hadn't occurred to her before then. Perhaps that was one of the reasons why Caroline seemed so irritated with her from time to time.

It took only ten minutes to get to Castel del Piano by a

smooth, tree-lined road that curved and twisted in a way she was starting to expect.

Parking in the shade of a large lime tree, she walked in the direction of some shops. As she approached, her heart sank. They were all shuttered. Looking around her, Rachel realised that there were no cars on the move, no pedestrians either. She looked at her watch. Not quite one fifteen. Hopefully, she followed a side street, emerging into another, broader one, lined with butchers' shops, delicatessens and bread shops. She noticed a cake shop with the shutter half pulled down over its entrance. Hesitantly, she stooped and stuck her head under it.

A pleasant-looking woman was wiping crumbs off a glass counter top. She looked up and smiled, greeting her in rapid Italian. Rachel couldn't understand one word of what she'd said.

"I'm sorry, I don't understand. Do you speak English?"

The woman smiled again.

" A little . . . shop closed. Sorry!"

"Is it siesta time already?"

"Is time for food. After, we make siesta."

"Do all the shops close so early?"

"*Sì, sì.* Everybody close shop now. You come . . . after *la siesta, no?*"

"At four?" asked Rachel. Then, thinking that even four o'clock might be too early, she added, "At five o'clock?"

"Come at five o'clock. Then all shops is open," said the woman, with the same, friendly smile.

In spite of her disappointment, Rachel managed to smile back.

"Grazie, signora."

"Prego! Arrivederla, signora."

While she was in Castel del Piano, Rachel thought she might as well take the opportunity to wander around the town. At one end of a street stood a fountain, bubbling and splashing into a large circular pond. Lethargic goldfish hung, almost motionless in its tepid water. There seemed to be plenty of shops around, she noted; even if they were all shut. At the other end of the town there was some sort of public park with benches scattered around under the trees. Quite a few of the balconies on the surrounding buildings were full of terracotta pots containing geraniums or basil. She passed a couple of shuttered houses with white-flowered honeysuckle clinging to wooden trellis. The scent was so strong that she stopped and inhaled deeply before moving off again along the street. Nothing she'd ever grown in her garden in Ireland had ever smelled so potently fragrant.

The only sign of life seemed to be a young couple; he sitting on the brown grass, leaning against a tree-trunk, she with her head in his lap. From time to time he would bend and gently plant a kiss on her upturned face. A dog, tethered to the leg of one of the park benches by a short length of rope, watched them with the resigned air of an animal that knows he must wait until his master is ready to take him on the longed-for walk.

Rachel turned away from the man and girl. Would *she* ever be part of a pair again? she wondered. Unexpectedly, Francesco's dark brown face came into her mind. Why? she wondered. He wasn't particularly attractive and anyway, she hadn't looked at another man since Simon's death. And after that first morning, when he'd fished the chairs out of the pool, she'd seen the wary look he'd given her. She wouldn't blame him if he thought she was a complete nutcase!

On her way back to the car, trying to keep in the shade as much as possible, she felt hot and uncomfortable. The skin on her arms and on the back of her neck was quite pink and tender from yesterday's excursion. Rachel was just about to cross the road when she noticed a small shop with its door wide open. The sign above the window said 'Gelateria.' Thinking that she might as well make the journey worthwhile, she decided to sample some Italian ice cream. It was supposed to be very good.

She sat outside the shop under a green awning and ate the lemon and almond ice. It was delicious and bore no resemblance to anything calling itself ice cream that she'd ever eaten in Ireland. Scraping up the last traces from the bottom of the glass, Rachel decided on a return visit in the near future.

As she got up to leave, a black car drove slowly past the gelateria. There were two things about it that caught her attention. The first was the fact that it seemed to be the only car on the move in the whole of Castel del Piano that lunch-time; the second was its darkened glass windows, making it impossible to see inside. She wondered why anyone would not want to be seen? Unless they were famous and craved anonymity of course. Rachel doubted that anyone *that* famous would bother to hide away in a small, black Golf. Anyway, why go for black? What a mad colour to choose for a car in this heat, she thought. As she hesitated at the edge of the footpath, the car accelerated smoothly away from her. Thoughts of going back to the house for a cool drink and a swim stopped any more speculation about the Volkswagen Golf with the Siena registration.

When she got back to Podere Vecchio, Rachel was greeted by Percy on the path up to the house. He gave short, gruff little meows as he padded towards her over the carpet of fallen chestnut tree flowers. It was obvious that he was delighted to see her back and allowed her to stroke his head and neck. When she tried to continue towards the house, Percy stood firmly on her right foot with his two front feet, while thoughtfully gazing into the middle distance. She crouched down, laughing and petted him again, telling him how handsome he was. It was pleasant there on the path in the dappled shade of the trees. As usual, the air hummed with the clamour of the cicadas. The scent of roses drifted down from the terrace above her.

Just as Rachel was about to remove the surprisingly solid cat from her foot, she felt him stiffen. His tail started to lash from side to side. She looked in the direction in which he was staring, at the long grass at the side of the path. There was the slightest hint of movement. Then the head of a bright green snake appeared, swiftly followed by, what looked like, yards of rippling body. It crossed the path only a few feet from where they watched. To Rachel, the animal seemed to flow over the stony ground without the slightest effort. Its appearance was so unexpected and the colour so vividly green, she felt intrigued rather than alarmed. She thought that it looked almost like a length of slithering green garden hose. A very long length of green garden hose. Percy made no attempt to approach the snake, she was relieved to see. She wondered, was it instinct or had he tangled with one before and learned his lesson? When the snake had disappeared, she lifted him up and, draping him across her shoulder, continued up to the house.

As she turned the key in the lock, she heard the phone ringing. Hurriedly pushing open the door and dropping her handbag onto the table, she picked up the receiver. Percy still lying across her shoulder.

"Hello?" she said, then remembering where she was, added quickly, "*Pronto?*"

There was a short silence, followed by a click.

She replaced the receiver and rubbed her cheek against the side of the cat's soft neck before lowering him gently to the floor. Perhaps her 'hello' had made someone think they'd dialled the wrong number. Well, if it were important, they'd ring again. She'd remember to answer correctly next time.

Rachel went through to the bedroom to change into her swimsuit. For a moment she considered the idea of swimming naked. Then she remembered the dignified Francesco's silent approach of the day before and decided it was not a good idea. After the chairs in the pool incident, if he came and found her cavorting in the nude, he would definitely think that she was mad. She remembered reading somewhere that Italians, especially in the country, were rather rigid in their ideas about what was acceptable and what was considered inappropriate behaviour – especially where women were concerned.

Before slipping into the swimsuit, she looked at her reflection in the long mirror. The slightly distorted glass made her look thinner than she was. Her hips appeared narrower and her breasts smaller. Blotches on its surface made it seem rather like looking at herself through a piece of spotted chiffon. Well defined areas of pink glowed on her arms and neck. All in all, not very attractive, she decided, turning away. Though losing so much weight meant that at least she could indulge herself in the eating department. She thought of the recently enjoyed lemon and almond ice cream and wondered if there was anything similar in the kitchen fridge or perhaps in the freezer downstairs. Caroline had told her to use what she wanted until she'd got her own supplies in.

Having drawn a blank in the search for more ice cream, Rachel settled for a long, ice-filled gin and tonic. Percy followed her out onto the terrace and proceeded to stretch out under the table beside her chair. The hoopoe called again – the same haunting triple call she'd heard before. She wondered if it ever made a mistake and added an extra one or was it always three? Why had it evolved in that particular way? She lay back in the chair, her towel folded to make a cushion behind her head and sipped the cool drink. She watched a couple of large cream and black butterflies hovering around the spiky heads of lavender flowers. They waltzed close to where she sat and the sound their wings made was almost like silk brushing against silk as they spiralled away over the terrace railing. Could they be swallow-tails? she wondered, making a mental note to see if Guy had a book on butterflies. He seemed to have an enormous number of reference books lining the shelves in the larger of the two sitting-rooms at Podere Vecchio.

Both he and Caroline were avid readers, although their tastes were very different. He liked facts; she liked novels. In the past, she'd sometimes lent books to Rachel, who had been surprised at how similar their choice of favourite writers had been. Caroline had always been generous about lending things, whether it was books, clothes or a recipe after Rachel had complimented her on a dessert eaten during one of the Haywoods' lavish dinner parties.

She had found herself thinking about Caroline quite a lot since she'd arrived in Italy. The woman was such a strange mixture – sometimes friendly, sometimes glacial, a combination of generosity and apparent spitefulness, a willingness to occasionally laugh at herself and extreme intolerance when it came to Guy. From what she could remember of the early days of the Haywoods' marriage, Rachel had always thought that Caroline was as much in love with her husband as he was with her.

"He's a dark horse, is my husband," Caroline had confided in her shortly after their marriage, with a smug look.

Rachel had understood from the remark that, while he might not appear to be the epitome of suave manhood, he more than made up for it in other ways. She had been glad for them both.

She speculated as to what might have happened to bring about the change? Had Guy done something to turn his wife against him? It seemed to her that he was a philanderer more in the mind than in practice. But perhaps he had only stayed relatively faithful because the beautiful women he fancied had been put off by his unattractive appearance and sometimes crude manners. Rachel hadn't heard her friend say a kind thing about her husband for years now – and yet he still seemed fond of her.

She gazed towards the chestnut-clad slopes above the garden and reminded herself that no one knew what really went on in another's marriage. She thought of Simon. Sometimes people didn't even know what was going on in their own. Before she could climb back onto the merry-go-round of wondering if Simon had been unfaithful or, if he'd had a sister, why had he hidden the fact, Rachel got up, walked swiftly over to the pool and dived in.

She decided she would be better organised the next day and would go shopping early in the morning. That way, she would avoid the worst of the heat and Angelica could crash and bang around the house in happy isolation.

Rachel spent a lazy afternoon beside the pool, smothered in Factor 20, deeply into the latest novel by Jennifer Johnston, one of her favourite Irish writers. If I ever write a book, I want to write like her, she thought, lazily swatting away a large black bee from the pages of *Two Moons*.

Later that evening, Rollo didn't turn up for his night-time snack of biscuits. So Rachel ended up feeding Percy a double measure. She was growing really quite fond of the stately Siamese. Everywhere she went in the house or garden, Percy shadowed her. If she stayed for more than a few minutes in the same place, he would walk over to her and place both front feet on one or other of her feet. She'd never once seen a cat behave like that and she found it an endearing habit.

Before going to bed that night, she stood on the terrace and called Rollo while she enticingly rattled some of the biscuits in his food bowl – but with no success. Assuming he was off hunting and would use the cat-flap when he'd had enough nightlife, she turned off the outside light, locked the doors and went to bed.

She was woken once in the night by Percy, scratching at her door. When he persisted, she let him in. He immediately jumped up on the bed and went to sleep. Rachel lay awake for some time, amused by the fact that he snored quite loudly. She wondered if it would keep her awake and if she might have to evict him from the bedroom. The next thing she knew, bright light edged the individual slats of the shutters and it was morning.

Chapter Seven

Angelica had already arrived by the time Rachel went through to the kitchen. All the kitchen chairs were stacked outside and the woman was in the middle of washing the tiled floor. No change there, thought Rachel, taking in the heavy frown and wild hair. It looked even spikier today, almost as if she'd stuck her finger into an electric socket by accident while hoovering. Refusing to be put off by her manner, Rachel smiled and greeted her in her best Italian with a 'Good morning' and a 'How are you?'.

The previous evening, she had repeated various phrases over and over again, in the hope that they might come in useful in breaking down Angelica's defences.

The effect was immediate and remarkable. Angelica's face lit up as though a light bulb had been switched on somewhere inside her. She nodded vigorously in Rachel's direction and returned the greeting. Rachel pointed to the dictionary lying on the kitchen table and various pages covered in the notes she had made the day before.

"Non capisco bene Italiano. Io devo studiare."

Again, Angelica nodded, seemingly impressed by Rachel's obvious desire to speak her language.

"Sì, sì!"

She gave another brief smile and returned to her mopping, her face once again taciturn but it seemed to Rachel, with somewhat less of a frown.

Rachel had been surprised at the sweetness of the other's smile – however transient. Obviously, expansiveness was not one of Angelica's traits. She was apparently the sort of person one got to know gradually.

While Rachel prepared the cats' food, she noticed that the woman still banged and crashed a lot but with perhaps less force than on the previous day. She hoped that the other would come to accept her presence and promised herself that she would work hard at the Italian – not just for the sake of peace and quiet at the Haywoods' but to make life easier all round.

Francesco appeared at the far end of the house just as she was finishing her coffee on the terrace. She saw him lean in through the French doors to greet Angelica. Although his end of the conversation was audible from where she sat, it was also completely incomprehensible. It would take a lot more sessions with the dictionary and grammar book before she could begin to understand what was being said.

The conversation lasted several minutes and involved, what sounded like, the man answering quite a few questions. Rachel was pretty sure that she was the subject of that questioning. She wondered whether Francesco had told the woman about finding the chairs in the pool. He raised his hand in a farewell salute to the invisible Angelica and stepped back from the doors.

"Good morning, *signora* Martin," Francesco greeted her as he walked towards her. "No trouble with chairs, no?" he asked, with a slight inclination of his head in the direction of the pool.

She responded to the definite twinkle in his eyes with a smile.

"No trouble at all, Francesco, thank you!" She gestured towards a chair. "Please sit down. You look hot."

"For one minute, thank you." He lowered himself onto the chair and wiped the back of his hand across his perspiring forehead. "All is OK for you? No problems?"

Rachel assured him that there were no problems, except for the fact that Rollo had not come home for his night or morning feed.

Francesco shrugged. "He make . . . how you say? . . . *Fare la caccia?*" Seeing Rachel's blank face, he thought hard. "He is animal . . . so he wishes to kill . . . to . . ."

"To hunt? You think he's gone hunting for small animals?"

"Is possible." He shrugged again.

She could see that Francesco was not in the least interested in Rollo's activities. Hardly surprising when the cat had only been missing for twelve hours, she thought. Having offered him coffee, which he declined, she asked him what work he did, other than helping out the Haywoods.

When he'd finished telling her in his broken English,

with pauses, while he searched his mind for the correct words, she was not surprised that he looked hot.

He got up at six every morning, Francesco said. After a quick breakfast, he was on the road to check out the animals he owned, that were scattered around the area in different locations. He had to feed and water his eight horses, his one hundred and twenty 'sheeps' and oversee the milking of his twenty-six cows. As well as the farming side of his work, he and his mother owned a butcher's shop in Castel del Piano. On top of all of this, Francesco, his mother and his brother and brother's wife also ran a small guesthouse locally.

She noticed that he didn't boast but spoke with quiet pride about his many achievements. His father had died when Francesco was still at school and the family had struggled to make a living. In true Italian fashion, he talked of his seventy-year old mother in almost reverential tones. Rachel got the impression that *Mamma* was quite a force to be reckoned with and that Francesco adored as well as respected the old lady.

As he talked, Rachel found herself watching him closely. She had been too flustered at their first meeting to recognise the fact that there *was* something attractive about him. There was a quiet strength under the unprepossessing exterior. She instinctively felt that he was a good person; the sort of person who, if he liked you, would never let you down. She reckoned that there was more to this stocky, weathered man with his thick mane of black hair that was already streaked with grey, than met the eye.

While they talked, Rachel noticed Angelica walking through the garden in the direction of the horses' drinking trough. She was carrying some over-ripe apples from the kitchen dresser. Rachel had noticed how quickly fruit went off in the heat. The bowl of cherries on the kitchen dresser that looked delicious the day she arrived had been almost inedible forty-eight hours later.

Although she knew from what Caroline had said that Francesco was in his late thirties, he looked older. The lines around his eyes and mouth were already deeply grooved. Rachel noticed that, although he didn't look particularly tired, all his movements were deliberate, as though he were pacing himself for the long day ahead. She asked him if he ever had time for a holiday. Francesco looked amused.

"Una vacanza? Sempre domani! Always, tomorrow!"

Rachel was just wondering if it would seem too pushy if she asked him if he was married when there was a piercing shriek from nearby, immediately followed by a high-pitched wailing that only a woman could make. It seemed to come from the direction in which Angelica had been going a few moments earlier.

Before she had time to get to her feet, Francesco was out of his chair and running across the lawn. Rachel hurried after him, wondering what could have happened to cause anyone to make such a terrible sound.

Francesco's white shirt disappeared into the trees bordering the field in which the horses were kept. Following as fast as she could, she saw that he had turned off the path and cut through the long grass. Fleetingly, Rachel wondered if there were any snakes lurking in the cover of its dried stems as she ran after him. The grass seemed to hiss at her as she pushed her way clumsily through it. She could feel the sun burning through the hair on the crown of her head and sweat beginning to trickle down her face and under her arms.

The wailing had stopped by the time she reached the electric fence by the trough. Angelica was huddled, sobbing against the trunk of an olive tree with her hands covering her face.

She was moaning, repeating the word "*Madonna, Madonna . . .*"

Just beyond the tree, Rachel could see Francesco on one knee with his back to them. He seemed to be trying to untangle something from the electric fence. It looked to Rachel as though the wire had been broken in a couple of places. Wondering how this could have happened, whether it had malfunctioned and the horses escaped, she drew level with Angelica. Just as she put her hand out to touch the woman's shoulder, Francesco turned towards her, his face grim. Beside him hung the limp body of a small grey cat. A piece of the severed electric wire was wound tightly around his neck, so tightly that it cut into its flesh. A trail of ants was already busy in the blood-streaked fur.

Half-blinded by her dash through the sunlight that streamed down outside the deep shade in which she now stood, Rachel took in the grotesque sight in front of her. She felt suddenly cold and nauseated.

While Francesco finished the gruesome task of releasing Rollo from the wire, Rachel led a distraught but now mute

Angelica back to the house, her arm around the other woman. Once in the kitchen, she poured them both a glass of cold water. As she turned towards her, she caught Angelica staring at her with a questioning look, almost as if she expected Rachel to tell her who had killed Rollo and why. Rachel was very near to tears herself but couldn't help being surprised that Angelica, who'd seemed so tough and unapproachable, had reacted in the way she had. She'd not shown any particular interest in either of the cats – at least not when Rachel had been around. What little Italian Rachel had learned seemed to have evaporated, leaving her unable to comfort the woman with words.

She sat beside her at the kitchen table, sipping her water and feeling inadequate. What she really wanted to do was go to her room, shut the door and quietly mourn the little cat who'd been so cheekily independent. The last time she'd seen Rollo was when he'd been teasing Percy on the terrace the day before. He kept making sudden forays from behind a flowerpot, batting at the older cat with a front paw before dashing away again to hide.

As well as being miserable, Rachel was starting to feel alarmed. She looked at Angelica's bowed head and clasped hands and wondered what sort of person would do that to a harmless cat. She thought of what had seemed like a stupidly insignificant prank with the chairs in the pool. Was the same person responsible for both occurrences? If so, where were they at this moment? What would they do next?

Eventually, Francesco reappeared, his hands and shoes smudged with dirt. He went first to Angelica and stood beside her, speaking in a low voice. Rachel didn't know what he said but after a few sentences, the woman looked up and gave him a slight smile. Then he turned his attention to Rachel and motioned towards the sink.

"*Signora*, I make clean my hands?"

"Of course." Rachel's voice sounded choked. "Did you bury Rollo, Francesco?"

"*Sì, signora*. I put him in the ground."

He began to wash his hands, rubbing at the dirt with his strong fingers. Rachel noticed that there were spots of blood on his shirtsleeve. When he had dried his hands, she could see him hesitating, as if he wanted to say something but didn't know how to put it into words. He hung the towel back on its hook and then slowly walked over to the table where the two women watched him in silence.

Looking straight at Rachel, he said, "*Signora*, you know many people in Italy – here in *Toscana*?"

Startled, Rachel replied, "No! I don't know anyone, apart from Mr and Mrs Haywood. Why?"

Choosing his words with obvious care, the man spoke again.

"It never happen like this before." A pause, then, "Only when you come to Podere Vecchio."

"Are you trying to tell me it's because I'm here that this happened?"

Looking straight at her, he said, "*È possibile*. It is possible."

"But I've never been to Italy before. Why should anyone do this? I don't know anyone here," Rachel repeated.

"*Dunque!* Perhaps somebody come who is not a friend of *la signora*."

Feeling that the conversation was taking on the quality of a bad dream, Rachel said, "I haven't *met* anyone since I arrived, apart from Angelica and yourself. Could someone from here have done this – someone in San Lorenzo?"

"Why they do it now – not when *signore* and *signora* 'aywood is here?"

She was uncomfortably aware that they were both studying her closely. They couldn't be blaming her presence in Podere Vecchio for the horror that had just happened, she thought. That was crazy! Rachel was stung into silence.

Francesco started to move towards the garden doors, his expression serious. Resting a brown hand on one of them, he looked back at her.

"*Attenzione, signora!* Think if there is some people who not like you. Perhaps somebody who come from *Irlanda.*"

The idea was so silly Rachel didn't want to even consider the suggestion. She looked at Francesco – so capable, so solidly reliable. Suddenly she didn't want him to leave.

"Will you come back tomorrow, Francesco?"

"I come to see if everything OK. Also to make good again the fence," he said, before stepping out into the glare of the Tuscan morning.

Hurriedly, Angelica got up from the table. Grabbing her purse from a chair by the window, she hurried after him. It was as though she didn't want to be left alone with this woman from Ireland, who seemed to have brought the household such bad luck.

It was well after five before Rachel finally drove to Castel del Piano to do her shopping. She was still feeling shaky as she parked the car under the same lime trees as before. What if whoever was responsible for killing Rollo came back? How could she stop something happening to dear old Percy? For a moment, the thought crossed her mind that she herself might be in danger.

In spite of having dismissed Francesco's comment about someone following her from Ireland, Rachel sat in the car and considered the idea for a moment. What enemies had she made? The only person she could remember having any sort of confrontation with in the recent past was Phyllis Dillon when Rachel told her that she would be leaving Greene and Rowntree. It was hardly likely that the acerbic Ms Dillon had either the time or the inclination to track her down. She could think of several people in the publishing world – and outside it – whom she didn't particularly like and who, as is the way of the world, probably felt the same about her. There was certainly no one she could think of who would be likely to follow her all the way to Italy and kill Rollo in such a cruel manner. She decided she was just being foolish. Perhaps Caroline with her high-handed manner had upset someone locally. What had happened was coincidence and had nothing to do with her own arrival in Podere Vecchio, she told herself firmly.

She got out of the car and walked briskly over to the nearest small vegetable shop. The display of fruit and vegetables both inside and outside was tidily arranged on tiered wooden racks. Glossy aubergines, twice the size of the ones back home, mirrored her face as she bent over to make a choice. Everything here looked so much brighter and bigger and more succulent.

Rachel emerged a good ten minutes later, loaded down with grapes, melon, oranges, tomatoes, lemons, tiny zucchini and aubergines. She'd also bought a large cellophane packet, tied with a red ribbon, of the locally dried porcini mushrooms. Another customer had seen her looking at the shrivelled-looking contents with a doubtful expression and had explained to her in careful English how to soak and prepare them for eating.

"They are a speciality of this part of Tuscany," she said. "You will like them – very delicate, very good! Mmm!"

Then the woman had bunched her fingers together, kissing them enthusiastically and making expansive movements with her hands to show Rachel just how good they were.

In the cake shop she had visited the day before, the woman greeted her warmly. Today, the glass shelves were covered with small, delicious-looking pastries; some topped with miniature marzipan fruit, others with fresh strawberries or golden slices of peach in aspic. In the corner stood a tall, glass-fronted fridge containing various fabulous-looking concoctions: swirls of meringue and pistachio, chocolate and almond confections decorated with rosettes of thick cream. On the top shelf sat a multi-layered cake with chestnut filling oozing invitingly from between the layers – another speciality of the region that had to be tasted.

She watched the woman wrapping each purchase in scalloped waxed paper, embellished in gold with the name of the shop. Then the separate parcels were carefully placed in smart boxes and tied with ribbon so they looked like expensive presents. It was very different from shopping in Moore Street in the rain. Rachel started to feel more cheerful.

By the time she'd visited a baker, a butcher's and a dairy shop with the most enticing collection of cheeses she'd ever seen, she could hardly carry everything back to the car. She had noticed a sign to a cantina just near the turning off to San Lorenzo. That should be a good place to try sampling some of the local wine. She'd do that on her way back to Podere Vecchio, she thought.

As she drove in the direction of San Lorenzo, the feeling of pleasure started to fade. It had been enjoyable to buy food from people who believed that what they sold and ate themselves was important and a subject worthy of lengthy and animated discussion. But the nearer she got to the house, the more the image of Rollo's limp body, hanging from the fence, filled her mind. By the time she reached the turn to the cantina, all she wanted to do was to get back to the farm and check that nothing had happened to Percy.

Chapter Eight

To Rachel's relief, Percy was lying in his favourite spot under the olive tree at the far end of the house. With her arms full of shopping, she couldn't make a fuss of him so she called his name softly, encouraging him to follow her.

As she walked along the path, she found herself checking out the garden to see if any chairs had been rearranged since earlier that morning. An unexpected movement in a flower-bed made her stop suddenly and stare at a patch of lilies. She wasn't sure if it had been a lizard. All of a sudden, a bird fluttered from one branch of a tree to another. The sound made her pause again for a moment, holding her breath. She glanced too at the doors and windows as she went past. Before going out, Rachel had made sure all the shutters were closed. Everything seemed to be all right. What exactly was she looking for? she asked herself, turning the key in the lock.

No sooner had she pushed the door open, than the

telephone began to ring. Dumping the parcels on the table, she hurried through to the sitting-room and answered it.

"*Pronto!*" There was no answer. She tried again, this time slightly louder. "*Pronto!*"

There was a click, and the line went dead.

Rachel made herself lower her tense shoulders as she walked back to the kitchen. She mustn't get into a state. This sort of thing happened in Ireland as well. People were constantly misdialling and then hanging up without bothering to apologise. All the same, her hands were shaking slightly as she undid the ribbons on the elegant white and gold boxes from the cake shop.

Rachel had promised Guy and Caroline that she would water the plants in pots around the terrace and swimming-pool. By seven o'clock, the sun had sunk low enough behind the trees for her to do the job. She liked watering. There wasn't often much need for it during an Irish summer. The sound of the water was soothing as it sprayed gently over the leaves of the geraniums, making them release a slightly acrid scent. She lazily waved the nozzle around in the air, drenching roses and herbs, washing the sun-warmed tiles on the terrace so that everything gave off a damp, hot smell that was almost tropical. Percy watched her from a safe distance, his blue eyes observing her every movement.

As she pulled the hose towards the flowers around the pool, the telephone rang again. For a moment, she was tempted not to answer it. But what if it were Caroline or Guy? She'd been putting off telling them about Rollo but she would have to contact them soon if they didn't get in touch first. Unwillingly, she closed the spigot, letting the hose fall with a thud to the ground and ran inside.

It was the same as before: she answered, there was a silence and then a click as someone at the other end of the line replaced the receiver. Rachel was starting to feel angry as well as alarmed. She was about to take the phone off its hook when it rang again.

Snatching it up, she shouted into the receiver, "I don't know who you are but stop playing bloody stupid games!"

She was about to slam it back down when she heard a surprised woman's voice asking, "Is that the Haywoods' house?"

"I'm so sorry," Rachel blurted. "Yes, it is . . . I . . ."

"Are you all right, my dear?"

The voice was not young and it sounded concerned. The accent was well educated and very English. Rachel tried to speak as normally as possible.

"I'm fine. It's just that some one's been phoning and then hanging up and it's spooked me a bit – that's all. My name's Rachel Martin by the way."

"Yes, I know. Caroline told me that you were looking after things for them while they're away. My name is Eleanor Digby-White, commonly known as Lennie. Not a very distinguished shorter version but much more manageable!"

There was a reassuring lightness in the way she spoke that had an immediate calming effect on the younger woman.

"Do you live nearby?" asked Rachel.

"Very close to you. Douglas and I live just at the turning

off to the cantina on the road in to San Lorenzo. We were thinking of paying you a visit if you're not too busy to entertain a couple of oldies!"

Relief filled her. She tried not to sound too eager as she reassured the woman that she wasn't busy at all and would welcome a visit.

"Would you like to come over now?"

"Well, I just have to change out of my tennis things and have a quick shower and then we'll be with you. See you in about forty minutes. 'Bye!"

Rachel didn't know how old Mrs Digby-White was but the idea of playing tennis, when the temperature was still in the mid-seventies, didn't appeal to her very much.

She went back to finish the watering. Long shadows lay across the surface of the pool now and the garden was quiet. Higher up the hill, the chestnuts were still bathed in the golden evening light.

Before going inside to change into something less crumpled than the dress she'd been wearing all day, Rachel called Percy. Taking his time, he came up to her, giving one of his short, gruff meows before following her into the house.

The Digby-Whites could be heard coming along the path outside the front of the house – or rather Mrs Digby-White could be heard. She seemed to be having a loud and very one-sided conversation. Rachel went out onto the terrace to greet them.

The elderly couple approaching her didn't look as though either of them were in good enough condition to have been running around a tennis court on a hot afternoon. The man was rather stooped, making him a good six inches shorter than his imposing wife, who held herself very erect. They both had white hair and looked to be well into their seventies. Mrs Digby-White had a slight limp, Rachel noticed. She was wearing a brightly coloured dress, covered in a busy purple and green floral pattern and the sort of old-fashioned thick-strapped sandals Rachel's English aunt used to favour twenty years earlier. A bright yellow bandanna held her hair in place, making her look a bit like an eccentric Indian squaw. Her husband's clothes were more low-key: grey slacks and a faded, short-sleeved pink shirt. He also wore sandals but over a pair of grey socks. They climbed the two steps up to the terrace carefully, the woman holding his arm.

As Rachel walked towards them, they both smiled pleasantly at her. The man said something to his wife that made her laugh. She held out a hand to Rachel.

"Douglas just told me that you are the prettiest girl he's set eyes on for days!"

Rachel smiled. "Well, I don't know about that. I've seen some gorgeous-looking women in Castel del Piano today."

"Ah, but my husband has a very short memory. He's a bit like the goldfish in the garden pond. As soon as he sees something new he likes, he gets all excited and forgets what he saw only a couple of minutes before. I think they call it attention-span disorder!" There was affection in her eyes as she glanced at the slightly hunched man at her side. Then she turned back to Rachel. "But he's perfectly right. You *are* very pretty indeed and it's lovely to meet you."

She shook Rachel's hand enthusiastically. There was

real warmth in her voice. The younger woman couldn't help liking her immediately.

"I thought we'd sit outside if you'd like. I've got some dessert wine and a delicious-looking cake from the cake shop in town. I'm so glad you came because I would have felt guilty eating it all on my own."

"What she say?" asked Mr Digby-White, leaning towards his wife.

She shouted into his ear. "We're going to have some cake and wine outside in the garden."

"Oh, splendid!"

Mr Digby-White smiled contentedly and followed the two women over to the table.

"He's very deaf," his wife confided to Rachel as they seated themselves. "Try and shout into his left ear. It's the better one of the two. He absolutely refuses to wear a hearing aid so don't worry if he can't keep up with the conversation. It's his own fault for being such a stubborn old fool!"

Rachel thoroughly enjoyed the evening with Lennie and Douglas as they insisted she call them. At one point, the conversation turned to Ireland, which they had once visited and liked.

"I got the feeling that people still made time for each other over there. Not like what's happened in England. Everyone's far too busy making money to stop and enjoy life and really look and listen to what's going on around them. Very sad really," said Lennie, taking a good swig from her wineglass.

"What's that?" said Douglas.

"I said we both liked Ireland very much. You know, that time we went over to Dublin and then visited your third cousins, twice removed, in Connemara."

"Beautiful place!" agreed her husband. "Nice people too! They talk to each other in trains."

It was obvious that they were devoted to each other, even though Lennie confided in Rachel that her husband had always adored attractive women and old age didn't seem to have dampened his ardour one bit.

"Mind you, it's usually been more a case of him flirting outrageously and enjoying the chase. If he'd actually caught any of them, I suspect he wouldn't have known what to do – with himself or them. At least his triple by-pass has slowed him down a bit!"

"What did you say?" said Douglas, looking at his wife through surprisingly blue eyes.

"I said you were a lecherous old rascal."

"Very true!" replied her husband amicably. "Any more of that delicious cake going?"

Laughing, Rachel cut him a third slice.

Lennie explained that they'd retired to San Lorenzo fifteen years earlier, when Douglas had been given a 'not so golden handshake' by the bank. They'd met Guy and Caroline when the Haywoods had first bought Podere Vecchio. It turned out they knew both Angelica and Francesco.

"She's a funny little one," remarked Lennie. "Not surprising when you think of what she's had to put up with over the years. Her mother died when she was a young child and she's been nothing but a servant to her wretched father and two brothers ever since. They give her a terrible time."

That explained Angelica's taciturn manner. Rachel asked her how well they knew Francesco.

"Oh, we've known him since we first came here. Nice chap. Very reliable. If he says he'll do something for you, you know it'll be done. No messing about! Very unusual in a warm climate!"

"What's that?" asked her husband, leaning precariously to one side.

"I said Francesco's hot stuff," bellowed Lennie. "Very reliable!"

"Couldn't agree more. Extremely nice chap," said Douglas.

It was nearly eleven o'clock when they got up to go. Lennie took Rachel's hand in her own freckled ones, roughened by years of gardening.

"I haven't asked you about the phone calls, my dear. If there's anything bothering you, just give us a ring. Would you like me to pop in for a chat tomorrow afternoon while Douglas is having his siesta? I get the feeling you were very strung-up when we arrived this evening. I might be able to help. I'm a bit psychic. Nothing spectacular but it comes in handy sometimes."

"I'd love you to come," said Rachel. "Thank you very much."

"What she say?" asked Douglas.

"She said 'Good night', dear," said his wife without a

hint of irritation in her voice. "Thank you for the lovely cake and wine, Rachel. See you tomorrow."

As she carried the glasses and plates in from the garden, Rachel started to feel nervous. Where was Percy? She hadn't seen him since Lennie and Douglas arrived at eight o'clock and it was now quarter-past eleven. Her heart sank. If anything happened to him, she'd never forgive herself. Just as she was going out to look for him, the cat appeared. It was almost as though he knew she wanted him to stay close to the house and not go off hunting. After making sure that Percy joined her on the double bed, Rachel slept soundly that night.

She woke early the next day and lay on her back, her hands behind her head, feeling the cat's warm weight against her leg and listening to the birdsong from the garden. It was too early for Angelica. Rachel wondered if the woman would come after what had happened on the previous day. Judging by her hasty departure, she'd given the impression that she thought it would be bad for her health to be around the Irish woman any longer than necessary.

Climbing out of bed, she knew that she couldn't put off getting in touch with Caroline and Guy any longer. As soon as Percy and she had breakfasted, she would ring them and tell them about Rollo.

As it turned out, Caroline was surprisingly sympathetic.

"You poor thing! What a horrible shock for you! It was lucky that Francesco was there to bury him."

"But Caroline, who would *do* such a thing?"

"Oh, some of the locals are a bit strange. You know – inbreeding and incest. It's quite prevalent in some of the smaller towns. I wouldn't put it past one or two people who think they have a claim on the land and that we have no right to live in Podere Vecchio. It's like Ireland still is in some places. Owning a certain scrap of land assumes frightful importance once anyone feels they've been cheated out of it. It doesn't seem to matter if the land is worthless or valuable. It's the principle of the thing. It brings out the worst in them."

"Francesco seems to think that Rollo was killed by someone who had a grudge against me."

Caroline gave a small laugh. "I find that rather hard to believe! What do you think, Rachel?"

"I think it's highly unlikely. I've only been here two minutes."

"Well then! Have you had any visitors yet?" Caroline's tone was casual.

"Yes. The Digby-Whites called in yesterday evening."

"I suppose you realise they're both quite mad. Especially her. Be careful or she'll be reading your tea leaves."

"I thought they were rather nice."

Caroline sounded scornful. "They're not the sort of people we mix with very often. Has anyone else called?"

"Only Francesco."

"I suppose you've guessed that Angelica's madly in love with him! Isn't that hilarious?"

Rachel didn't think it was the least bit hilarious. She was beginning to feel more and more sorry for the girl.

Angelica's life seemed hard enough without her suffering from unrequited love on top of everything else. Having seen the way Francesco talked to the woman in the kitchen after he buried Rollo, Rachel didn't think the feeling was mutual. He had been gentle and sympathetic with her, nothing more.

Angelica still hadn't arrived by ten o'clock. While Rachel tidied the kitchen and washed up, she thought over her conversation with Caroline. Guy had been out when she'd rung. Rachel reckoned that he would be more upset about Rollo than his wife had seemed. She'd seen the little cat allowing Guy to stroke him. When she'd tried, Rollo had skittered away from her and hidden in a flower-bed.

Just as Rachel decided she would have a swim, the phone rang. She picked it up. No one spoke. She stood silently for a moment with the receiver to her ear. She got the impression of traffic noise, muted and distant. Then she hurriedly replaced it and went through to her room to change into her swimsuit.

As she undressed, she fought down a feeling of panic that was threatening to make her run round the house, locking all the doors and windows.

She'd have her swim and then she'd go and look at the monastery that she'd glimpsed through the trees on her way to Castel del Piano. That would take her mind off the phantom caller until Lennie arrived after lunch.

The small road to the monastery climbed through a large olive grove. Rachel noticed black nets under some of the trees. She supposed they were for catching the olives when they were ripe. The track was rough and covered in a layer of dust, like the track down to the river near Podere Vecchio. The sunlight, slanting down amongst the trees, was filtered by the canopy of leaves, speckling the rocky ground in a delicate tracery of shade and light.

After driving for ten minutes, she rounded a corner and, suddenly, the monastery appeared in front of her. It was set on the edge of what looked like a giant cornfield. The walls were honey-coloured, sweeping up to a dome at one end of a large chapel. She guessed that the smaller building to one side must be where the monks lived. One enormous cypress stood near the entrance to the chapel. Rachel thought it must be at least forty feet high – possibly even taller. She wondered how old it was.

As Rachel walked towards the open doors, she could hear unaccompanied singing coming from the building. The sound seemed to float through the hot air. She slipped inside, walking carefully so that her sandals made no sound on the stone floor. Here too, the effect was golden – like the walls outside. Light shone through the clear glazed windows onto the worn stone slabs. A simple altar with a tall wooden crucifix and six candles in unadorned iron candlesticks stood on a raised platform of stone. Arched colonnades ran along each side of the chapel and behind the altar. Above these colonnades there was a gallery. There were no paintings, no flowers – no decoration of any sort. Standing in front of the altar, on either side, twelve, white-robed monks sang their liturgy. Rachel sat down in a pew near the back of the chapel and shut her eyes, letting her thoughts melt into the music.

After a while, she found herself thinking of Simon. Although she felt sad, the ebb and flow of the singing made the sadness bearable. In this lovely, tranquil place, where, apart from the monks, she was the only other person there, she felt strangely detached from her grief. It was almost as if everything that had happened over the past months was diminished by her being there. The feeling of contentment, with all her problems for the moment forgotten, was extraordinarily powerful. She couldn't bring herself to pray – that was something she'd not done since she was a small child, terrified by the idea of spending an eternity in Hell – but she thought that what she was experiencing was probably the next best thing to praying.

When the last echo of chanting died away, she reluctantly made her way out into the midday heat, screwing up her eyes in the intensity of the glare as she fumbled in her bag for her sunglasses.

She took her time driving back to Podere Vecchio, putting off the moment when she knew reality would have to kick in again. She wanted to hold on to her sense of wellbeing for a little while longer.

As she followed the road back to San Lorenzo, she became aware of a car a little distance behind her. The reason she'd noticed it was that any cars she'd seen in her rear-view mirror up until then had always been intent on zooming up to within inches of her back bumper, before overtaking on the first dangerous bend that presented itself. This one, however, seemed to appear out of nowhere and then stay well back from the Audi. The gap between the two cars neither increased nor lessened after travelling for three or four miles. As far as she could make out, it looked like a small, black car.

Rachel was aware that the muscles of her face and neck had become tense. Feeling she was probably being paranoid, she put her foot down, driving as fast as she dared on the twisting road. The black car stayed in the same position. Each time she went into a corner, it was still behind her. Each time Rachel increased her speed on a straight stretch of road, it was there – visible in the rear-view mirror.

Grit sprayed from the verge as she flung the car into the turn for San Lorenzo. Sweating in spite of the air conditioning, she slowed down on the narrower road and looked in the mirror. A black Volkswagen Golf accelerated past the turning. It was impossible to see the driver through the car's darkened glass windows.

Chapter Nine

Rachel glanced at her watch as she hurried along the path up to the house. It was only just after one and Lennie wasn't due until about two. She would stay inside, out of view with the doors locked. She'd make sure Percy stayed with her so that she could keep an eye on him.

What made the hair prickle on the back of her neck when she got back to Podere Vecchio was the white carnation, lying on top of the bonnet of Guy's covered car. The flower was fresh and the stalk had been cleanly cut at a slight angle. She knew that there were no white carnations in the Haywoods' garden. Rachel also knew that the flower had not blown or fallen onto the car. It had been deliberately placed where she would see it on her return. She couldn't bring herself to pick it up. Walking quickly away, she left it lying there.

This meant that not only had she been followed by the black Golf, but also someone else had been in the garden while she was out. Were there two people, determined to make her life a misery? What had she done to deserve this?

Inside the locked house with Percy sleeping unconcernedly on a kitchen chair, Rachel waited for Lennie. She looked at her watch again. Half past one. She was near to tears as she paced back and forwards, her headache getting worse by the minute. A rapping on the front door made her freeze in the middle of the room.

It was too early for Lennie. She doubted it was Francesco. He always went round the house to the French doors in the kitchen. He hadn't come back as he said he would the day Rollo was killed. Rachel felt disappointed and let down by that. Lennie had said how reliable he was. But he was also busy and perhaps he felt that the cat's death, strange and horrible as it was, didn't come top of his list of priorities.

Another rap on the door. If she stayed quiet, perhaps whoever it was would go away. Rachel crept to the window and peered down through the nearly closed shutters to the path below the front of the house. The jasmine was so thick under the window, she could see nothing.

"Hello? Rachel, it's Lennie!"

Rachel realised that she'd been holding her breath. Filled with relief, she ran down the steep steps that led to the front door. Her anxiety made her clumsy as she unhooked the security chain and wrenched the snib off the catch. Eventually, she managed to undo the double locking system that Guy had installed when he'd first arrived at Podere Vecchio. Throwing open the double doors, she stood, flushed and trembling in the opening.

Lennie took one look at her face and quickly stepped inside. Closing the doors behind her, she motioned to Rachel to go back upstairs.

"Don't worry. I'll lock the doors and follow you up."

When she reached the top, Lennie took Rachel by the arm and led her into the sitting-room.

"You sit down there and I'll just open the windows and shutters. It's like an oven in here."

"You came earlier than I expected."

"Yes. I felt you might need me. I've been talking to Francesco. He's doing some checking up and he'll be here later on."

Rachel looked puzzled.

"What sort of checking up?"

"He says that a friend of his has noticed a car hanging around down by the gates." Lennie saw Rachel stiffen. She sank thankfully onto the cushion beside her. "I think you should tell me all about yourself. I want to know why you decided to come here and what happened before you left Ireland." Seeing the doubtful expression on Rachel's face, she continued cheerfully. "Indulge me and we may be able to get to the bottom of why, on a day with the thermometer at eighty, I find you locked inside the house and shaking like a leaf. There are lots of things I'd like to know, including why on earth didn't you tell us about poor Rollo yesterday?"

So Rachel told Lennie about Simon's death and the two sprays of flowers with the attached notes. She told her that, since arriving in Podere Vecchio, chairs had been moved around outside and that some of them had been thrown into the pool. She told her about the numerous silent phone calls. Rachel described how Angelica had discovered Rollo's corpse on the electric fence and that she hadn't wanted to talk about it at the first meeting with Lennie and her husband. She said she'd seen the black car twice; that today, it had followed her as far as the turn off to San Lorenzo. Finally, Rachel told her about finding the white carnation on the bonnet of Guy's car when she got back from visiting the monastery.

Lennie didn't say anything until the young woman had finished. Her eyes never left Rachel's face while she was talking. She'd noticed on the previous evening how drawn the girl looked – and how thin.

Just then, the phone shrilled on the table near them. Rachel gave a start, looked at it and then at Lennie. Seeing her hesitation, Lennie leaned over the end of the couch and picked it up briskly. She listened for a moment. Rachel watched, her whole body tensed, unconsciously leaning slightly back against the cushions, as though wanting to distance herself as much as possible from the instrument. Lennie's wrinkled brown face broke into a sudden smile. Covering the mouthpiece with one hand, she whispered over to Rachel that it was Francesco. Rachel was impressed by the other woman's Italian. She seemed to be completely at ease with it, talking deliberately, with no pauses. Lennie had obviously come to grips with the language but not the accent. She sounded so very English in her pronunciation that, in spite of everything, it made Rachel want to smile.

After a short conversation, Lennie replaced the receiver and turned her attention back to Rachel.

"Well, it seems that the black car is rented from a small garage in Siena. Francesco's cousin in the police has even come up with a name – an Irish woman – a Diana Forde. Does that ring any bells?"

Rachel shook her head.

"I don't know anyone with that name."

"Well, the car's been spotted near the gates by local people several times since Caroline and Guy left on Saturday. Francesco's cousin says that they will keep an eye open for it and they hope to talk to the driver. He says he will come up this evening to finish mending the fence and he'll pop in to make sure you are all right." Lennie regarded Rachel's pale face for a moment and then asked, "*Are* you all right? Or would you like to come and stay with us for a few days until this nonsense blows over?"

Rachel gave her a small smile.

"I'm fine . . . really I am. I'm not usually such a drip. I think it's the combination of the calls, the car and the chairs being moved around on top of Rollo's death. It was just so horribly cruel and senseless. I promised the Haywoods I'd look after the house and their cats and now look what's happened. I really should be able to cope with the other stuff. I'm just being stupid. I'm sorry."

"I don't think you're being the least bit stupid, my dear." Lennie looked at her thoughtfully, "I think that maybe you are right to feel a little alarmed."

"Why do you think that?" asked Rachel, swallowing anxiously.

Lennie opened her battered handbag and produced the white carnation.

"I picked this up on my way past Guy's car. I knew immediately that something was wrong here an hour ago. I had one of 'my strange turns' as my dear and utterly unpsychic husband will insist on calling them. So I came down just after you must have got back. I spent some time in the area surrounding the car." She gave Rachel's knee an encouraging pat, "A lot of people, Caroline included, think I'm a batty old woman. Perhaps I am. Mind you, Douglas maintains they're the best sort to live with. He says he never gets bored when I'm around to surprise him with my weird ways! Anyway, my dear, I did get a strange feeling while I was down by the cars. What's more, there are definitely unhealthy emanations coming from this poor flower that I don't like. I think the person who left it for you to find is . . . well, how shall I put it? . . . a little unsafe perhaps."

"Unsafe?" Rachel tried to keep a slight quaver out of her voice. "By unsafe, do you mean unstable – or just plain dangerous?"

Lennie chose her words with care. "The last thing I want to do is to be melodramatic. Let's just say that I think whoever left it is a little . . . disturbed or unbalanced. If there is a connection between what's been happening here and the driver of the black car, then it will be a good thing if the police can talk to them and find out exactly what is going on. Once that's done, you'd be surprised how it will all seem like a storm in a teacup! Now, how about making me that cup of tea you promised? And how about unlocking the doors and enjoying it out on the terrace?"

They'd taken their tea into the garden, accompanied by Percy.

"It's good that he's taken such a liking to you," remarked Lennie casually as she bent down to stroke him.

"Why?" Rachel spoke more abruptly than she'd meant. "I mean, do you think he's in danger?"

"No, my dear," said Lennie quietly. "I just think it's good for you to have his company. He's obviously taken a liking to you and that's a great compliment coming from a cat like Percy. I've never seen him be particularly friendly to anyone else before – certainly not with Douglas or me."

Lennie made Rachel laugh with stories of how she and her husband had gone about renovating the house in which they now lived. At the beginning, they'd hired a local builder to do the work for them, not knowing that he was renowned in the entire region for his dishonesty and laziness.

"Of course, neither of us could speak much Italian fifteen years ago and so he always had a marvellous excuse to misunderstand us. So when I thought I'd told him to get hold of one lot of materials, he would appear days later with something entirely different. It was all rather wearing! Eventually, we bumped into Francesco and he told us the right man to go to. We lost quite a lot of money we couldn't afford but it all ended well and my Italian improved very quickly in the process. I can now discuss gable-end walls, drains, soffits and barge-boards with the best of them!"

"Are you happy living here?" asked Rachel. "You don't miss England?"

Lennie's eyes wandered over the garden before she replied.

"Douglas hasn't got very much longer to live. The doctors tell us that his cardio-vascular system is more or less kaput. He loves the heat and he has his books and his piano – and me. He's very content. The last thing he needs is the upheaval of moving back to England and the English climate." She chuckled. "And I can't say that either of us relishes the idea of being within reach of a handful of rather dismal and distant relatives. So I shall stay here until he goes and then I shall probably continue to stay put out of sheer sloth." She took a sip of tea and then enquired, "Why do you ask?"

Rachel was struck by how serene this elderly woman was, with the maze of fine lines criss-crossing her face and her untidy hair, just about held in place today by a pair of tortoiseshell combs. Lennie Digby-White appeared to completely accept whatever fate dished up. Rachel supposed that she'd asked the question because, at the moment, she felt so disturbed by what had happened at the Haywoods'. She'd started to wonder if this sort of thing was endemic. Even though she had fallen in love with the countryside and Podere Vecchio in particular, something strange was going on. Although Lennie had managed to make her laugh, Rachel still couldn't stifle her sense of deep unease at the situation in which she found herself.

When the older woman eventually said she ought to go, she repeated the invitation for her to stay with them. But Rachel couldn't help feeling that it would be somehow wrong to leave. She shouldn't just run away – and she *was* supposed to be looking after the house after all. It would be like admitting defeat. The police were on the lookout for the car and Francesco was calling in that evening. She had Lennie's phone number, which was reassuring.

It was odd, but right from the beginning, Rachel had felt strangely at home with Lennie; as if she'd known the other woman all her life.

"I feel as though I've known you for ever," she said impulsively, as they walked down towards Lennie's dented Fiat.

"We were great friends in another time and place. I have a feeling that you saved my life, my dear."

This was so surprising, Rachel was at a loss at what to say. Before she could respond to this extraordinary statement, Lennie gave her a quick kiss on the cheek.

"Remember to ring me if you're bothered about anything at all. I can be with you in a few minutes. And remember too what I said about coming to stay. You'd be more than welcome." She laughed. "Douglas would be in seventh heaven!"

She climbed into her car, swatting a resident wasp out of the window with a casual wave of her hand. It took several attempts before the woman succeeded in getting her door to close properly.

Rachel watched her bump down the driveway. She could just make out, in the travelling veil of dust accompanying the car, an arm that appeared suddenly through the driver's window and gave a brief wave.

For the rest of the afternoon, Rachel kept herself busy. If Angelica wasn't going to make an appearance for a while, she'd better do some housework. After Lennie's visit, she felt more like herself, although she still had flashes of the dead Rollo if she didn't concentrate on the task in hand.

By six o'clock, when she was beginning to run out of steam, she saw Francesco walking past the sitting-room window. He carried a toolbox in one hand and a roll of wire over his shoulder. Determined not to behave like the superstitious Angelica, she went outside and greeted him cheerfully. She was rewarded by an approving smile.

"*Buona sera, signora!* I come to make good the fence."

"Good evening, Francesco." She wondered if she should ask him if there was any more news from his cousin in the police and then decided against it. He would tell her if he had any new information. "Can I help you at all?"

He looked amused. "No, no! Is OK. I manage, thank you."

"Well, when you've finished, come back and have a cold drink."

"Thank you, *signora*."

As he walked away, she wondered if it would be inappropriate to ask him to call her Rachel. At home, anyone doing a job for you usually called you by your first name within five minutes of arriving on the doorstep. It was a habit that always drove her shy mother mad.

"*I* should be the one to decide on whether a person calls me Jean or Mrs Kerrigan – not some creature who's barely left school and who's young enough to be my grandchild," she'd say, thoroughly annoyed.

"What does it matter, if they do the job properly?" Rachel had asked once, amused that her mother should get so worked up about something she considered trivial.

"It's got something to do with good manners, other people's dignity and having one's private space not invaded," her mother had replied firmly. "Unfortunately, the way the world's going, we will soon no doubt be referred to by numbers – like the poor cows. I wouldn't be at all surprised if they stick ear-tags on us next!"

Rachel remembered that she had been taken aback by how strongly her mother felt on the subject.

Although his manner was formal, Francesco had a way of looking at her that made Rachel wish she'd had time to at least comb her hair and wash her face with cold water. She felt hot and sticky after her sweeping and hoovering. But it would look too obvious if she disappeared and changed into something less limp now. However, she could have a wash and do something about her hair. As she went inside, Rachel realised that, for the first time since Simon's death, she was bothering about whether a man found her attractive or not. She felt first of all stupid and then a little shocked. Then she told herself that to be shocked was pretty foolish. As if Simon were in any fit state to care what she said or did or, indeed, to mind how she looked. Suddenly, it seemed as though he had died a lifetime ago. She had never experienced the comforting feeling of his being somewhere close by – like some people said they did when a loved one had died.

As she dried her face, Rachel asked herself if the woman in the black car could possibly have anything to do with her dead husband. What was the name Lennie had told her? Diana Somebody-or-other? She was absolutely sure she'd never heard it before.

113

Feeling a little more presentable after the wash and brush-up, Rachel squeezed fresh oranges and a lemon into a jug of lime and Perrier water. She mixed in plenty of ice and decorated it with leaves of mint and borage flowers. Putting out glasses and a plate of savoury biscuits, bought the day before, she carried the tray into the garden and sat down on the terrace to wait for Francesco.

Percy was hunting a lizard by the pool. She watched him as he crouched beside a pot of frilly-edged pink and white geraniums. He was totally immobile, except for the tiniest twitch at the end of his dark chocolate tail. Her eyes strayed to the roses at the far side of the pool. There were some really beautiful ones that were the deepest red, side by side with an abundantly flowering rose of the palest apricot. As she admired them, Rachel suddenly became aware that, out of the corner of her eye, something pale moved under the trees behind the far rose-beds. She quickly turned her head and was just in time to see a shape withdraw into a swathe of bamboo. Rachel heard the dry, rustling sound it made as it parted and closed behind the figure. She looked again. Nothing was visible but she'd definitely seen someone standing there, watching her, a second before.

Fighting down the desire to immediately bellow as loudly as she could for Francesco, she walked as calmly as she was able in the direction of where he was working. The minute it took to reach him felt like an age. As she approached, he looked up. As soon as he saw her agitated face, he let go of the fencing post and moved towards her.

"*Signora?* What is wrong?"

"Francesco, there's a man down by the swimming-pool. I saw him just now. He's hiding in the trees. I know I saw someone there!" she insisted, fearing that he would think her imagination had got the better of her.

Without any hesitation, he said, "Come! Show to me where is the man."

When they reached the spot where Rachel had seen the man slip in between the striped stems of bamboo, Francesco glanced at her, putting his finger up to his lips. Then he too slid through the whispering curtain and disappeared from view.

For several minutes, she heard nothing: no footsteps, no rustling of leaves, no sounds of fleeing or of pursuit. Then there was a sudden shout and a noise of running feet. She stayed rooted to the spot, straining to work out in which direction they were going.

All of a sudden, there was the sound of someone approaching and a snapping of branches. The bamboo parted and Francesco reappeared, holding tightly on to the shoulder of a pale-faced man in mud-coloured shorts and shirt. The first thing that struck Rachel was the haunted look in the man's eyes. He was panting. His brown hair was streaked with sweat and a bramble had made a long scratch like a slash from a red biro down the side of his narrow face.

Francesco shook him none too gently, then fired several sentences at him in Italian. The man ignored him. The only thing that seemed to be of interest to him was Rachel. He stared at her intently, refusing to answer the increasingly infuriated Francesco's questions. Francesco shook him again – this time more roughly. Still the man stayed mute, his eyes boring into Rachel. As she looked at him, she wondered if it were he who had been responsible for leaving the carnation. Had this rather miserable, scrawny specimen of manhood crept into the garden in the middle of the night to throw chairs into the pool? Why? And, more importantly, who was he?

With a sudden movement, the man drew forward his right leg and kicked back hard against Francesco's shins. Knocked off balance, Francesco gave a grunt of pain and let go of the other's shoulder. Before he had time to renew his grip, the man was running like a hare along the poolside and over the grass. By the time Francesco had started after him, he had reached the house. Rachel watched, stunned, as first one and then the other disappeared out of sight around the end of the building.

Eventually, she saw Francesco making his way back towards her, breathing hard and shaking his head.

"*Mi dispiace, signora*. Sorry! He too fast."

"Don't worry, Francesco. You gave him a fright. I'm sure he won't come back." He didn't look as if he'd understood her. "It's OK. Really it is."

She smiled at him but even as she smiled, Rachel knew that she was more alarmed now than she'd been before this latest incident had happened. The man had looked at her in such a strange way – intent and yet somehow dispassionate – the way a hunter might sum up an animal before delivering the *coup de grâce*. Even Francesco being there didn't stem the flow of panic she felt rising inside her like a tide of acid.

Sensing her distress, he moved nearer to her.

"Come!" he said, taking her gently but firmly by the arm. "You sit and take some cold drink. Then the *signora* feel more calm."

She didn't argue but let him guide her back over the grass to the terrace. The feeling of his hand on her arm was reassuring and, she had to admit, pleasurable.

Chapter Ten

The storm started at one in the morning. Rachel heard the first stirrings of the trees below her window as she lay in bed, annoyed at how awake she felt. It sounded like the sea.

She got up to check a shutter that was rattling somewhere in the house. The temperature had dropped quite considerably and for the first time in a week, she felt chilly. A sudden flash of lightning lit up the kitchen. It was followed by a loud clap of thunder that sounded as though it was immediately over her head. Percy, who'd followed her through from the bedroom, made an uncharacteristically undignified dive underneath the dresser. No amount of cajoling would convince him to come out.

Hugging herself, Rachel stared into the garden through the French doors. She wished they had shutters on them or at least curtains to block out the scene outside. The

118

brilliant white flashes lit up the terrace. For second time since her arrival, it seemed to take on the appearance of a stage with the table and chairs in readiness for the actors. Olive trees danced in a swaying backdrop beyond. Although she'd not put on any lights, all of a sudden, she felt terribly exposed in the flickering glare. It was almost like being too close to a malfunctioning giant neon light.

She decided the best thing to do would be to make herself a cup of tea. There was no point in going back to bed. Sleep had evaded her before the storm started. No way would she be able to drop off in this racket. She smiled slightly to herself as she put the kettle on the hob. Why did the Irish always think that making a cup of tea was a cure for all problems – even storms?

As she pulled on jeans and a sweater, she remembered how kind Francesco had been earlier on. He'd stayed for nearly two hours, walking the boundary with her, showing her the carefully mended electric fence and checking through the surrounding woods for signs of the intruder. Then he'd sat at the kitchen table and told her a little more about his work. He talked of his horses with such passion that Rachel was intrigued and forgot how frightened she'd been.

"The most beautiful animals in the world," he insisted. "I win *il primo premio* many times with my Constanza. She *very* fine horse. So strong! Plenty *coraggio!*"

Rachel found herself wondering if he ever talked about a woman with such fire in his eyes. He liked women well enough. She'd seen the way he often looked at her but it seemed as though it was always with a detached sort of regard; certainly fairly well down on the Richter scale of true interest and arousal.

It transpired that Francesco was unmarried. From what he told her, a wife wouldn't get a look in. It seemed that all his remarkable energies were directed into his horses, his other work and keeping in Mamma's good books. Reading between the lines, his mother sounded rather a handful.

"There is sometimes problem with my brother, brother's wife and *mia madre*," he admitted to her with a rueful smile. "Is not always so easy!"

"You all live together?"

"*Certo!*" He looked surprised. "Mamma is not happy for her sons to go away. She like very much the children of my brother also. *Problemi, sempre problemi nella casa,*" he added with a laugh.

She thought he seemed very content with his life, even if there were 'always problems at home'.

Eventually, he'd gone, telling her that he would call back in the morning and would close the gates behind him now. They were normally left wide open but it might make '*signora Martin più sicura*' – feel more secure.

In fact, Rachel was feeling far from secure, even though Francesco had warned her of an impending storm, saying that with 'plenty rain' the man was not likely to be standing around in the garden during the night. She'd pretended that she agreed with him and had no need to be worried. Even as she reassured him, she could still see the intruder's pale blue eyes boring into hers with disturbing intensity.

She had sat for hours, watching, or trying to watch,

Italian television. Channel after channel seemed to transmit nothing but audiences participating in mindless game shows. Reading had not made her feel any less nervous. She found that she kept going into the unshuttered kitchen, to look out into the garden, to check if there was any sign of the pale-faced watcher among the trees.

Now, as she sat, nursing her mug of tea, legs curled under her on the sofa in the bigger of the two sitting rooms, Rachel found herself wishing that she hadn't let her pride get the better of her. What an idiot! Why the hell hadn't she accepted Lennie's offer to stay?

There was a particularly loud crackle of lightning, followed instantly by a deafening thunderclap and the lamp on the table beside her flickered and went out. For a moment, she stayed motionless, numbed by the sheer force of the storm. The feeling of being completely alone was frightening. Rachel reached out for the phone, tentative fingers probing the darkness until she found the receiver. It was the middle of the night but Lennie had told her to ring at 'any time'. She then remembered that the number was jotted down on a slip of paper in the kitchen. About to put the receiver back, she realised she couldn't hear the dialling tone. Rachel put it to her ear again and listened. The line was dead. Shivering involuntarily, she got up and, groping around with two hands, she managed to replace it. Was this because of the storm? Or had the line been deliberately cut?

The rain started so unexpectedly, the roof seemed to be under attack – as if the contents of a whole dam had been suddenly tipped out on top of the house and surrounding garden. One moment, all she could hear was the trees thrashing around in the wind and the thunder; the next, a whole new dimension had been added to Mother Nature's arsenal. The drumming sound was so loud, Rachel could hardly hear her own thoughts.

However, the rain didn't quite block out Percy's plaintive meow from somewhere near the door. She called him and was comforted by the feeling of his soft coat touching her leg, then the pressure of his weight on her right foot. Sitting down, she picked him up and held him close to her. But Percy didn't seem to want to be held. He struggled determinedly until she released him back onto the ground where he again meowed. Reluctantly getting up again, Rachel followed the cat's progress from one room to another, guided by his increasingly persistent yowls until he reached the top of the stairs. She'd put the catch onto the cat-flap to stop him going out at night and perhaps coming to grief like Rollo. He certainly seemed to want to be let out now – rain or no rain, storm or no storm.

Awkwardly, Rachel felt her way down the steep stairs and undid the catch. Percy, ears back, tail twitching, hesitated a moment, then vanished through the opening into the roaring darkness outside.

At regular intervals in what remained of the night, Rachel opened the kitchen window that looked down onto the front garden and called the cat. As the hours went by, the thunder and lightning died down to the occasional rumble and flicker over the distant hills. The torrential rain continued unabated.

She'd wrapped herself in a blanket from the wardrobe in her room and dozed fitfully and uncomfortably on one of the couches. A little while after half past five, Rachel got up. She felt stiff as she walked to the window. Looking out into the grey curtain of rain, she stretched her arms and rolled her head around in an effort to loosen the muscles. The wind had dropped but the rain all but obliterated any object further than the nearest trees. There was no sign of Percy. He hadn't come in through the cat-flap or there would have been telltale footmarks and anyway, if he'd come back, she was sure he'd have come straight to her.

She tried the light switch by the kitchen door. There was still no current. Thank goodness that the stove was gas. Rachel decided she couldn't wait any longer before she tried to find the Siamese but at least she'd be able to make herself a cup of coffee when she got back. She might even light the fire in the kitchen to make things a little more cosy.

Unhooking a waterproof jacket from the stand, she put it on. She unlocked the French doors and stepped out into the wet, thankful that it was daylight now. If you could call it that – everything looked so dismal in the half-light that filtered through the low clouds shrouding the top of the hill. Closing the doors behind her, she decided to make a circuit of the house before searching further afield.

She splashed her way round to the end of the building. There, the steps down to the lower part of the house were awash with water. It had gouged out a channel in the path at the bottom and a small stream now snaked its way down to the fig-trees. Somewhere in the oaks and chestnuts beneath the house, she could hear the sound of cascading water where yesterday had been silence. She hoped the horses had found enough shelter to protect them from the worst of the storm.

As she started to wade past Percy's favourite olive tree, Rachel spotted a padlock lying in a puddle at the edge of one of the flowerbeds. She bent over and picked it up. It was broken, with a short length of chain still attached to it. Nervously, she peered at the old door in the end wall of the house. Even from where she stood, with rain dripping from her hood, Rachel could see that the padlock was missing and the door stood slightly open. Her heart missed a beat. She knew that, before going out the day before, she'd locked the kitchen doors behind her and checked all the outside doors carefully: the main double doors in the front that were locked on the inside and the one at each gable end that led into the storerooms. She also knew that, yesterday, both of them had been securely padlocked.

Her instinct was to turn and run – but what if Percy was inside one of the shadowy rooms and for some reason couldn't get back out? As quietly as she could, Rachel pushed open the door and stood for a moment on the stone threshold. She started to shake from a mixture of cold and fear. It was so dark inside, she could hardly see anything at all. As her eyes became accustomed to the gloom, she took a tentative step and then another into the first room. In here, the sound of rain was less deafening. Through a narrow, arched window to her left, she could see the leaves of plants quivering as they were battered by the constant stream of water.

Cautiously, she approached the first archway, looking to

left and right as she went. Nothing had been moved or disturbed as far as she could make out. Leaning forward, Rachel peered around the rough edges of the wall. A sudden low growl made her stop abruptly, heart thumping. The sound was repeated, this time more loudly. Her eyes searched the shadows for the source of the menacing growling. It seemed to be coming from somewhere above her. She twisted around and looked up.

Crouched on a small section of shelving in between the antique farming equipment, was a wild-eyed Percy with his fur standing on end. He looked twice his normal size. The cat was staring at something to her right.

Just as she was in the process of turning her head, an arm shot out of nowhere and caught her around her neck. For a moment, she could hardly breathe. The sleeve was unpleasantly wet against her skin. She could smell the sour reek of an unwashed male body as she was pulled back against the other's chest. The man was breathing rapidly. The exhaled air from him tickled the side of her neck unpleasantly. What was it she'd once read? she thought frantically. If you are attacked, go limp and lull your attacker into a false sense of security before trying to break free. Rachel did her best to give an imitation of a rag-doll, as though she'd just fainted from shock.

Immediately, the hold around her neck was loosened. She managed to force herself to wait a couple of seconds before spinning round and pushing against her attacker's chest with all her strength.

Released, Rachel backed away from the figure in front of her. Grabbing the first thing within reach, a rusting fork lying against the wall beside her, she pointed it at the man.

"You move and I'll stick this into you," she yelled at him, making violent jabbing movements with the fork.

Her yelling and threatening mime with the implement had an instant effect. The man's hands dropped to his sides as he flattened himself against the clutter of woven baskets hanging behind him.

Rachel, still breathing hard, looked at him carefully. Even in the dim light of the storeroom she could tell that it was the same man who had frightened her in the garden the day before. His previously pale brown shirt and trousers were so sodden that they looked almost black now and clung to his thin frame. The scarlet scratch down the side of his face showed up clearly in the poor light. He seemed to be shivering with fright as much as with the cold. In fact, she thought he looked more terrified of her than she was of him. Rachel lowered the fork slightly.

"Who are you?" she demanded in a quieter voice.

He didn't answer; just stared at her with his pale blue eyes. Then he gave a quick glance in the direction of the archway beside them. Rachel immediately raised the fork and her voice.

"You needn't imagine I won't use this if you try anything. You're not moving until I find out who you are and what you are doing here. So, don't think about running away again because, I swear to God, you'll regret it."

Just for a moment, Rachel was rather surprised and appalled at the surge of violence she felt towards the interloper.

She sounded so vehement, the man pressed himself

back even harder against the baskets so that they creaked and rustled behind him. Rachel noticed that his eyes kept flickering from her face, to the fork, to the cat and back again. She heard Percy shift on the shelf above her, dislodging a shower of pellets of rat droppings and chunks of plaster. Calling to him softly, Rachel kept her eyes glued to the shaking man in front of her. She could hear the cat making his way along the shelf. As Percy moved, the man's shivering seemed to increase and a look of horror spread over his face as he watched the animal edge his way past the stacked flowerpots and tins.

In spite of the bizarre situation, Rachel found herself watching the stranger, fascinated. When the cat eventually dropped to the floor beside her, he flinched as though a poisonous snake had just materialised in front of him. He gave her a beseeching look. She watched him carefully, fork still poised.

"What's the matter?"

For the first time he spoke, eyes darting from her face to the cat.

"Please, send it away."

So, he was able to speak after all! She immediately recognised his accent as Irish – perhaps, she thought, from Donegal. His voice was unusually pitched – rather high, like a woman's. His fear made the man speak softly and it was difficult for her to hear him clearly. Rachel stared back at him. He swallowed hard and made a slight movement with his head in the direction of Percy.

"Make him go. Please!"

Rachel didn't know what to do next. The man was

obviously scared to death of Percy, who was now hiding behind her legs. Every now and then, the animal let out a small growl. If the man was frightened of the cat, he in turn must have scared Percy into behaving like this. For him to be hiding on the shelf made her suspect he had been chased or threatened. Rachel had never seen him look or sound the way he had a few minutes ago. If she turned her attention to Percy, then the man would make a break for it. She was sure of that.

Playing for time, she stood her ground, trying to look thoroughly in command of the situation. What could she do with this wretched creature, who had a look about him that was more frightened boy than adult man?

"Why were you in the garden yesterday afternoon?" she demanded.

Unwillingly, he raised his eyes to her face.

"I wanted to see you."

"Why?"

"I needed to see you better."

"What do you mean, 'better'? Had you seen me before somewhere?"

He nodded slightly.

"Where?"

"When you were shopping in the town."

"Where were you?" He didn't reply. Rachel raised her voice. "I said, where were you?"

"In the car."

"A black car with darkened windows?"

He nodded slightly again. Rachel knew instinctively that he'd not been the driver of the car.

"Who was with you in the car?"

He stayed silent, lips compressed, his mouth forming an obstinate line.

"Were you following me?"

The man's eyes slid away from her to where Percy lurked, half-hidden behind her. He obviously wasn't prepared to answer that question either. Rachel tried again.

"Do you know my name?"

"It's Rachel," he said quickly.

"So, if you know my name, it's only fair that you tell me yours."

For a moment, the man's eyelids descended and his eyebrows drew together in a slight frown. He looked, Rachel thought, like someone who was incapable of spontaneous response. It was as though he were checking his mind to see if his instructions allowed him to divulge his name. She wondered if he was completely normal.

After a pause, he opened his eyes and said, almost in a whisper, "Frank."

Rachel was relieved. Part of her fear up until now had sprung from the fact that, whoever was watching her, had been an unknown quantity. Now that she could see him up close and knew his name, he suddenly seemed less threatening. She lowered the fork slightly.

"Right, Frank. I don't think this is a good place to talk. If I take you up to the kitchen, do you promise not to do anything, like trying to escape – or throttling me? My neck still hurts from when you grabbed me."

His look of instant remorse made Rachel pretty sure that he had not meant to cause her any harm.

Almost timidly, he said, "I'm sorry, so I am."

"Well then, I will trust you. Walk ahead of me and we'll go inside and see about getting you a hot drink." Then she added, "But if you try to make a run for it, I promise I'll stick this into you."

Before moving, the man hesitated, as if puzzled at her trust, his eyes searching her face as though he were trying to work out what sort of a person she was and if she really meant what she said. Rachel indicated the way with a wave of the fork. After another nervous glance at Percy, he started to stumble towards the outer door.

Chapter Eleven

Sitting at the kitchen table, Rachel watched the man called Frank drink his tea. He held the mug with both hands and made sucking noises as he thirstily gulped it down. His hands and nails were dirty and there were a couple of rips in his shirt that looked as though they could have been made when he was trying to get away from Francesco the day before.

Rachel lit the wood-burning stove in the kitchen and sat him down at the table as close to it as possible, with the result that his clothes now steamed in its heat. The unwashed, acid smell she noticed when he had pinioned her with his arm reached her in unwelcome waves. She gave him a towel and suggested he dry his hair but he seemed happy to leave it the way it was. He'd fidgeted around with it while she made the tea and now it lay across his knees, unused.

She found herself examining the man's face. There was

something about it that was familiar and yet she was
certain that, until she'd seen him in the garden the
previous day, she had never set eyes on him before. Still,
there was something about the shape of the nose, the slight
hollow in the chin, even the hairline that she recognised
from somewhere or sometime in the past. It made an
already strange situation even more disquieting. And after
the fright he'd given her in the storeroom, she still couldn't
think straight.

He had refused to sit down until Percy was banished
from the kitchen. When Rachel had shooed the cat into
the next room and shut the door, she asked what is was
about cats that made him afraid. He looked surprised by her
question.

In his almost woman's voice, he replied, "They're evil
creatures, so they are."

"Evil?" she queried.

He would say no more on the subject, just shaking his
head and staring at her.

Rachel returned to asking him why he had been standing
in the garden, watching her on the previous day. When he
refused to answer, she became angry. After all, he was
obviously in league with the person in the black car and
even if he was only doing as he was told, he was hardly
innocent. He must know something.

She leaned forward with a sudden movement, clenching
her hands so that her nails dug into the palms.

"You had no right to spy on me like that. The police are
looking for you, you know."

He paused in the middle of draining the mug and

withdrew it from his lips. Then he held it in midair with his mouth still open, lips unpleasantly wet-looking. If he hadn't been so pathetic, Rachel could almost have laughed – he looked so ridiculous. But seeing him like that, she suddenly didn't want to make him any more upset than he already was.

"It's all right," she said in a gentler voice. She sat back slightly in her chair. Lacing her hands around her mug to warm them, she added, "They don't know you're here. But they are keeping a look-out for the car."

He said nothing as he slowly lowered the mug to the table. She noticed that his hand trembled as he put it down.

Rachel wondered what it was exactly that made her feel sorry for him. Was it because there was something simple and vulnerable about him as he sat there in the grey morning light, in his half-dry clothes with his hair still plastered down against his narrow head? Was it those pale eyes that seemed so full of doubt and anguish? She thought that he didn't look like the sort of person who was equipped to deal with the tough world outside.

A gust of wind buffeted the chimney and a log shifted noisily in the stove, making a flurry of sparks. The man flinched as though the sound were unbearably loud. He looked, she thought, like a frightened wild animal, always listening for and scenting danger, always on the verge of taking flight. She reminded herself that wild animals, when cornered, had a habit of becoming dangerous.

It was his fear that made her decide that he posed no real threat. Indeed, out of the two of them, he seemed to be the weaker.

Rachel stirred some sugar into her tea, allowing herself to relax a little in the heat from the fire. The feeling of panic at how she could get in touch with the outside world began to fade. If only she could somehow persuade him to tell her about the driver of the car.

She smiled at him. "Look . . . Frank, I don't want to upset you. You will be free to go as soon as the rain stops – if you promise not to come back. But you *must* tell me about the other person in the car." She looked at him encouragingly. "You know, it's not nice to be followed or watched. It made me feel frightened. Especially when I found things moved around in the garden during the night. Did you throw the chairs into the swimming pool?"

He quickly lowered his eyes, avoiding her gaze.

Then he said, in a whisper, "I didn't mean to frighten you, honest!"

"So, why did you do it? Why did you put the flower on top of the car? It *was* you, wasn't it? *Why?*" Rachel's voice rose slightly as she leaned towards him, agitated.

He flinched again. His left hand moved up to his mouth, like a child that is afraid of giving the wrong answer to a difficult question.

Briefly, he looked straight at her, then he blurted out, "Di said I had to put the flower on the car. She said I had to or she'd make sure I went back in."

"Who is Di?" she persisted, at the same time wondering what he meant by going 'back in'. Surely to God he hadn't escaped from prison?

For a moment, she thought he wasn't going to answer, then in a troubled voice, he said, "Di's my sister."

Rachel remembered what Francesco had told Lennie over the 'phone about the car having been hired out to a Diana somebody-or-other. Suddenly she remembered the signature accompanying the two lots of flowers that had been left on Simon's grave. Both cards had been signed with the letter D.

Telling herself that she must not sound aggressive, she asked, "Do you always do as your sister tells you?"

Frank frowned at the empty mug in front of him for a moment, pondering the question.

"Mostly I do."

"Is your sister a lot older than you?"

"Ah, no!" he beamed at her, his whole face lighting up suddenly. "We're twins, so we are! Mammy said I came first though." The fleeting expression of satisfaction disappeared as he added, "Di forgets I'm thirty years old too." His face clouded. " She's always telling me what to do."

"And you don't like that?"

"I do not!" This was said with an emphatic shake of the head. "She thinks she's so clever, so she does. Knows it all does my sister."

For a moment, Rachel caught a look of real anger in the blue eyes that was masked by him hurriedly turning his head away as if he realised he'd dropped his guard. Instinctively, she understood that she had to exploit this sibling rivalry if she was to find out more.

Rachel glanced at her watch and then out of the window. Half past six and the rain seemed finally to be easing off.

"Would you like another cup of tea, Frank?"

"Aye, if it's not too much trouble."

"No trouble at all," she replied, getting up from the table.

The effects of a sleepless night were catching up on her and she was beginning to feel really tired now. She told herself that she had to keep her wits about her. She must not let him off the hook. One way or another, he had to tell her more about this sister of his.

Rachel kept him in view as she boiled the kettle and made a fresh pot of tea. Frank swivelled round in his chair so that he faced the fire. He looked much less tense. She noticed that the tremor in his hands, as he held them out towards the heat, had almost disappeared.

She turned off the gas and carried the pot over to the table.

"Are you feeling warmer now?"

"Thanks. I am." As she poured out the tea, he looked up at her and said in a timid voice, "You're a nice woman."

The compliment took her by surprise.

"I only gave you some tea and lit the fire to warm you up. That's not much."

"I didn't mean to frighten you, you know."

She smiled slightly.

"I know that now, Frank. I'd just like you to tell me why you were in the garden and why you broke into the room downstairs." She sat down again, giving him an encouraging smile. "I want to understand, that's all."

He was looking worried again, as though he wanted to tell her more but was afraid. His sister must have tremendous power over him, she thought.

Pointing in the direction of the garden and speaking softly, Rachel said, "Look, Frank! The rain's nearly stopped.

You'll be able to leave soon. But first, you must tell me why your sister asked you to do these crazy things. I need to know. I really do."

Perhaps it was the gentle tone of voice or the wording of the request that made the man's eyes suddenly brim with unexpected tears. Although taken aback, Rachel stayed silent, waiting for him to answer.

"Di said that you're wicked. She said you had to learn to be sorry for what you did," he said in a voice, so choked with emotion, she could barely make out what he was saying.

She stared at him. "What have I ever done to you or your sister?"

He looked at her accusingly. His voice grew suddenly louder.

"You know!"

"I most certainly do not!"

"You married *him*, so you did."

For a moment, Rachel looked blank. He means Simon, she thought. Why on earth would being married to Simon be a crime?

"You *are* talking about Simon, my husband?"

He gave her a swift sideways look that was impossible to interpret.

"He's gone now. It's just you – on your own. You're the only one left, so you are."

A frisson of fear travelled down Rachel's spine. Perhaps he had escaped from prison and in spite of his appearance, was dangerous. Suddenly she remembered Rollo's body dangling from the electric fence.

Even though she was aware that she should be careful, Rachel found she couldn't stop her voice from sounding accusing and angry.

"Did *you* kill the cat? Was it you who did that horrible thing?"

An ugly red flush spread over the man's face. There was a clatter as he dropped his nearly full mug onto the teapot on the wooden table. The next moment, he was on his feet, shouting, waving his arms in the air like a mad thing.

"She told me to do it. Di said I had to do it. I didn't want to. But the things she said . . . terrible things . . . Di told me I'd feel better after. It was all part of the plan. Anyway, cats are evil . . . creatures of the devil. She said it had to be like that. She said you had to be shown that she meant business."

He was yelling at the top of his voice now. Sweat poured off his face and neck, down onto the partially dried shirt. Frank's chair toppled over with a loud crash as he backed away from the table. His eyes looked glazed. Rachel realised that he had lost control and immediately she was paralysed with fear. She could feel the blood draining away from her face and, all of a sudden, she felt extremely cold. The other, gentler Frank had been replaced by this gesticulating, panting creature, who looked as though, at any moment, he would attack her. I must do something, she thought frantically. But Rachel found she couldn't move. It was like being glued to her chair. The only thing half-functioning was her mind – and even that didn't seem to be of any help to her.

Then he stopped shouting. All she could hear was the sound of his breathing that seemed to erupt from him in gasping sobs. Dear God! she thought to herself, he's going to kill me. As the man started to move along the other side of the table, his eyes staring through rather than at her, Rachel watched, terrified and fascinated like an animal trapped in the headlights of an approaching car. She knew that she had no chance of getting away. He was now between her and the closed doors. She was helpless, frozen; her feet and hands strangely leaden. By the time Frank had reached the other end, she had almost resigned herself to inevitable death. Even if she could find the strength, there was no time to grab anything to use as a weapon. All the heavy saucepans were out of reach and the kitchen knives were tidied away into the drawer. She found herself muttering the words of a half-remembered prayer.

She involuntarily spoke out loud. "Holy Mary, mother of God . . ."

Frank halted for a moment, his face slightly tilted to one side, curious.

She searched her mind for something that might make him back off. The words of the prayer seemed to have stopped his approach – for the moment. Perhaps he had been brought up as a good Catholic boy. But Rachel's confused brain refused to allow her to dredge up other prayers that she'd once known by heart as a small child.

As she desperately searched her mind for the right phrase or even just a word, there was the sound of a man's voice calling from the front path that ran beneath the kitchen window.

The effect of the call was immediate. Without hesitation, Frank spun round and started to run, wrenching open the doors into the garden and bursting out onto the terrace so fast, she hardly saw him go. Rachel could hear his footsteps pounding across the terrace – and then silence.

Suddenly dizzy, she collapsed into her chair and slumped forwards, supporting her head in her hands. She didn't feel the lukewarm drips falling into her lap from the small river of tea that flowed from Frank's fallen mug. All that mattered was that he had gone.

She was still shaking when Francesco walked through the open doors.

It took a little time before Rachel was able to explain to him what had taken place during the previous hour. He listened carefully while she described finding the broken padlock, the opened door and the terrified cat. When she told him how Frank had grabbed her round her neck, his look of concern changed to anger.

"But why you go inside when you see the door open? Is very dangerous for you to do this."

She liked the fact that he was so anxious. She smiled wearily at him, feeling better by the second. Francesco had that effect on you, she thought. There was something so good and solid about him that she began to forget that only a little while earlier she had feared for her life.

"I was worried about Percy. Especially after what had happened to Rollo."

He looked at her, incredulous.

"So, you do this dangerous . . . foolish thing because of a *cat*?"

"Yes!" said Rachel, annoyed that he seemed to be

missing the point completely. She added irritably, "Where I come from, animals matter."

"In Italy animals matter – *if* they are useful. You should not put yourself in danger like that, *signora*."

Again, Rachel wished he would call her by her first name. Perhaps, if she'd given in to her impulse to sob on his shoulder when he had come into the kitchen, he would be calling her Rachel by now. On the other hand, as she looked at Francesco, Rachel thought that, if she had thrown herself into his arms and sobbed, he probably would have found her behaviour enormously embarrassing.

She remembered how kind he had been to Angelica after the discovery of Rollo's corpse: kind but still distant. This man, who caressed his horses' necks with such a delicate hand, had never touched the woman's arm or made physical contact of any kind. Instead, he expressed his compassion with words – and in that way, he had succeeded in calming and reassuring her.

Thoughts of Simon filled her mind. *He* would have instinctively known what she needed. He would have wrapped his arms around her and let her bury her head against him, hugging her to him, stroking her hair while she cried away her fear. He had always known what to do in a crisis or when she was upset.

Then a small voice inside reminded her that Simon was not bloody well there to comfort her, that he was dead – that he might well have been involved in some way with that madman's sister, Diana. The sister, who, from what Frank had said, was manipulative and possibly even more dangerously deranged than her twin brother.

141

Rachel rubbed her tired eyes, aware that Francesco was watching her every move. *Perhaps he's worried that I might have a delayed attack of hysterics,* she thought. Part of her wanted to have a good bawl, part of her wanted so much to be held. *No, I won't let myself behave like a gibbering idiot.* With an effort, she turned away from him and walked over to the sink for a cloth to mop up the spilled tea.

"Would you like some tea, Francesco? It's still hot."

"No, thank you, *signora.*" He watched her face, slightly puzzled by her suddenly brisk manner. "There is more you not tell me. Please sit and say to me what happen with this man Frank. How he come in the house? You bring him in here?"

"Yes . . . ," Rachel hesitated, feeling foolish. "I suppose I felt sorry for him." Seeing the look of disbelief on Francesco's face, she added hastily, "And I thought I could make him tell me about his sister . . . and that would be useful to the police perhaps."

She looked at him, helplessly.

Staring at her, unsmiling, he asked, "What happen when this Frank is here in this room?"

Reluctantly, Rachel sat opposite him at the table and told him the rest. She left nothing out, including her feeling of terror that the man had been about to kill her when Francesco called up to the window.

He listened attentively, occasionally asking her to repeat something that he had not understood.

When she finished, he was silent for a moment. When he eventually spoke, he sounded grave.

"*La signora* must not stay in Podere Vecchio."

"I promised to look after the house for Mr and Mrs Haywood. I can't just leave!"

Francesco got to his feet.

"But you have no telephone, no electricity." He was starting to sound exasperated. "You do not know where is this Frank. Perhaps he come back," he said, stating the obvious as far as Rachel was concerned. She never wanted to see those pale blue eyes and long, anaemic face ever again.

"The police will have to catch him. They know the number of the car. Surely it wouldn't be too difficult for them to find it!"

"*Certo!* But perhaps they not find the car so quick. So, *signora*, is necessary for you to come with me to the house of *signora* Lennie. The storm make much damage. No electricity in Podere Vecchio for many days. Also much water on the road. Trees also. I come with my feet," he said, gesturing towards his sodden boots.

He was obviously determined that she should go with him. His concern had almost made him speak English more fluently – even if it were still at only half the speed the locals used when talking amongst themselves.

"But what about Percy?" asked Rachel, at the same time wondering how Lennie had managed to persuade him to call her by her first name. Perhaps Digby-White was just too much of a mouthful for the Italian. Then she remembered that Lennie and her husband had known Francesco for more than fifteen years.

"The *signora* said the cat come too," Francesco persevered. "I talk with her today. The *signora* is worry that you not

OK. She is waiting for you. There you will be more safe I think." Seeing that Rachel was about to argue, Francesco added with an air of finality, "Until the police find this car, is not good to stay in Podere Vecchio, *signora Martin*."

Suddenly, it all became too much for her and, in spite of promising herself that she wouldn't, Rachel burst into tears.

He moved swiftly around the table. "*Signora!* Do not be sad! All is OK," he insisted.

She struggled to her feet, tears coursing down her cheeks. "I am frightened, Francesco!"

Taking her by surprise, he suddenly pulled her towards him, kissing her wet cheeks and holding her firmly.

"There is no reason to be frightened. I promise," he said. "No harm will come to you."

As they stood close, her cheek touching his, Rachel felt a glow spreading through her, warming and calming her. And, all of a sudden, with his arms around her, she no longer felt helpless and hopeless and impossibly alone.

She pulled away slightly, looking into his face. Then she gave him a watery smile. "Please don't call me *signora* any more. I'm Rachel."

He let go of her gently and, wiping a tear away from under one of her eyes with his finger, he said quietly, "If you wish it, I call you Rachel."

Chapter Twelve

The rain had stopped by the time Rachel and Francesco left the Haywoods'. None the less, it had taken nearly an hour to wade through the fast-flowing rivers of brown water that poured over the steep road from San Lorenzo. Even though Rachel rolled up her jeans, they were damp and uncomfortable by the time they had negotiated the worst of the flooding. Francesco had parked his jeep on the approach road to the village, knowing the likely state of the track leading to Podere Vecchio. He was well used to the sudden storms that swept over that part of Tuscany from time to time and knew that, even with a four-wheel drive, it was virtually impossible to negotiate some of the minor roads without running the risk of driving over the edge. There was always a local farmer with a tractor who'd willingly come to his aid but he preferred not to have to resort to asking for help.

Prudent as well as reliable, thought Rachel tiredly as she

sloshed her way over the sometimes invisible ground. The warm glow she'd experienced in the kitchen earlier had evaporated, leaving her feeling uncertain and weary. Perhaps she'd read more into his behaviour than was wise. She had nearly fallen a couple of times into submerged potholes but somehow managed to keep her balance. The overnight bag on her shoulder made the going more difficult.

Francesco had his hands full, carrying a disgruntled Percy who was swathed tightly in a towel to stop him struggling free. Rachel thought he looked rather like a mummified Egyptian cat. From time to time, he gave a low growl; but it was not the same furious sound she'd heard him make in the storeroom – more a protest at the indignity of the situation. She caught him looking at her as though he feared she would disappear, leaving him in the clutches of the not-so-sympathetic Italian. Perhaps Percy guessed that Francesco considered him not worth the effort. She was pretty sure that the man thought the animal should have been left to fend for itself.

By the time they reached the jeep, there were breaks in the thick grey clouds and the air was starting to warm up. As Francesco turned the vehicle, Rachel noticed that the steeply climbing road up to the church had taken on the appearance of a small river – almost a waterfall. There seemed to be nobody around and most of the houses still had their shutters closed.

She wondered where Frank was at that moment. Had he made it back to his sister? Where was the black car now? It occurred to her that she hadn't seen a single member of the police anywhere near San Lorenzo since she arrived. There had been quite a few in Castel del Piano but they had seemed far too busy chatting to each other or admiring themselves in shop windows to chase criminals. And she'd spotted one handsome young policeman occupied in eyeing up a pretty girl sashaying past on the other side of the street. He'd ignored the fact that an impatient van driver, blocked in by a parked lorry, had roared off along the pavement, making a sedate elderly woman, dressed in black, dive for cover behind a tree. The woman had re-emerged, shaking her fist and shrieking insults at the disappearing van driver. It was almost as if she'd not expected any help from the policeman in the first place.

From San Lorenzo, it was only a two-minute drive to Lennie and Douglas's house. Rachel admitted to herself, if not out loud, that she was thoroughly relieved that she would soon be safe in the elderly couple's home – away from Podere Vecchio.

Parking the jeep at the side of the road, they climbed out. Holding tightly on to a struggling Percy, Francesco drew Rachel's attention to a small wooden sign. *Villa Fiorita* it read, in crooked, bright red letters.

"My brother's son make this name for the *signora* Lennie," he explained.

"How old is he?" asked Rachel.

"Armando is six years. He very much like the *signora* and *signore*. They very kind to him. They kind to me also. *La signora* give me lessons so I can speak with her in English," Francesco said, smiling.

He looked so nice when he smiled, she thought.

Obviously the Digby-Whites weren't the sort of blow-ins who just used the amenities in their adopted country; they had become part of the local scene. Rachel wasn't at all surprised.

As soon as Francesco and Rachel opened the sagging gate, they saw Lennie standing in the open doorway, smiling. Deep purple was her chosen colour of the day – with matching bandanna. She beckoned them up the steps.

"There you are at last! I was starting to think you'd got lost. Come on! You look a little wet and muddy, the pair of you!"

Rachel wasn't surprised that they looked muddy. As well as muddy, she felt exhausted. The drama of the last couple of hours had left her feeling emotionally as well as physically drained. Added to that was the confusion she now felt at the way Francesco had behaved. She couldn't work out if his unexpected show of concern had been because he thought it was the only way he could calm her and get her to leave the house or whether it was because of a genuine interest in her on his part.

Lennie welcomed them, kissing Rachel warmly on the cheek and giving her a quick, quizzical look that made the younger woman wonder if the other knew that all was not well at the Haywoods' house. They followed her thankfully inside.

The woman sat her down on a battered couch in the sitting-room next to an armchair where Douglas dozed, a newspaper spread across his lap. He had slipped down in the chair so that he looked in danger of being eclipsed by the cushion behind him. The remains of an early breakfast lay on a nearby table.

"I'm going to make you a cup of coffee and then you can change out of your damp clothes and go to bed for a while, my dear. You look a little the worse for wear!" Giving her husband a gentle nudge on the shoulder, Lennie said in a loud voice, "Wakey-wakey, dear. We have guests."

Douglas stirred, opening his eyes and peering up, trying to focus on his wife's face.

"What was that?"

"I said we have guests. Can you talk to Rachel for a minute while I make some coffee?"

Douglas's gaze switched to Rachel, his face lighting up.

"Of course, of course! Be a pleasure," he said, hauling himself into a more upright sitting position and pushing his glasses into place. "Forgive me for not getting up," he said, "but the old legs are playing up a bit in this damp weather."

Rachel thought how pleasant he looked. His deeply tanned face was, like his wife's, covered in a maze of wrinkles. His white hair was ruffled and his reading glasses sat slightly crookedly on the bridge of his nose, giving the impression of a rather befuddled owl, suddenly woken from a deep sleep. He had a kind face, she thought. The sort of face she'd have liked her father to have. She thought of how withdrawn and tense he so often looked. The expression on Douglas's face was contented. She suspected that his contentment was in no small measure due to the fact that he had spent the last fifty odd years of his life with Lennie. Rachel also thought how very tired he sounded, in spite of his welcoming smile.

Leaving her husband to look after Rachel, Lennie led Francesco through to the kitchen.

While Rachel talked to Douglas, she could hear his wife speaking rapidly in Italian as soon as she was out of the room. I bet she's finding out what's been going on at Podere Vecchio, she thought. Then she heard Francesco replying even more rapidly. The word 'pericoloso' – which she knew meant dangerous – cropped up a couple of times. There had been signs in the train, warning passengers not to lean out of the windows – 'È pericoloso sporgersi.' With all the recent drama, that train journey to Grosseto seemed to have taken place in the distant past. Leaning out of windows didn't sound all that dangerous when one had been scared half to death by the wild-eyed Frank in the kitchen at Podere Vecchio.

Rachel tried to concentrate on what Douglas was saying in his mild-mannered voice. He was telling her about a storm, a decade earlier, that had caused a landslide, washing away many of the small, local vineyards and burying several houses.

"All the men worked together to dig out the survivors. They were lucky – we got there in time and no one died. Of course, I was a lot fitter then."

Even though he smiled at her, his voice sounded wistful.

Rachel slept deeply until woken by Lennie at midday.

"I thought it was best not to let you sleep too long or you'll be wide awake tonight," she said, pulling back the curtains and unhooking the shutters.

Steamy heat and sunshine immediately filled the room. Rachel got a whiff of hot, damp vegetation from the garden outside.

She sat up, blinking in the bright light. From the bed, she caught a glimpse of what appeared to be a jungle. Climbing plants framed the window, their leaves washed clean by the rain. The view was filled with a tangle of greenery, intermingled with roses, lilies and jasmine that flowed around and over a rickety-looking summerhouse. The building looked in danger of disappearing completely into an embroidered backdrop of scented colour.

"It's like looking at a painting by Rousseau," she exclaimed. "All it needs is a tiger, peering out at us from the undergrowth. I feel I've woken up to a new world. I can't believe it's the same place when I think what it was like just a few hours ago."

Then it all came crowding back. Rachel's smile faded abruptly and her expression changed from one of delight to anxiety as she remembered what had happened at Podere Vecchio earlier in the day. Lennie, seeing her troubled face, pointed to Percy, sound asleep at the foot of the bed.

"Well, that's the nearest thing to a tiger you're likely to come across in this neck of the woods! I put my head round the door earlier and you should have heard the racket he was making. Bit of an eye-opener! I didn't know cats snored." She smiled cheerfully at Rachel. "How about having a shower and then after lunch we'll have a chat. Do you like fish?"

"I love fish."

"Good! I got some from Castel del Piano yesterday. I use a delicious and extremely easy recipe that Clara, that's Francesco's sister-in-law, taught me – more or less foolproof, even for a woman with my limited culinary skills! It'll be ready in about twenty minutes. That suit you?"

"That would be lovely," replied Rachel. "Thank you, Lennie," she added, managing an answering smile.

The simple meal of fish in a rich tomato and basil sauce with brown rice, eaten with a salad that included crisp lettuce and scarlet radishes from the garden, and made glossy with the local, green olive oil, was delicious. They finished up with cherries and pears so succulent that Rachel found it nearly impossible not to end up with sticky juice liberally dribbled on fingers and chin.

Afterwards, she and Lennie took mugs of herbal tea out on to a small terrace.

"More calming for the nerves than the old coffee," said Lennie.

She explained that Douglas would join them later. He was lying down for a while. He'd had a fall on the previous day and had not slept well because of the storm and needed to rest.

"He's more shaken by his tumble than he likes to pretend. But he keeps forgetting that he's nearly eighty. Douglas thinks that he's still in his mid-twenties some of the time. Mind you," Lennie laughed, "I regularly forget my own age – so, I'm just as bad! Very annoying – all this crumbling that takes place on the outside – when inside one still wants to dance tangos and sing at the top of one's voice and climb trees!"

During lunch, Lennie had carefully steered the conversation away from any mention of Podere Vecchio. Instead she had brought up a number of diverse topics:

food, books, music, art, the delights and difficulties of gardening when one is 'not in the first flush of youth' to the awfulness of Italian politicians. Rachel gathered that Lennie didn't think much of politicians in general. She was especially scathing on the subject of the Italian variety.

"I've lost count of how many elections there have been since we first moved here. It doesn't seem to matter who's in power – nothing much changes. The poor stay poor and the rich get a little more rich and little more corrupt. In many ways, San Lorenzo is very much the same as it was when we first arrived fifteen years ago. Now, people have televisions and electricity and those ghastly noisy strimmer things but all that doesn't seem to have made them any happier. The young ones still drift away to the cities," she commented regretfully.

"I had noticed that the local population seems to have an average age of about seventy-five," said Rachel.

Lennie gave her an amused glance. "Well, that makes Douglas and me a typical example then!"

Rachel laughed. "I'm sorry! I didn't mean . . ."

"No, my dear. You're perfectly right. This is a village of geriatrics I'm afraid. Thank goodness there are people like Francesco and his brother's lovely family around to liven us up from time to time." Lennie looked directly into Rachel's eyes. "Although, I gather, things got a little lively this morning at the Haywoods'."

Rachel tried to keep her voice even but it was not easy. An image of Frank, standing opposite her in the kitchen at Podere Vecchio filled her mind: the mad eyes, the mouth wide open as he shouted at her, spittle collecting at the side of his lips, arms flailing, his knuckles white as he banged the table in front of him.

Without being able to stop herself, she started to shake. Suddenly all the tension and fear she'd felt and had been trying so hard not to think about since waking, came tumbling back into her mind. The whole thing was intolerable – Frank, the spying, the very real sense of malice emanating from the unknown and invisible sister. What distressed her most was not knowing their connection with Simon. She didn't feel she was coping with it at all adequately.

Instinctively, she moved closer to Lennie. There seemed to be a well of serenity and quiet strength at the heart of this tall, elderly woman with the untidy grey hair. During lunch, Rachel found herself thinking that she was rather like a cross between a Duchess and a bag lady, with her clipped accent and wildly inappropriate clothes.

Two arms encircled her and she found herself sobbing on Lennie's shoulder like a child. Rachel felt that she'd burst if she didn't get rid of all the pent-up emotion inside her. She hadn't cried, really cried, like this since those first terrible weeks after Simon's death.

Lennie said nothing – just held the younger woman, with her cheek resting lightly against the mass of chestnut hair until the shaking stopped and the tears ceased.

"I'm sorry, Lennie," Rachel said eventually, wiping her eyes with the back of her hand. "I don't know what got into me. I thought that losing Simon had made me stronger, more capable – but it seems I was wrong."

Lennie put a gentle hand up to the girl's face.

"It sounds to me that you had a lucky escape this morning, my dear. I blame myself for not insisting the other day that you come here. Unfortunately, with the way things are with Douglas's health, it wasn't possible for me to come down to the Haywoods' to stay with you. Francesco too was concerned but I persuaded him that you were at the other end of a phone and you would be fine if we kept in touch. However, we hadn't bargained for the storm being so bad and the telephone lines not working." She smiled at Rachel. "Sometimes, I forget to follow my instincts and it's nearly always a mistake."

"Do you think that the phone line was deliberately cut?"

"I'm not sure. Our line is working but Francesco said that there were a lot of branches down so it could have been storm damage. Anyway, the important thing is that you *are* here now and until the police get cracking and find the car and this Frank fellow, I think that this is the best place for you to be. Don't you?"

"I would like to stay here until they find him and his sister – and the car," said Rachel, gratefully. "To be honest, it's the idea of the sister that's scared me even more than Frank. I think that without her there in the background, he probably wouldn't be a threat. He's unbalanced but she seems to be able to make him do what she wants, even though it sometimes makes him angry. I think he knows perfectly well that his sister is manipulating him but, for some reason, he doesn't seem capable of resisting. It is possible that he's really a gentle soul who's being led dangerously astray."

Lennie nodded slightly.

"From what I've gathered, I think that's a very perceptive summing up of the situation. He said they were twins, didn't he?"

"Yes and he seemed delighted with the idea that he was born first. That was important to him. It was as though he could just about pretend her bullying him didn't matter because, whether she liked it or not, he is the older of the two."

"Sometimes, even when twins aren't identical, they have a very close bond, occasionally, a sort of sixth sense with a highly developed ability to communicate over long distances and to know when something is wrong when they are apart from each other. Perhaps this young man is frightened that if he doesn't do what his sister tells him, she will know immediately and be angry."

"Yes," agreed Rachel quietly, "I got the impression that, in spite of the bravado, he is very afraid of her. He said something about her 'sending him back in' if he didn't do what she wanted. What do you think he meant?"

"I'm not sure, my dear." Lennie's face was thoughtful.

She was just about to say something more when the telephone rang in another room. Rachel could hear Douglas's voice as he answered it.

"That will be Francesco," said Lennie, getting to her feet. "He may have some news for us. I won't be a moment, Rachel."

After she left the room, Rachel wondered how Lennie could be so sure it was Francesco on the other end of the 'phone. On reflection, she wasn't all that surprised really.

There was a lot more to Lennie than met the eye. I'm glad she's on my side, she thought, thankfully.

A few minutes later, Lennie returned with a preoccupied expression.

"What's the matter? What did Francesco say?"

The older woman went over and sat down beside her on the couch. She took one of Rachel's hands in her own.

"Francesco said that the police have found the car."

"Well, that's good, isn't it?"

"Not really. It had been abandoned behind the hospital in Castel del Piano. They've been keeping an eye on it but they seem to be pretty sure that it's been dumped there, that no one is coming back for it. There were no belongings left in it apparently."

Rachel stared down at Lennie's hands holding her own. She saw that they were freckled with age spots, the nails short and uneven, the skin roughened from working in the garden. Her head buzzed, making it difficult to think straight.

Somehow, she found it difficult to accept what she'd just been told. She'd been so sure that today – or at least by tomorrow – Frank and his sister would be found and she and Percy would be able to go back to the Haywoods' again.

Apprehensively, she looked at Lennie. "So, what do we do now?" she asked.

Chapter Thirteen

"Come and sit down and have a chat with me," said Douglas from the veranda of the summerhouse.

He watched as Rachel walked towards him, followed, as always, by Percy, carefully picking his way through the still wet grass. The man thought how lovely the slender young woman was as she crossed the lawn in the morning sunlight that streamed through the trees. The light caught the glints of chestnut in her dark brown hair. She looked more rested than on the previous day – although there was still tension in her. He could see it in the way she held herself. Her shoulders were very slightly hunched and a slight frown creased the smooth skin over her brown eyes. As she got closer, Douglas was reminded of his wife when he had first seen her at a party in a friend's garden, all those years ago. Then, Lennie had walked with the same, slightly swaying step and her brown hair, from what he could remember, had been swept up on top of her head in a similarly untidy arrangement – and just about kept in place by an assortment of grips and combs. Nothing much had changed in the hair department, he thought. His wife had never managed to tame her coiffure!

Rachel smiled as she sat down in the other battered cane chair. Wind chimes, hanging from the eaves and half-hidden by jasmine and roses, made a slight sound. It wasn't the usual silvery tinkle that Rachel had heard from most garden chimes – perhaps, she guessed, more like the rounded, resonant chime of distant temple bells that one might hear in somewhere like Tibet. She glanced up at them.

"What a beautiful sound."

Douglas leaned towards her, turning his head a little to one side.

"I'm sorry, my dear. You'll have to speak a bit louder, or enunciate more clearly. I'm getting a little bit deaf in my old age."

"I said that the chimes make a beautiful sound," she repeated more loudly, looking straight at him.

"Yes, I seem to remember that they do. I haven't heard them for some time now, I'm afraid. If we had a hurricane, I might just manage to catch a hint of them." He beamed at her. "Did you sleep well last night? Lennie tells me that the cat snores!"

Rachel laughed.

"Yes, thank you. I'm getting used to it. It's rather companionable really."

It flashed through her mind that Simon had always slept soundly and silently. They had laughed when

Caroline and Guy were first married and she'd said he'd snored so loudly, it had been like trying to sleep beside a mechanical digger on a building site. After a fortnight of tossing and turning, she'd come to the conclusion that a building site would have been more restful – he ground his teeth as well as snoring.

Douglas took off his dark glasses and put them on the veranda railing beside a newspaper.

"I'm sorry I didn't keep you company yesterday but I wasn't at my best. I have days like that every now and then. As Lennie says, 'Old age really is a bugger!'" He chuckled. "I should have been put down long ago. You'd shoot a terminally sick dog when the vet's bills become too absurd. Unfortunately, I haven't been able to persuade my wife to put me out of my misery yet – but I'm working on it!" Douglas leaned forward. "Lennie told me what happened yesterday at the Haywoods'. Most unfortunate, the whole thing. I'm sure that Francesco and his pals in the police will have it sorted out pretty smartly. I expect you've gathered that we think very highly of our Francesco?"

"Yes," replied Rachel, nodding. "I think with good reason. He seems a very capable man and he's been very kind to me over the past few days." To her horror, she felt a blush, spreading up from her neck to her face. "I expect you've made a lot of very good friends since you came to live here," she said, hurriedly.

Noting her pink cheeks, Douglas spared her further embarrassment and went along with the conversation's sudden change in direction, wondering at the same time whether his wife realised Rachel was carrying a torch for the Italian. Of course she would! He smiled to himself. Lennie knew about things almost before they happened. It was one of the things about her that still kept him fascinated after fifty years of marriage.

"Yes, we've met a lot of people and we've made a handful of friendships that are especially good. Extraordinary people, the Italians! I know it's rather an obvious observation but they're so very un-English the way they set about life . . ."

Rachel waited for him to finish the sentence. A slight spasm crossed his face and for a moment the blue eyes closed.

Concerned, she leaned closer to him.

"Are you all right?"

There was no response. Just as she was wondering if she should go and fetch Lennie, he opened his eyes again.

"So sorry, my dear. I didn't mean to startle you. Sit down. Sit down!" He flapped a hand at her, insisting she sit down again. Taking a small pill-box from his shirt pocket, he placed a white tablet in his mouth. There was silence for a few minutes before he spoke again. "Take that worried look off your face, please. I'm supposed to be cheering you up – not the other way round!"

"You looked as though you were in pain just then. Are you really all right or would you like me to get Lennie?"

With an effort, the old man pulled himself up in his chair and wagged a finger at her.

"I am as right as rain, young lady, and don't you dare go and tell my wife anything or you'll have her more worried about me than she is already."

Although he smiled as he spoke, she knew that he

161

meant what he said. He didn't want Lennie knowing about what had just happened. Reluctantly, Rachel agreed. She wondered how much he was able to keep hidden from his perceptive wife. Not much, she thought.

At that moment, Lennie called them from the kitchen window.

"Lunch is ready, if anyone's interested in eating it!"

Cautiously, Douglas got to his feet, motioning Rachel to precede him. That way, she thought, it made it difficult for her to offer him a helping arm.

What was it Lennie had said to her, with a shake of her head and a hint of a sigh, the previous evening when he had insisted on getting out of bed, only to have to go back a few minutes later?

"Stubborn as well as deaf! You'd think after all this time he'd have cottoned on to the fact that I know what's good for him, wouldn't you?"

Although she'd been speaking to Rachel, her eyes had followed her husband's slow retreat back to the bedroom with a look of such sadness that the younger woman had not known what to say. Then Lennie had turned back to her with a cheerful smile.

"You can love them to death but you can't change the blighters! They're always convinced they know best."

After lunch Rachel helped wash up the dishes and stack things away. There didn't seem to be much order in any of the cupboards. When she asked what went where, Lennie shrugged.

"Doesn't really matter, dear. Wherever you can find a

space. That way, when I'm rooting around for something, I discover plates and serving dishes I'd forgotten I had. It makes the daily routine of cooking just a little more interesting." Lennie absent-mindedly dried her hands, as she looked out into the garden. "I'm afraid I was never a good cook – not like Clara. That's Francesco's brother's wife. She's an absolutely amazing young woman. It's quite extraordinary what she can produce with a few simple ingredients. Still, I'm better than I used to be. When Douglas first married me, we lived on boiled eggs and toast and hot chocolate. On high days and holidays, I could just about manage to fling a chicken in the oven and throw together a dish of stewed apple and lumpy custard. There always seemed to be so many more important things to be doing than standing over a hot stove, prodding something in a pot! Poor Douglas had to take his important clients out to dinner rather than risk bringing them back to the house. I'm sure they thought I was a complete disaster as a wife. Still, he never complained, bless him!"

"You both seemed to have married the perfect mate," said Rachel, rather wistfully.

"Well, it wasn't all good luck you know. I went to an old woman who read Tarot cards. She put me on the right track. Mind you, the first time I clapped eyes on Douglas, I think I knew I'd got a winner! There was this lovely aura he had. All the right colours and no bits missing – to his aura, not Douglas," she added, chuckling.

"I don't know anything about Tarot cards or auras but I felt the same way about Simon. He just seemed right for me . . ." Rachel's voice trailed away.

"And now you think that, for some reason, you may have been wrong about him – that he wasn't the man you thought he was. Is that why you're so unhappy?" asked Lennie gently.

"Oh, Lennie! I don't know what to think any more." Rachel put down the dish she was holding. "I was so sure of Simon. After a little while, I think I took him for granted. I don't think he realised how much I loved him or how happy I was for those six years we had together." Her frown deepened. "Now, with all this weird stuff going on down at Caroline and Guy's, I just feel I have no control over my life any more. I seem to be drifting along and things are happening to me that I don't want to happen. It's like a horrible game of snakes and ladders. Just as I think I'm making progress, something awful happens and I'm back where I started. I feel sort of disempowered – if that's the right word."

Looking at her forlorn expression, Lennie said briskly, "Cheer up, most things are never quite as bad as one imagines them to be. Francesco will be here any minute now and we will have a council of war; see if we can't sort out a few things and make you feel as though you are back in the driving seat again." She propelled Rachel gently towards the garden door. "While Douglas is having his siesta, we'll wait for Francesco out in the summerhouse."

As they walked over to the precarious structure, Rachel wondered how many more storms would be needed to level it to the ground. One side of the roof looked decidedly lower than the other. It appeared as though the greenery was all that was holding it up.

She suddenly stopped, looking around anxiously for Percy.

"Don't worry, my dear. The cat's over there, persecuting lizards behind the camellia." Lennie pointed to a twitching chocolate-coloured tail that stuck out from under a shrub to the right of the summerhouse. "That animal hasn't let you out of his sight ever since you got here. I don't think you need worry about him. Percy's a wise old thing."

As Rachel sat down, she stared at the few inches of tail and said, almost shyly, "It's funny, isn't it, how very occasionally you meet an animal or a person whom you sort of bond with almost immediately. I felt it with Simon – and now with you and Percy."

"Yes, it's rare enough to feel completely at ease with someone. The fact that you had that feeling with Simon should reassure you, Rachel. Don't make the mistake of prejudging any possible involvement with him and the woman leaving flowers on his grave. Has it crossed your mind that he may be entirely blameless?"

"I *want* him to be entirely blameless, Lennie. But I find it difficult to understand. If he had a sister, why should he pretend he was an only child?"

"Perhaps he didn't know he had a sister. That's always a possibility to consider." Lennie's attention was distracted by the sound of the side gate creaking noisily. She smiled as Rachel twisted round in her chair. "Well, here's Francesco. Perhaps he will have some information that will start you on the road to finding out what it's all about." Lennie waved energetically at Francesco as he walked across the grass towards them. *"Ciao, Francesco! Come stai?"*

"Bene, grazie, signora Lennie!"

A broad smile lit up his face, making him look almost handsome, Rachel thought with surprise. She suddenly realised that her heart had skipped a beat. She remembered how he had held her in the kitchen at Podere Vecchio. Had that moment of intimacy made any impression on him? Or had he forgotten about it already?

She could see that he looked at Lennie with real affection. Then he turned to Rachel. *"Buongiorno, signora Martin.* How are you?"

To Rachel, his greeting was, as ever, politely formal. She couldn't help feeling a stab of disappointment. He'd already forgotten that she'd asked him to call her Rachel. Her expression must have given her away because Lennie gave Francesco a quick glance.

"I think it would be in order for you to call *signora* Martin, Rachel. Don't you agree, Francesco? After all, she's almost one of the family."

The man hesitated before giving a slight nod.

"Certo! If the *signora* wishes."

Rachel felt that perhaps she'd have preferred it if Lennie had said nothing. At the same time, she couldn't help feeling curiously disappointed in him. It wasn't such a big deal, surely, to ask to be called by one's first name? Especially after what had happened a couple of days earlier. Perhaps she was being foolish – allowing herself to read too much into the occasion.

"What news do you have, Francesco?" she asked, as calmly as she could.

It turned out that the only news he brought them was

negative. Frank and his sister had apparently disappeared into thin air. No one had come back to claim the car before the garage insisted it be returned to them. Neither the police nor any of the local people had seen anyone answering Frank's description.

Francesco had been back to Podere Vecchio and all appeared normal. The horses were well and the sudden rivers that had sprung from nowhere and made the driveway almost impassable had gone. He had cleared away the fallen branches. As for the electricity! He shrugged expressively.

"Perhaps tomorrow it is mended."

He hadn't sounded too sure of that, Rachel thought.

"What about the telephone?" she asked.

Francesco held up both hands, palm upwards and gave another, more exaggerated shrug.

"Perhaps also tomorrow."

Judging from the expression on his face, that sounded even more doubtful.

"Well, that settles it!" said Lennie firmly. "You most definitely can't go back there with that Frank one still on the loose and with no phone or electricity. Quite out of the question! You can ring Caroline and Guy and tell them you've moved in here, plus cat, for a few days until the phone and electricity fellows get their act together. No need to go into any details. We wouldn't want Caroline worrying about you."

Rachel couldn't help smiling at the implication. That particular lady was far more likely to worry about the house being broken into and rifled or damaged while empty than the house-sitter being scared out of her wits by a dangerous intruder.

"I will go each day and look that everything is OK," said Francesco.

"See, see, Francesco, not look," Lennie interrupted gently. "You will go and *see* that everything is OK."

"*Certo, signora* Lennie," he replied with a grin. Turning to Rachel, he added, "Sometime I think I have two mammas."

"What would I be doing with another male around the place? I've quite enough to do as it is with the one I've got already," said Lennie, laughing.

Rachel felt that it was quite possible that Lennie would love Francesco to be her son. Neither she nor Douglas had ever mentioned having had any children of their own.

"I tell you if I have news of the man and woman," he promised, turning to go. "Now I go to *see* my Constanza. *Ciao!*"

Rachel's heart sank. Who was Constanza?

"Yes, you go and talk to your beloved horse, Francesco," said Lennie, smiling as she watched him go.

Relieved, Rachel sat back in her chair, pushing up a strand of hair that had fallen down over her face. Of course! What an idiot she was! He'd mentioned his favourite horse only the other day.

"I swear he talks about that horse as though she were a woman."

"Rachel! You sound quite annoyed. Don't tell me you are jealous of the beautiful Constanza?"

"Of course not!" Rachel replied quickly, hastily bending

over and stroking Percy, who had come over to stand on her foot. Unblinking, he looked up at her with his wide periwinkle-blue eyes. "Although, I can quite understand why some people think that animals are more rewarding than humans a lot of the time."

"Yes, but you have to agree that it's infinitely more rewarding to have a really good relationship with a man than an animal – even a splendid cat like old Percy here. If you'll excuse me saying so, Percy," Lennie said with a chuckle. "I know ancient mythology tried to prove otherwise. Those Greeks and Romans had some strange ideas about some of their deities' ancestry. Imagine going to bed with a swan!"

Later that evening, before it got dark, Rachel read to Douglas while Lennie did some of what she referred to as 'emergency weeding' in the vegetable garden.

"Otherwise, after all that rain, anything edible will have completely disappeared under a sea of weeds," Lennie muttered, gardening fork in one hand, as she hunted around for the secateurs.

Douglas watched his wife as she ransacked first one and then another cupboard.

"Can't you close your eyes and let your mind tell you where it is? Visualise it or something?" he suggested helpfully.

"You know perfectly well that it doesn't work like that, Douglas," Lennie shouted over her shoulder. "You have to keep your special powers for the important things in life."

"I thought your vegetables *were* important. You certainly spend enough time watering them and murdering any intruders. I feel quite sorry for the slugs and snails when you're on the warpath!" He turned towards Rachel with a twinkle in his eye. "Talks to her plants, she does. Just like that Prince Charles character. Quite batty, the pair of them!"

Lennie ignored him.

Suddenly she gave a triumphant "Got them!" and dived headfirst into the far corner of the cupboard, emerging with a pair of secateurs. "I swear the blessed things move around the place when I'm not looking!"

"Perhaps you're not the only one with special powers around here, my darling!"

Lennie looked at him, eyebrows raised. "You just work on a method of finding your glasses without getting me to hunt for the wretched things all over the house umpteen times a day and leave me to concentrate on life's mysteries!"

"Can't hear a word," replied Douglas, sitting back in his chair with a smile, his eyes following his wife as she strode purposefully out of the room.

Rachel was glad that Douglas felt well enough to tease Lennie. She'd thought at lunchtime that there was a disturbing pallor lurking under his tanned face and there was a frailty to him that she hadn't noticed during their first meeting at the Haywoods'. Perhaps Lennie was right and the fall he'd taken the day before she came to stay at Villa Fiorita had done him harm.

He'd asked her to read out a letter from the paper – a two-day old copy of *The Times* – because his eyes were tired. When Rachel had finished shouting out the letter, he looked at her admiringly.

"Not only beautiful to look at but also beautiful to listen to, with that lovely Irish accent of yours."

Lennie, who'd come back to hunt for some potion she needed for the welfare of her *zucchini*, pulled a wry face at her. Then she shook her head, surveying her husband with a pitying look.

"Be careful, Douglas, old thing. You've steam coming out of your ears!"

"What was that?" he asked, cupping his ear with his hand.

Rachel laughed. "Would you like me to read out anything else?"

Again she was aware of Douglas watching his wife as she marched briskly back into the garden with a large brown bottle bearing a label apparently depicting slugs and snails in their death throes.

In a quiet voice he said, almost as though he were speaking to himself, "The best thing that ever happened to me in my life was marrying that marvellous, mad woman."

Chapter Fourteen

Rachel was starting to feel that what Lennie had said to Francesco about her being one of the family was becoming true. Her affection for the elderly couple increased as the days passed. However busy Lennie was, looking after Douglas or working in the garden, she always made sure she was there for the younger woman.

She seemed to know when Rachel wanted to be left quietly on her own. Sometimes they talked together as they sat side by side on the veranda of the summerhouse; sometimes they cooked or gardened in companionable silence. Little by little, Rachel found herself telling the older woman more about her life in Dublin. She described her parents and the regret she felt at her inability to please them, her work in the Dublin publishing firm, her marriage to Simon.

Lennie asked her if she and Simon had wanted to have children.

"Simon wasn't in a rush but I'm sure we'd have got round to it sooner or later," Rachel answered in a quiet voice. "It's a shame we left it too late. It would be lovely to have a little bit of him living on in a child."

Lennie paused in the middle of deadheading some roses, "Sometimes these things happen – or don't happen – for the best. Having a child when you are trying to manage on your own can be very difficult." She scooped up some dead rose leaves, stuffing them energetically into the cardboard box at her feet. "Douglas and I would have loved children but it wasn't to be. Perhaps it's just as well we didn't; I'm hardly a conventional sort of a woman. I'd have probably mislaid them – and certainly would have embarrassed the poor things to bits! My own mother embarrassed me like mad when I was a teenager and thought that keeping up appearances was all-important. She used to sing in the street when we went out shopping. I just hated that! I'd turn crimson and pretend she didn't belong to me. She also refused to stand up for *God Save the Queen* on important occasions. She said the woman was fine and didn't need saving from anything, thank you very much!" She smiled at Rachel. "I think that from what I've seen of Clara's little ones, enchanting though the pair of them are, parenthood is jolly hard work!"

On her fourth night at the Digby-Whites', Rachel dreamed of Simon. He was standing in the shadows at the end of a long, narrow street. The houses were tall and grey and leaned towards the street in a way that was somehow menacing. She saw that all the windows were blank, as if they had been covered in black cloth. Walking as though her limbs were made of lead, she struggled in slow motion towards him. As she got nearer, she tried to call to him but was unable to make a sound. Then Simon's face started to change, dissolve, so that his features slowly rearranged themselves. She watched in horror as the man that had been her husband metamorphosed into the watcher in the garden. She realised that she was holding out her arms to Frank. In her dream, she screamed a long, soundless scream.

She woke, terrified. It had been so real, so extraordinarily vivid. She lay, curled up in the bed, knuckles pressed against her lips, trying to stop herself from thinking the unthinkable. But she couldn't stop remembering the fleeting recognition she had felt in the kitchen when she watched the man at the other side of the table: the nose, the slight dimple in the chin, the way the hair parted to the right over a high forehead. Although so deceptively different in over-all appearance, there was no getting away from it. Frank must, in some way, be related to Simon.

Lennie surveyed Rachel's pale face at breakfast next morning. She noticed how puffy-eyed the girl looked as she handed her a plate with lukewarm scrambled eggs reclining soggily on a piece of over-cooked toast.

"Bad night?" she enquired, gently.

"Bad dream." Rachel stirred her coffee listlessly. "Lennie, I think that Frank and Simon are related in some way."

"What makes you think that?"

Rachel described the dream that had been responsible for her not sleeping again until dawn, and then only for a short time.

"I knew there was something about Frank that was familiar in some strange way but there was too much going on and I was too tired to think it through properly. It was only after the wretched dream that I realised how alike some of his features were to Simon's."

"If he is related, does it make you more worried?"

Rachel looked at her. "Oh, Lennie! If you could have seen the way that man was staring at me in the kitchen. He terrified me. I can't believe . . . I don't want to believe that there could be any connection between that madman and his sister and Simon." Her voice dropped. "Simon was always in control of himself; he never lost his cool for a moment. Yes, he could be moody at times and get annoyed, of course, but I never felt in the least bit threatened by him. Simon made me feel safe."

There was a rustle and she was suddenly aware that, at the other end of the table, Douglas had lowered the paper onto his lap. His blue eyes were looking at her with concern.

"You all right, my dear? I missed most of the conversation but you look a little out of sorts."

Lennie leaned towards him, placing her hand over his, and spoke in a clear voice.

"Rachel had a bad night, dear. A nasty dream. She'll be fine when she's eaten a bit of breakfast."

Her husband nodded slightly. He smiled at Rachel. "I expect it was Lennie's cooking that did it. You need a cast-iron gut to make it through the night after one of her 'specials'!" He patted his wife's arm. "Good thing I spent some time in the army in my youth. The soldiers' Mess in the Gambia and Gold Coast stood me in good stead. Set me up for a life of the cuisine of the adventurous and unlikely."

Rachel couldn't help laughing. The curry Lennie had thrown together on the previous evening, while describing the delights of the poetry of Charles D'Orleans, had been a little strange. It was as though she'd become bored with what she started out making and so had chucked in a little of anything that she could lay her hands on. She'd assured Rachel that marmalade was a very good companion to banana, cayenne pepper and ginger.

"Never follow a recipe," she had cautioned her. "Then people don't know when you've lost the plot and done your own thing. It's worked a treat so far, even though Douglas swears I've tried to poison him on a couple of occasions!" She'd given Rachel a wicked smile. "And it doesn't half put off people one doesn't terribly like – mostly quite ghastly relatives from Bognor and the wilds of Yorkshire – from landing on one at mealtimes! I used it several times over the years before Douglas retired – to marvellous effect." She smiled happily at the recollection.

"If we'd lobbed Lennie's version of beef dumplings at them, my wife could have wiped out the entire German army in one fell swoop," remarked Douglas.

"So very unkind and only possibly true," Lennie said, looking at her husband with mock severity.

"What was that?"

"Don't you 'what was that?' me, you old so-and-so. You know perfectly well what I said. I saw you reading my lips."

"Lovely lips they are too, my darling," said Douglas, retreating back to his paper.

Shoving into place some escaping strands of grey hair with a bright yellow clip, Lennie turned to Rachel.

"What would you do with him?"

"I don't think I'd be able for him at all," Rachel said with an answering smile.

There was a knock on the door behind her.

"Permesso?"

Lennie's napkin fell to the floor as she got up from the table with a welcoming, *"Francesco, caro mio!* Come in, come in – and have some coffee."

Rachel watched as the man greeted them both. She noticed how comfortable he seemed to be with them as he sat down at the table beside her. He looked thoroughly at home in the small kitchen. She saw too how his eyes searched Douglas's face, as if he were making sure that the old man was all right.

When Lennie went to fetch him a cup, he turned to Rachel. "How is the *signora* Rachel?"

Well, she supposed that was an improvement on just *signora!* She smiled at him. "The *signora* Rachel is very well, thank you, Francesco."

Lennie bustled back into the room and filled a cup with coffee, handing it to him with a questioning look.

"Any news, Francesco?"

He shook his head. "No news, Lennie. Nobody see nothing. Nobody hear nothing."

For a moment, it looked as though she would correct his errant grammar but decided against it. She sat down and sipped her own coffee thoughtfully.

"Everyone well at home? We haven't seen Clara and the little ones since before the storm," said Douglas.

"She send you her greetings and say she come on Sunday with the family after church finish," replied Francesco. Adding, "If that is OK."

Rachel noted how he spoke loudly and clearly but not in the patronising way in which so many people talk to those who don't hear well.

Douglas looked pleased. "Excellent! Excellent!" He looked over to Rachel. "That baby Rosa of Clara's will make all the lads dizzy when she's a little older! Quite enchanting! She's got her mother's eyes."

"Give her a chance, Douglas! The child's only fourteen months old," said Lennie, with a chuckle.

"Oh, these women!" continued her husband, undeterred. "They start pulling at your heartstrings right from the moment they're born." He looked at Lennie. "And some of them manage to dazzle a fellow all the way from cradle to grave."

There was a poignancy in the quick look that Douglas gave his wife across the table that made Rachel catch her breath. Something passed between the two of them that hinted at a profound regard and affection and the certain knowledge that Douglas's ill health meant that the time would arrive, and soon, when it would all come to an end.

She wondered if her marriage to Simon would have

developed into something as rich and contented in old age. Passion and delight in each other when young is one thing but how many of us manage to take pleasure in our partner when we're unwell and struggling along in our seventies or eighties? she asked herself. Her parents' faces floated into her mind: her mother's anxieties, her father's look of bitter disappointment at the way his life had turned out. It was sad. Her parents were financially so much better off than Lennie and Douglas but she couldn't remember the last time she'd heard them laughing or enjoying a joke together, let alone exchanging an affectionate remark. She promised herself to ring them in the next couple of days and see how they were.

Rachel was suddenly aware that Francesco had asked her a question and was looking at her, apparently waiting for a response.

"Sorry! What did you say?"

"I ask if the *signora* like to come to look if the horses are well."

"At Podere Vecchio, you mean?" said Rachel, not able to stop herself from sounding cautious.

She was aware of Lennie whispering to him, "*See*, Francesco. See, not look!"

"We will go to *see* them and to *look* at the house," he continued, with a slight smile.

His brown eyes took in her reaction to his suggestion and she saw that he knew perfectly well how nervous she felt at the prospect of going back to the Haywoods'. Still, she was responsible for the place while they were away. Rachel felt Percy's tail brush against her leg under the

179

table. It was strangely comforting. As were the deep brown eyes watching her.

"Right!" she said, with a cheerfulness she didn't feel. "When do you want to go?"

"We go now, if you like."

"Right," said Rachel again, but with less enthusiasm. She wished she could think of a credible reason for putting it off until later.

Francesco unlocked the gates and as they drove along the shaded driveway approaching the house, Rachel glanced towards Guy and Caroline's cars, parked side-by-side under a large chestnut. Apart from the Audi looking a little dusty and both being liberally scattered with chestnut flowers, all seemed well. To her relief, there was no sign of any cut flowers of any description decorating either vehicle.

After Francesco switched off the engine, she looked out of the window as the eddies of dust settled around the jeep, trying hard to pull herself together. What she wanted to do at that precise moment was to ask to be taken straight back to Lennie and Douglas. Villa Fiorita seemed more like a sanctuary than ever. Francesco looked over at her, a hand on his door handle.

"Is OK?" he asked in a gentle voice.

Rachel hastily opened her door.

"Yes, I'm OK."

They started to walk up the steep path to the front of the house, both looking around them as they climbed. Neither spoke. Rachel assumed Francesco's silence was because he was shy. She wondered if it had been Lennie's idea to revisit the scene of the crime. Perhaps she thought that Rachel, seeing it in sunshine again, would feel better about the place.

All doors and shutters were closed. Rachel saw as they went round the end of the building that he had replaced the broken padlock with a larger one. At the rear, chairs and table sat tidily on the terrace, the swimming-pool sparkled invitingly, the flower-beds looked freshly hoed. Everything appeared to be in its rightful place. There wasn't the slightest sign of there having been a storm only four days before. She guessed that Francesco had worked hard, clearing away debris from the pool and surrounding area. The grass, which had been brown and brittle when Rachel arrived, was now covered by a mist of miraculous green.

"You have done a lot," she said.

"Angelica also is here yesterday. She make everything good in the house and make clean the table and chairs outside," he replied, pointing to the recently swept terrace.

Rachel was surprised that he had managed to persuade the woman to come back.

"I thought that Angelica didn't want to be here at the house. I think she believes that all the bad things that have happened are because of me – and it seems that she might be right."

"I tell her she must do her work. *Signora* 'aywood will not be happy if she find out Angelica not here to clean for *signora* Martin . . . Rachel," he corrected himself. "It is good for her to come here. Her father and brothers are not kind to her so she need to have time away from them."

181

"You mean, they are cruel to her?"

Francesco made the gesture with his hands she'd seen him make often during conversations with Lennie and Douglas.

"They not good people," he said emphatically.

Then he moved away, as if not wanting to continue the conversation any further.

She watched as he went to the edge of the terrace and glanced towards the bamboo at the far end of the garden. Seeming satisfied that all was as it should be, Francesco walked back to her. Rachel liked the way he moved, effortlessly, unhurried. She thought he looked, if not exactly handsome, attractive with his brown face and arms, his large capable hands and the greying dark hair that grew over the top of his blue shirt collar just a little. She'd always liked the fact that Simon had been over six feet and this man was barely an inch taller than she was. But there was something compelling about him all the same. She knew that she wanted him to touch her, to put his arms around her again.

He stopped in front of her and she became aware that he was looking at her a little strangely, almost as if he guessed her thoughts. Embarrassed, Rachel turned away and started walking towards the horses' paddock.

"The *signora* can see everything is well at Podere Vecchio," he said, drawing level with her.

Rachel came to an abrupt stop, turning her head to look at him.

"I don't know if all is really well, Francesco."

He looked at her questioningly.

"What is not good here in this beautiful garden?"

"Oh, the garden is beautiful, especially after all that rain. I didn't mean that." She hesitated, wondering how best to describe the way she felt. "It's rather like being in the Garden of Eden. It all looks marvellous until you remember that there is a serpent in the grass." She knew that it was unnecessary to add: and people who wished you harm, possibly hidden somewhere nearby.

"Garden of Eden?"

"Yes. Heaven. Paradise. You know?"

His face broke into a smile.

"*Paradiso! Sì, sì.* I know what it means." He started to walk slowly along the path. "Signora . . . Rachel, there are always serpents in beautiful places." He gave a small shrug. "You are careful they do not bite but you do not . . . allow . . . them to make ugly the beautiful garden. You can not live always with *la paura*."

"Fear?"

He nodded.

"It is fear that make a man weak. Is not good."

She wondered if he were ever frightened of anything.

They reached the newly mended fence and climbed carefully under the wire. Francesco put both hands to his mouth and called to the horses, a long, drawn-out, rolling shout, deep and resonant. The sound echoed around the hillside. Almost immediately, Rachel heard answering whinnies and the sound of cantering hooves. First the chestnut stallion appeared. Rachel stepped back. He was going so fast, it looked as though he were going to charge past and jump the fence behind them but he skidded to a halt, blowing and snorting with his nose only inches away from Francesco's chest. The grey mare then trotted up and she too moved close to where he stood.

As he talked to them in a low voice, their ears flickered backwards and forwards as though they understood everything he said. He kept his voice low and caressing. All the time he spoke, his hands gently worked over their necks and throats, rubbing under their manes, stroking their noses, tickling their velvet chins. It was quite apparent to Rachel that, for the moment, he had forgotten her existence. Even though large numbers of flies made the surface of the horses' skin quiver in little spasmodic ripples and their tails swish all the time in a vain attempt to keep the persistent insects at bay, they too seemed oblivious of her. She noticed the way the chestnut pushed his head against the side of Francesco's neck so that his heavy chin rested on the man's shoulder while the grey's eyelids drooped as he petted her.

The light under the trees was diffused and although it was very hot, Rachel felt she could stand like this forever, enjoying the gentle scene in front of her.

A sudden loud bang from a nearby field made her jump. The horses threw up their heads and backed away. The spell was broken. She looked at Francesco in alarm.

"What was *that?*"

He laughed. "*Un canone.*"

"A cannon?" she asked nervously.

"To make afraid the birds." Seeing that the noise had frightened her, he moved closer. "Not to kill, not to make afraid *la signora*," he said, with a small smile.

Francesco's step towards her meant that she was closer

to him than she had been since he'd held her in the kitchen after Frank's escape. He smelled of horse and sweat on a clean body. He smelled of man. Suddenly Rachel was overwhelmed with the need to kiss him. Without thinking, she moved close enough for the skin on his arm to touch her own. It was warm and firm. Her whole body seemed to be tingling from the surge of electricity that shot through her. Reaching out, she put a hand behind his neck and drew him towards her, her lips searching for his. For a second, she felt him resist and then his arms were around her, pulling her against him and he was kissing her hard, holding her so tightly she could hardly breathe. She heard herself give an involuntary moan.

Rachel didn't know how long that kiss lasted. It seemed to go on forever. It was like drinking from a deep well after a long, debilitating illness. When they drew apart, she felt aroused, exhilarated – and appalled. What *had* she done? All her mother's careful reminders on how nice girls behaved had obviously been wasted. Civilised young women didn't go round the place grabbing men and insisting on kissing them. Unlike last time, when he had comforted her, she didn't have the excuse of having just been scared to death. Would he think she was a complete trollop? She couldn't bring herself to look him in the eye.

Instead of withdrawing, Francesco took hold of her arm and with his free hand, raised her chin so that she had to look into his face. She didn't know quite what to expect. Rachel consoled herself with the knowledge that at least he had kissed her back so it wasn't all one-sided. His expression was difficult to read. Troubled, serious? It was hard to know what he was feeling as he looked at her.

"I'm sorry, Francesco. I hope you are not angry," she said in a low voice, aware that he hadn't let go of her arm yet.

He seemed about to say something, his hand half-lifted as though he were going to touch her cheek but his eyes suddenly clouded over and he stepped hastily back from her. For a moment he stared at Rachel, then drawing a deep breath, he ran his fingers roughly through his hair. There was almost a feeling of desperation in the way he did it.

"I think is good now I take *la signora* to Villa Fiorita." Rachel opened her mouth to speak but he held up a warning hand. "I promise . . . is better I take you."

She held a hand gently against the side of his face. "You do like me, Francesco, don't you?"

"Of course! I like you, Rachel. I like you too much."

Quickly, he turned, ducking under the wire in a fluid movement. Before she could think of anything to say, he was walking towards the path without looking back to see if she were following.

Slowly, she bent down and climbed through the strands of wire. What was wrong with him? It was obvious that he found her attractive. So, why did he have to run away like this? She hoped that, by her making the first move to kiss, she hadn't put him off. As she watched him hurrying away from her, Rachel experienced a feeling that was almost desperation. He was the first man who had engaged her, either physically or emotionally, since Simon's death. She couldn't just pretend to herself that what she felt for him was casual lust. It wouldn't be easy but, somehow, she would have to get him to talk to her, to tell her how he really felt.

Chapter Fifteen

The veil of dust settled around her as Rachel stood at the side of the road and watched Francesco drive away in the mud-spattered Jeep. Although she'd been longing for them to talk, he had started the engine immediately she'd climbed in and they hadn't said anything to each other during the short drive back to Villa Fiorita. Although she wanted desperately to break the silence, she hadn't even dared look at him, after glimpsing his face at the start of the journey. He'd looked so remote and unapproachable. She was certain now that she had made a complete fool of herself and that the man would never allow himself to be left in a room alone with her ever again. The knowledge that he had returned her kiss with a passion that appeared to equal her own did nothing to diminish her embarrassment.

She found Lennie in the little sitting-room that looked out over the back garden. The shutters were half-closed, making the woman's face and arms eerily zebra-striped. Untypically, Lennie was lying down on the couch, her head resting on a pile of cushions. She was wearing what looked like some sort of brown and black caftan. A Mozart piano concerto filled the room.

Rachel was about to pick up Percy, who had been waiting for her in the hall, and tiptoe out when the other woman lifted her head, squinting at the silhouetted figure in the doorway.

"Hello! I didn't hear you come in. I'm drowning in Mozart and thinking positive thoughts! Was everything all right at the Haywoods'?"

Thankful that her own face was in semi-shadow, Rachel tried to sound as casual as possible.

"Everything seemed fine. Where's Douglas?"

"Probably having a snooze in the garden. I persuaded him that he needed to make up for lost sleep."

He wasn't the only one to have had a bad night. Rachel had heard Lennie moving around in the early hours. She realised that, because the other woman was always so busy, her face animated and interested by whatever she was doing, her own tiredness was hidden most of the time.

"Can I get you a cup of coffee? I was going to make one for myself."

"Lovely, dear! I'm just being self-indulgent, lying here like a dozy old pasha but I'm enjoying every minute. What's the point in giving in to temptation and then not relishing it? By the way, where's Francesco got to?"

"Oh, he remembered something he had to do. He said

he would see you soon," lied Rachel as she carried a purring Percy through to the kitchen.

When Rachel returned with the coffee, Lennie had opened the shutters so that the room was bright again. A faint breeze stirred the pink and green curtains so that the cabbage roses on them undulated slightly. Although none of the furniture seemed to match either in style or colour, Rachel liked this comfortable room with its walls covered in bookshelves and paintings and the baby grand piano, half-hidden under crooked piles of sheet music that looked like tipsy skyscrapers.

She had heard Douglas playing a couple of times since her arrival in Villa Fiorita and she had found herself immensely moved by his gentle, unfussy touch. Not for him the mannerisms adopted by so many pianists, professional and amateur: no head-swaying or hands poised above the keys before descending dramatically, no look of intense suffering that she'd noticed on soloists' faces at past concerts. He sat very straight, head tilted a little back as he peered down at the music through his bifocals, his face serene and concentrated. He seemed to have a special fondness for Brahms. Rather than tiring him, the music seemed to give him strength so that at the end of a piece, he looked exhilarated. Rachel had watched Lennie looking at her husband while he played. She couldn't help seeing that, although she smiled slightly with pleasure at the music he made, her eyes were sad.

Now, regarding her with a cheerful smile, Lennie said, "I know you said that everything was fine at the house but *you're* anything but fine. Tell me to mind my own business.

I won't be in the least bit put out but I'm going to do my impersonation of the Wicked Witch of the West and meddle! Even without having to resort to using my crystal ball, I do know that there's something bothering you. Is it Francesco perhaps?"

Rachel handed her the cup of coffee and sat down in Douglas's sagging armchair before answering. She should have known better than to pretend with Lennie.

"Is he gay, Lennie?"

An amused chuckle bubbled from the other woman.

"Not in the least! A sophisticated young woman like yourself must have known he wasn't when you first met him. What on earth makes you ask that?"

"I don't know! It's just that he seems uncomfortable when he's with me. I've seen him look at me but when he sees I've noticed, he looks all embarrassed and turns away as though it's bad manners or something."

"Well, in my limited experience of what happened way back in the mists of time, I seem to remember that when a man was interested in a woman, his interest could make him appear clumsy and awkward. Especially if the man were shy. Women seem to forget that sometimes men find doing the right thing at the right moment just as excruciatingly difficult as women do – perhaps even more so."

For some reason that thought hadn't occurred to Rachel before. Somehow, sexual shyness had always seemed the prerogative of the female of the species. She considered the possibility. Could Lennie be right? She remembered how much she had wanted to kiss him and how she had taken matters into her own hands.

"I do believe you're blushing, Rachel." Lennie's voice was gently teasing.

With a sigh, Rachel said, "I'm afraid I made a bit of a fool of myself this morning. I couldn't stop myself and I kissed Francesco."

"I'm delighted to hear it! And did he kiss you back?"

Rachel looked at her and laughed. "Yes, he did."

"So what makes you think you made a fool of yourself?"

"It was such a marvellous kiss. It just felt right, you know? But after we'd kissed, he almost ran. Francesco couldn't get away from me fast enough. In the Jeep, he wouldn't look at me or even talk. Then it felt as though what we'd done was something dreadful."

Lennie shook her head. "Silly, silly man! I wonder what all *that* was about." She smiled at Rachel. "Anyway, whatever's the matter with Francesco, I'm delighted that you forgot about all your worries long enough to let your passions guide you. Very healthy!"

"Don't say anything to him will you?" Rachel said, suddenly worried.

"No, my dear, of course not." Lennie gazed down into her cup of coffee. Then she looked over to where Rachel sat, cup in hand, absent-mindedly stroking Percy who had installed himself on one of her feet. "There's one thing I've noticed about our Francesco that might have some bearing on his behaviour. I think he's a little in love with his brother's wife, Clara." Seeing Rachel's shocked expression, she continued, "But because he is an honourable man, I doubt that she even knows. He's also very proud; proud of his family, what they have achieved, proud of his mother

191

who is a difficult old soul, and proud of his brother's family. He would certainly never do anything to jeopardise any of that – it's far too precious. Also, Francesco's been strictly brought up and although he's very independent in many ways, he wouldn't want to upset his mother."

"Do you think it could have anything to do with him considering it . . . inappropriate behaviour because our backgrounds are so different, our cultures, habits . . . whatever?" Rachel paused, then added tentatively, "Do *you* think that it's inappropriate?"

"What is it they say? Love conquers all. If you and Francesco are meant for each other, it will work itself out." Lennie scrutinised Rachel's face. "Of course, you may have just kissed him because you have been lonely and you, very understandably, needed to feel a man's arms around you again. If that is the case, I very much doubt that any harm has been done. It would be good for Francesco to remember he's nearly forty and if he doesn't get married soon, his mother will have kittens. She's been giving him a hard time on that particular subject over the last few years. She says she wants more grandchildren and that Clara and Bernardo's two aren't enough. The fact that Clara happens to believe that two are more than enough really infuriates her!"

"I certainly wasn't thinking of marriage or anything like that," said Rachel, hurriedly. "It's just that I really like him so much – and I'd have preferred it hadn't ended the way it did, that's all. I feel a bit like a scarlet woman, trying to lead the upright man astray."

For a moment, Lennie regarded her with a solemn expression. Then, her face crinkled and she broke into a broad smile. "I think that's very far from the truth, my dear Rachel!" She burst out laughing. It was so infectious, Rachel couldn't help joining in.

At that moment, Douglas walked slowly into the room. Rachel couldn't help noticing how out of breath he seemed as he sank onto the arm of the couch beside his wife. He looked from one to the other.

"What are you two ladies laughing about?"

"Men," said Lennie in a clear voice, eyebrows raised comically.

"What's that? Did you say men?"

She nodded. "That's right. The mystery and madness of men. Rachel has decided that they're difficult to make out."

"Difficult to make out? Rubbish!" said Douglas, turning towards Rachel. "We're very simple beings, us men. We are all engaged in the same thing – looking for the perfect woman. It's just that it sometimes takes a long time and, sadly, some of us never find her. So that makes us seem mad or bad but really any strange behaviour is because we're disappointed that we haven't succeeded yet. Was there any man in particular you were thinking of? Some one I might know perhaps?" he asked artfully.

"No!" said Lennie and Rachel in unison.

"What was that?"

Rachel laughed. "No!" she repeated.

"Couldn't be Francesco then."

"Douglas, be quiet and behave!" commanded Lennie.

That evening, just as it was beginning to get dark, the telephone rang in the hall.

"Can you get that, Rachel?" shouted Lennie from the kitchen.

Rachel made her way out of the sitting-room and picked up the phone.

"*Pronto!*"

She thought she caught the sound of someone giving a short sigh or an exhalation of breath that could have been stifled amusement. Her stomach lurched. Not again! Not here where she'd thought she was safe.

"Who is it?" she demanded, trying to keep her voice from shaking.

This time, there was definitely a throaty sigh of amusement from the other end of the phone. Then the connection was broken.

She was suddenly aware of Lennie's presence beside her. She turned to her, one hand nervously massaging the back of her neck, the other still gripping the receiver.

"It was them! I know it was. How did they find out that I was here?"

"I'm sorry I asked you to answer the wretched phone! It was only after you picked it up that I'd a premonition that it was the wrong thing to have done," said Lennie, taking the phone from Rachel and putting a comforting arm around her. "Come into the kitchen and we'll talk it over." She followed Rachel through the sitting-room and into the kitchen. "Now sit down while I dry my hands and get us a glass of wine each."

Rachel saw that Lennie had been in the middle of washing lettuce for the evening meal. Splashes of water lay on the tiled floor and water still ran from the tap. A half-filled salad drainer lay on its side on the wooden draining-board. Two saucepans bubbled on the old-fashioned electric cooker. Through the open window, she could see Douglas sitting on the summerhouse veranda as the shadows deepened around him. Some kind of antique paraffin lamp hanging on a hook above his head gave off enough light to make his mass of fine grey hair look like a sort of silvery halo. He appeared to be talking to Percy, who gazed steadily back at him from the other chair.

Carrying two generously filled glasses over to the table, Lennie put them down and pulled out the chair opposite Rachel. Once sitting, she took a couple of gulps from her glass, looked pleasantly surprised and twisted round in her chair to have another look at the label on the bottle behind her.

"Good stuff this! I must get some more of it. Far superior to the dreadful gut rot they produce in the local rat-infested cantina. Drink up!" she raised a glass to Rachel. *"Salute!"*

Rachel obediently took a sip of the red wine. It *was* good. It reminded her of blackcurrants and elder flowers and oak. But, however pleasant the wine was, all she could think about was the fact that Frank and his horrible sister knew where she was hiding.

"What are we going to do now?" she asked, anxiously.

Lennie held her glass in front of her for a moment, lost in admiration of the fiery glow that the kitchen light made as it shone through the plum-coloured liquid.

"It's almost dark and supper will be ready in ten minutes. Tomorrow is Sunday and Francesco will be coming over with his mother and the rest of the family. I think the best thing to do is ring him and ask him to contact his cousin so that the police know we've had a call that could *possibly* be from those two troublemakers. Francesco may be able to persuade them to trace the call. I don't know. But for the moment, we will have a pleasant evening together. Now Rachel, stop looking so worried and see if the pasta is nearly ready while I finish the salad."

If Lennie herself was worried, she was hiding it well, thought Rachel.

At supper, Douglas ate very little. He excused himself by explaining that he'd polished off too many chocolate biscuits with his tea earlier on. As far as Rachel could remember, he'd not eaten anything with his tea either. She could tell that Lennie was concerned over her husband's lack of appetite but that she didn't want to make a fuss. As it was, Rachel found it difficult to pretend that all was as it should be. She didn't think that Lennie had mentioned the phone call to him and she was glad of that. Douglas was looking far from well. The ivory pallor underlying his tan seemed more pronounced this evening but she knew how stubborn he could be when it came to his own health.

He had confided in her the day before that there wasn't much that could be done for him.

"You see, my dear, the doctor and I have an understanding. He's told me that they've done all they can; they've juggled with the cocktail of pills I have to swallow every day until they got it as near to being right as they can be. The consultant at Castel del Piano said I should

consider myself as being in 'injury time' now." He'd laughed.
"It's rather a good way of putting it, I think. When I told
Lennie what he'd said, I'm afraid she got rather cross – with
him and with me." He'd looked at her with a tired smile. "If
I were to be completely honest, apart from the idea of leaving
Lennie behind, I'd be more than content to go now. I do feel
as though I've rather run out of puff."

"Like a dozy old steam train," said Lennie, materialising
suddenly through the door. Rachel wondered how much of
the conversation had been overheard by her. Her voice
was cheerful but underneath, she could see the strain. It
showed in the way she kept looking at Douglas, always on
the alert for tell-tale signs of some sort of crisis looming.
Usually she radiated contentment but there was a tension
in her today especially that made the younger woman wish
she'd not added to her problems by landing on them with
all her own worries.

Now, this evening, as they settled into the comfy
armchairs in the cluttered sitting-room, it was obvious that
Douglas was not up to playing the piano. Lennie suggested
that they listen to a record instead. Searching among the
jumble of ancient vinyl discs in the cupboard beside the
couch, she unearthed a record in its old-fashioned cardboard
cover. Rachel could see that the centre of the disc was bright
red with a dog, listening to what looked like a giant horn.

Carefully putting the needle down at the start of the
second track, Lennie said, "This is one of our favourite
pieces of music. It's the slow movement of Samuel Barber's
string quartet. Douglas once had a girlfriend who was a
gifted viola player and, on their first date, she invited him

to a concert at which it was performed. He introduced me
to it years ago. It's quite lovely."

Rachel lay back in her chair and closed her eyes. It
seemed to her that the piece was played with great feeling
and tenderness. She had never heard it before. It was
beautiful and infinitely sad. Once, she opened her eyes for
a brief moment. Douglas and Lennie were both listening
intently. Lennie's hand lay on her husband's shoulder,
lightly covered by one of his own elegantly long-fingered
hands, the veins standing out blue under the rice-paper-
thin skin. She hastily shut her eyes again, feeling
overwhelmed by a sudden sense of loss. Thoughts of Simon,
of the frail old man opposite her and of an empty feeling
deep inside made her want to burst into tears. With
difficulty, she stayed dry-eyed and when the music softly
faded, she somehow managed to not give in to the urge to
weep for herself and for the elderly couple for whom she
felt such affection.

Although she'd felt emotionally exhausted a short time
before, Rachel could not get to sleep that night. Even
Percy, blissfully snoring at the end of her bed, didn't comfort
her. She knew that she was lying there, waiting for
something to happen. Each creak in the old house or rustle
of leaves in the garden made her tense. It felt as if all her
nerve-endings were tingling. After every sound, it took
several minutes of deep breathing before she could relax
again.

Needing to feel the night air on her face, she got out of
bed and quietly swung open the shutters. Fireflies and glow-

worms glimmered against the dark shapes of trees, making the garden look magical. A faint aura of light hung in the sky, marking the moon's position behind her duvet of clouds. Rachel could hear the wind chimes resonating softly in the slight stirrings of hot night air. Leaving the shutters half-open, in the hope that some current of air would enter the stuffy bedroom, she climbed back on to the bed, covering herself with the sheet.

She fell asleep after some time but it was only for a little while. Suddenly, she was wide-awake. She knew that a sound of some kind had disturbed her. A pulse seemed to be hammering in her temples. She held her breath. There it was again. It was like a piece of silk being waved around in the air. She could make out nothing in the dark room. Again and again, the sound seemed to come from first one side of her, then the other. In a panic, she finally summoned up the courage to fumble for the switch on her bedside lamp, fully expecting to see a figure on either side of the bed.

Light flooded over and around her, temporarily dazzling her. For a moment the room seemed quite empty. Then the rustling, fluttering, silky sound came again. She looked up, just in time to see a bat settling on the light that hung from the centre of the ceiling. It regarded her with beady eyes, set deep in its furry, pug-dog's face. Rachel could have cried with relief.

Chapter Sixteen

"They'll be here soon," said Lennie, as she put out little dishes of nuts and olives on the table that she and Rachel had set up on the lawn in front of the summerhouse. "You'll like Clara. She's a dear and puts up with a lot from that mother-in-law of hers. She only makes a stand occasionally and then she really digs her heels in. Very good for Mamma! As for the children! You'll see why Douglas and I are so besotted with them."

"And Clara's husband – Francesco's brother – what's he like?" asked Rachel, hoping to God Francesco wouldn't have told him what happened in the garden at Podere Vecchio on the previous day.

Lennie paused in mid-stride. Watching her, Rachel got the feeling that she was considering how best to word her reply.

"Well, let's just say that he isn't quite as special as Francesco has become for us." Adding, somewhat ambiguously, "He's nice enough, I suppose."

Then, in a flurry of scarlet and magenta, she rushed back to the house for more glasses.

Rachel turned to Douglas who was standing, leaning on his walking-stick, gazing at the lilac-blue haze of lavender, now in full bloom. The scent seemed to come in great waves, washing over them, mingling with the perfume of roses. He turned his head and saw her looking at the silk-winged cream and black clusters of swallow-tail butterflies feasting on the flowers.

"Quite gorgeous, isn't it?" he said.

Rachel nodded, smiling.

"You're so lucky to live here."

"What's rather queer?" he enquired, cupping his ear.

Rachel laughed. "Oh, life is rather queer," she said, speaking more clearly. "I think you're very lucky to live in a place like this."

"Absolutely! Couldn't agree more. But I seem to remember that you come from a lovely part of the world too. Very easy to think the grass is greener elsewhere. We all do it. Would you want to live in Italy rather than Ireland?"

"I think I might . . . if things were more normal."

Seeing her slight frown, Douglas, walking with care, moved to her side.

"Don't worry, my dear. It will all work out for the best." He gave a small chuckle. "Anything Lennie's involved in usually ends up with everyone well and truly sorted out."

Rachel smiled. "You're probably right. I've just been cursed with an over-active imagination, that's all."

Just then, a young boy with black curly hair came charging into the garden through the side gate. He ran full tilt towards them, grinning broadly. He made Rachel think of a small brown bird, swooping round the rose-bushes and in and out of the chairs.

"*Ciao, Zio! Dov'è Zia Lennie?*" he cried, in a husky, child's voice as he launched himself against Douglas's legs, making the old man nearly lose his balance.

Rachel hurriedly grabbed his arm.

Propping himself up with his walking-stick, Douglas leaned down towards the animated small figure and smiled at the upturned face.

"*Nella cucina, Armando. Nella cucina!*"

The child was immediately in full canter across the grass towards Lennie, who at that moment, emerged from the kitchen. Her face lit up as he flew towards her, arms outstretched. It seemed to Rachel that all worry drained out of her face as she picked him up and hugged him to her.

"*Ciao, bambino mio. Come stai?*"

Rachel's attention was caught by the arrival of a pretty woman in a bright blue dress, carrying a small child with the most enormous brown eyes she had ever seen. Behind her came a stocky, grey-haired woman in black, flanked on either side by Francesco and another man. He must be Bernardo, Francesco's brother, she thought. They looked very like each other but she could tell that Bernardo was several years younger. His face was plumper and there was no grey in his black hair. She saw his eyes sweep briefly over her before he turned to Douglas.

She watched as Douglas went forward to greet them.

"*Buongiorno a tutti. Siete tutti benvenuti!*" He made a little bow in the direction of Francesco's diminutive mother. Kissing her hand, he said, *"Signora! Sempre più elegante!"* Rachel could see that, although she immediately made protesting noises, she was thoroughly used to and enjoyed his light-hearted flattery.

Douglas called Rachel over and she shook hands with Francesco's mother. She was aware of the woman's small, jet eyes taking in every detail. Her interest did not appear in the least hostile but Rachel felt there would be very little that got by her unnoticed. Her grey hair was drawn back into a severe bun. She wore very little jewellery but Rachel could see that her simple black dress was well cut and beautifully made. Her black leather shoes looked expensive too although the stockings could not hide the knotted blue veins in her legs and swollen ankles.

She then shook hands with Bernardo, who smiled pleasantly at her and murmured *'Signora.'* Rachel didn't want to catch Francesco's eye but when she greeted him, he seemed relaxed enough.

"How is *signora* Martin?"

"Well, thank you, Francesco," she replied, equally formal. For a moment, she wondered if she had imagined their passionate kiss under the cherry trees in Podere Vecchio. "Do you have any news?"

"No, but my cousin, he try to find where the telephone call come from yesterday. I will tell you when I hear more," he promised, smiling reassuringly at her.

Then he turned towards his mother and, taking her arm, led her solicitously over to one of the chairs.

After she had been introduced to all the family, Rachel excused herself and went in search of Lennie to see if there was anything she could do to help. She found her in the kitchen, watching Armando pour freshly squeezed orange juice into a small jug. Already, his hands and face were slightly sticky-looking. He looked up as she came in and smiled a wide, gap-toothed smile.

Lennie introduced them and the boy solemnly shook hands with Rachel, leaving her fingers lightly coated with the scented orange. With great care he balanced the jug and a glass on a small tray and made for the door into the garden. Rachel watched apprehensively as he staggered down the two steps, the tray at an angle, making the glass collide with the jug with a clunk.

"Should I carry it for him?" she asked.

"No! For goodness' sake, don't! He'll manage. Very independent chap is Armando. He'd be most annoyed if you made it look as though he couldn't do it on his own. Have you met *La Mamma* yet?"

"I shook hands and was scrutinised from head to toe. She seems a rather formidable lady."

Lennie laughed. "She certainly is! That woman held the family together when her husband died. The boys were still small and she worked from home, taking in laundry, making clothes, picking olives, slaving away in the vineyard – anything – so that the family had bread on the table and her boys had an education. She had a tough time of it but she did a good job. Francesco and Bernardo admire her determination – and she's still strong. You should see her out in their vineyard or in the shop in Castel del Piano, working like a man half her age. I think her customers sometimes find her a bit daunting. She can be a little demanding but they put up with it most of the time with a good grace. It's sometimes hard on Clara though. She would love Bernardo and her to have a house of their own where it wouldn't matter if the children ran a little wild." Lennie handed Rachel two plates, loaded with cheeses, slices of melon and curls of translucent ham, and then scooped up two more. "Come out and I'll sit you beside Clara. Francesco's been teaching her some English – so with your bit of Italian the two of you should be able to hold some sort of a conversation!"

Rachel couldn't help noticing how lovely Clara was. The woman reminded her of a painting by Modigliani. With her almond-shaped eyes, creamy oval face and long neck, she looked like a young Madonna. She carried herself with the same dignity that was so evident in the rest of Francesco's family.

"Francesco help me to speak the English . . . a little," she haltingly confided to Rachel. She laughed. "I not very good but you speak to me slow and perhaps I understand."

"No, you speak very well. Better than my Italian," said Rachel, admiring the little girl on the other's lap. She couldn't stop looking at the child's happy face with its amazing eyes with their fringe of black lashes. "How old is Rosa?"

"She has more than one year. How you say . . . ?" Clara turned to Francesco. "*Francesco, come si dice quattordici mesi in Inglese?*"

As Francesco answered her, Rachel caught a fleeting expression crossing Bernardo's face. She couldn't make out whether it was annoyance that his wife had chosen to ask his brother the question instead of himself or irritation that she had interrupted their conversation. Whatever it was, for a moment it made him look far less pleasant than Francesco.

Clara seemed unaware of her husband's sour expression and determinedly battled on in her fractured English. There was something vibrant and warm about her that was most attractive. If Francesco was in love with her, Rachel could see why. She watched the way Clara handled her children; how Armando would, from time to time go to her, putting his hand on her arm, waiting until she'd finished speaking before asking her a question or telling her in elaborate detail about some discovery he had just made in the garden. Each time, she listened to him attentively while Rosa sat placidly in her lap like a happy little Buddha. The little girl alternately turned the narrow gold bracelet on her mother's arm, fascinated by the sunlight flashing on its faceted surface and made eyes at Douglas. She would peer around her mother's arm, then retreat in a fit of giggles when he made faces at her. Rachel wasn't sure who was the greater flirt – the man or the child.

Francesco's mother gave Rachel the occasional nod and smile but made no attempt to speak to her after her first question, delivered at breakneck speed when she first sat down. Rachel had not understood a word. She looked helplessly at Douglas who'd been amused by her puzzled expression.

"Don't worry, my dear. You'll soon pick it up. Complete immersion is what you need. We'll have to start having all our meals in Italian!"

206

Armando had been allowed to act as wine waiter. He took the job seriously. Very carefully, with a napkin clutched around the neck of the bottle and the tip of his tongue protruding slightly from between his lips, he poured out the fragrant wine into pretty, engraved glasses with a fine twist of gold enclosed in their stems. He had made several attempts to catch Percy but the cat was having none of it. With an indignant flick of his tail, he hastily disappeared under the summerhouse where he stayed, staring balefully at the intruders with eyes that were the colour of the Tuscan sky.

Once, when Clara was talking to Douglas, Rachel saw Francesco glance in the other woman's direction. It was only for a second but there was such intensity in that look she experienced a sinking feeling. She knew that he had never looked at her in that way and most probably never would. She told herself not to be a fool but she couldn't stop a sudden rush of disappointment and a brief stab of jealousy. She felt suddenly deflated and depressed.

When Clara talked to him, she seemed completely unconscious of any undercurrents. She laughed as she teased Francesco about something that had cropped up in the general conversation. Rachel couldn't follow what was being said most of the time. They all talked so fast, Lennie and Douglas included. It left her thoroughly confused.

The sensation of being alone, even in the middle of all the talk and laughter, returned. She wondered if she would ever really belong; become part of what was going on around her again. When Simon was alive, being his wife had given her confidence when she had to go to events without him. Just knowing he would be waiting for her at the end of the day had made her feel happy and secure.

As if she'd read her thoughts, Lennie got up and changed places so that she was next to Rachel.

"You should be concentrating on your Italian, not worrying about the future or regretting the past, my dear." She smiled at Rachel. "They'll be going in a little while and then you can get your breath back."

Soon after, Francesco's mother picked up her bag and rose from her chair. She thanked Lennie and Douglas for their hospitality with the same formal graciousness that Rachel had seen Francesco display in his dealings with herself. Almost immediately, Francesco and Bernardo also got to their feet. As they prepared to leave, Bernardo called to Armando to stop trying to wriggle under the summerhouse in an effort to join Percy, there was a sudden cry from Clara. Rachel turned to see her suddenly go down on one knee, Rosa on her hip, as she hunted for something in the grass. It appeared that she'd lost her gold bracelet.

Straight away, Francesco went over and crouched beside her, combing the grass with his fingers, peering under the table and chairs. Rachel heard him speaking quietly to her. She guessed that he was reassuring her that it would be found.

She noticed that Bernardo made no attempt to join in the hunt for the missing bracelet. He merely looked irritated by the delay. After a few moments, he fired off a couple of rapid sentences at his wife. This resulted in Clara giving him a glance but without saying anything in response. Rachel spotted the quick glare Francesco gave his brother, before turning away dismissively and continuing his search.

"It has to be close to where Clara was sitting. Rosa must have loosened the catch," said Lennie, now also on her hands and knees in the grass.

Again, an outburst from Bernardo but this time he was interrupted by his mother.

"*Silenzio, Bernardo!*" The expression on her face was severe.

Bernardo was silent. Good for *Mamma!* thought Rachel.

Armando, who had given up trying to catch Percy and had disappeared behind some bushes a few moments earlier, now re-emerged looking somewhat guilty. Giving his grandmother and father a wide berth, he went up to his mother. Pulling the bracelet slowly out of his trouser pocket, he pressed it into her hand and then planted a quick kiss on her cheek.

"*L'ho trovato io!*" he announced, turning towards the assembled group and shooting a defiant look in his father's direction.

Bernardo let out a snort of impatience but said nothing.

Ignoring him, Lennie got to her feet.

"Well, thank goodness for that!" She ruffled the boy's hair affectionately, giving him a conspiratorial smile. "*Sei molto cativo, bambino mio!*"

He smiled up at her, completely untroubled at the idea of being called a bad boy. Rachel could see that Armando was well aware of how fond Lennie and Douglas were of him. It was evidently an affection that was returned in full measure.

Lennie turned to Rachel and explained that the bracelet had been a wedding present from Bernardo to his wife. Rachel still didn't feel that explained the man's offhand manner. If he were so anxious about it being lost, why on earth hadn't he joined in the search too?

"*Vieni qui, Armando,*" commanded his grandmother.

The tone of authority was not to be ignored. Obediently, the child trotted over to her. She took his hand firmly in her own and set off in the direction of the side gate, followed by the rest of the family. Rachel watched, amused, as Rosa blew kisses over her mother's shoulder at Douglas and Lennie.

She noticed that although Francesco had greeted her when they first arrived and said goodbye before leaving, he had not looked her in the eye at any other time during the visit.

After supper that night, Rachel asked Douglas why there were no nightingales in the garden at Villa Fiorita.

"No nightingales? Oh, we have them but once their courting's done, they stop singing," he told her.

"Lazy lot!" chuckled Lennie. "Once they're sure that they've got their mate, they can't be bothered to serenade her any more!"

Douglas, who'd been watching his wife's lips carefully in the lamplight, turned to Rachel.

"Lennie wouldn't thank me if I tried to serenade her. It's a sad fact of life but I've never been able to sing. Make the most appalling racket! I sound something like a malfunctioning electric saw apparently." He eyed his wife over the top of his glasses. "Wasn't that your description, my darling, the first time you heard me attempting a hymn at Aunt Maude's funeral all those years ago?"

"True," said Lennie. "But then from what I remember of your Aunt Maude, it served her right! Anyway, you serenade me with your piano-playing."

The evening was especially warm and they had taken their glasses of wine outside. Rachel lay back in her chair and looked up at the clear night sky. Every now and then, she glimpsed bats wheeling above her, fleeting silhouettes against the backdrop of stars. She was just able to hear their calls, tiny pinpricks of sound in the darkness. The silken rustle that had alarmed her so much in the bedroom was indistinguishable out here in the garden with all the other noises of the night.

Untypically, Percy had decided that he wanted a lap on which to sit. He chose Douglas. The man looked down at him in surprise.

"Goodness me! I feel most honoured," he said as he stroked the animal's soft fur with his gentle pianist's hands.

Lennie got to her feet. "Shall we leave these two to keep each other company while we go and clear up the supper things?"

After the washing-up was done and coffee made, the phone rang. Rachel couldn't stop herself from giving an involuntary jump and then freezing in the middle of putting the last of the cutlery into the drawer. She looked at Lennie.

"Lennie . . ."

211

"It's all right dear. I'll answer it. I can tell you now that it's most probably Francesco."

She hurried out of the room. Rachel didn't move until she heard Lennie's voice as she answered the phone. She waited, hardly daring to breathe. There was a short pause before the woman continued speaking. It all sounded perfectly normal.

'Oh, Lord! What a neurotic idiot I've become," she thought, picking up the coffee pot and putting it onto the tray. Carefully negotiating the two steps down into the garden, she started to walk towards the summerhouse.

The first thing she noticed as she approached the group of chairs was that Percy was no longer ensconced on Douglas's lap. What she saw next made her stop dead, fingers gripping the tray tightly so that her knuckles turned white.

Douglas was still sitting in his chair but there was a subtle difference in the angle at which his body rested against the cushion behind him. His head drooped slightly towards one shoulder, his half-hidden face gleamed strangely in the little lamplight that filtered through the oleander leaves above. His eyes seemed to be open. Forcing herself to put the tray on the table before she dropped it, Rachel bent down and looked into his face.

"Douglas? Douglas?"

A slight sound, like a groan, escaped from him. Foliage rustled nearby, making her glance up quickly. A sudden tremor, as though a pulse of electricity passed through the man's body, drew her attention back to Douglas.

She touched the hand lying on his lap. It felt strangely

unresponsive. Then Douglas made the same sound again. Rachel looked into his face. The features seemed to have taken on the appearance of being only half human. One side sagged as if all the life had drained from it. The look of helplessness and fear she saw in his eyes hit her with such force, she spun around and started to run towards the house, calling frantically for Lennie, her voice cracking with panic.

It wasn't just the way Douglas looked that made her run. A white flower had been slipped into the flaccid hand that lay on the man's lap. Rachel knew beyond all doubt that he had not picked it himself.

Even before Rachel gave her first shout, Lennie had dropped the telephone in mid-sentence. Erupting from the house and running towards Douglas, her grey hair falling around her shoulders, leaving a trail of combs in the trampled grass, she passed Rachel as though the younger woman were invisible.

Chapter Seventeen

"Francesco is on his way. He'll be here soon. I have to go with Douglas now, Rachel."

Lennie's face looked haggard in the ambulance's lights, her eyes unnaturally bright.

"Of course! I understand," said Rachel, kissing her on the cheek. "I so hope everything will be all right. Don't worry about me. I'll be fine."

She watched as Lennie climbed into the back of the vehicle. Just before the doors closed, the older woman turned round and smiled slightly at her.

"He's a tough old bird. I expect he'll be chasing the nurses in a couple of days' time!

Then she was gone. Rachel could hear the sound of the siren, first on the narrow road leading to the cantina and then more faintly as the ambulance climbed the hill up to the main road to Castel del Piano. She could see its firefly beam flickering in and out of the gaps in the trees as it flew along.

'Please God, may he be all right,' she silently prayed as she stood in the dark at the road's edge.

When she could no longer hear its dismal wailing, Rachel became aware of just how dark the night was. The suffocating blackness of it pressed in around her. There was no moon and the stars were hidden behind a thick blanket of cloud. For a brief moment, panic flared in her, making her break out into a sweat. Rooted to the spot, to her every night sound had all of a sudden become amplified and threatening.

She had just started to force herself to relax when she thought she heard footsteps coming along the road towards her. She couldn't move. Eyes straining to make out a darker shape in the surrounding dark, Rachel wondered if it were Frank coming for her. Was this where she would die? Would it be at the side of the road? Would he strangle her? Knife her? Rape her? There was no mistaking it; the sound of footsteps drew nearer. Someone was approaching, walking stealthily, carefully, and inexorably closer to where she stood, like a doomed animal, waiting for the end. The man had frightened Douglas nearly to death. Now he was coming back for her. All her thought processes seemed to be in slow motion. Would his sister be there too? Would she watch while he killed her? Somehow, no scenario seemed too bizarre. She instinctively knew that anything was possible where Frank and his psychotic-sounding sister were concerned. They were different, anarchic and dangerous. She understood that people like them didn't obey the normal rules of logic or civilised behaviour.

Suddenly, she found herself pinioned in the white light

from a powerful torch. Involuntarily, Rachel let out a low sob of fright.

"Rachel? What are you doing on the road?"

The voice was Francesco's.

Immediately, she stumbled forward, half collapsing against him.

"Thank God! I thought it was them," she moaned, her face pressed into his shoulder, her fingers clutching his shirt.

She was aware that he had switched off the torch. She could feel his arms around her and, for a moment, it felt the safest place on earth. For a few minutes, he said nothing, just held her, waiting for her breathing to calm. Then, very gently, Francesco released her.

"Now, we go to the house," he whispered. "Is better not to be in the road. Come!"

Taking her by the arm, he led her through the gate and quietly along the path to the house. Once inside the front door, he drew the bolt and turned off the light in the front hall.

Rachel felt that some explanation for her behaviour was needed.

"You frightened me, Francesco. I didn't know that it was you on the road. Where is the Jeep?"

"I put the Jeep at the cantina and walk so nobody hear me," he explained in a low voice.

Then, putting a finger to his lips, Francesco motioned for her to stay behind him. Silently, she followed him as each room was checked and all the shutters were closed. The last room was the kitchen. When that too had been searched, Francesco made sure that the door into the garden was securely locked. Just before he pulled down the blind, Rachel caught a glimpse of the area in front of the summerhouse. The hanging light still illuminated the chair where Douglas had sat only an hour earlier. The shadowy dent his body had made in the cushions was still visible. There was no sign of the white flower. Lennie had snatched it from her husband's hand and hurled it into the night as though it were scalding hot.

Leaning back against the sink, she turned towards Francesco and asked, "What about Percy? He's disappeared."

Francesco pulled out a chair for her. When she was sitting, he took his place beside her.

"The cat will be OK. Do not worry about him. But for yourself, you must be careful."

His voice was calm but Rachel sensed that he was far from happy about their situation. He had changed out of his Sunday suit and was wearing his usual workday clothes – jeans and a green, short-sleeved shirt and dusty leather boots that looked as though he must have tramped many miles in them.

Now that he was there, her own terror had faded and all she could think about was Douglas. He had looked so frail under the grey ambulance blanket as the men carried him through the garden. Frail and so different, as if the Douglas she had come to know had gone, leaving behind a shell that only vaguely resembled him physically, a being without the spark that had made him so uniquely Douglas. She wondered what was happening in the hospital now. A sudden thought occurred to her.

"Did you tell the police, Francesco?"

He raised his hands from the table and grimaced.

"What I tell them? *Signore* Douglas is ill . . . and in his hand is a flower? They will laugh. There must be more to make them do something."

"But, what about what happened at Podere Vecchio? They know about the flower on the car don't they?"

"*Signora* Lennie, she tell them. But I think . . ." His voice trailed away.

"They think we have over-active imaginations. They think that she's not quite right in the head. Is that it?"

Francesco looked puzzled. "I not understand."

Rachel got up and reached for a glass on the shelf.

"It doesn't matter." She glared at him. "What do we do now if Frank and his lovely sister arrive?"

She started to fill the glass with cold water from the tap.

Francesco smiled grimly. "If they come, we shall see what to do," was all he would say.

Rachel woke with a start. Through the shutters, she could hear crickets chirruping in the night air outside. Then it all flooded back: Douglas, the white flower, the ambulance, her fear and the arrival of Francesco.

After she and Francesco had sat around for a couple of hours, making stilted conversation, waiting for something to happen, he had insisted that Rachel try and get some sleep. Not wanting to be alone in her bedroom, she had curled up on the couch in the sitting room. Now, she felt stiff and her mouth was dry. The light from the small lamp on the table barely reached the corners of the room.

Francesco must have turned off the kitchen light and the open doorway leading into it loomed dark and uninviting. She could not hear him moving around. Perhaps he too had fallen asleep, propped against the table.

Suddenly, all her senses were alerted. A plaintive meow sounded from outside the front door. She got up quickly, stumbling from the pins and needles in her leg, and hobbled out into the small hallway. Peering through the narrow strip of frosted glass that was set into the door, she could just make out the cat's shape on the other side. Then came another, louder meow, followed by a long, persistent yowl and the sound of scratching at the base of the door. Rachel hesitated, wondering whether she should find Francesco before opening it. On the other hand, if there were anyone lurking, Percy's crying would only draw their attention to the animal. She couldn't bear the thought of anything happening to him. As quietly as she could, she drew back the bolt and undid the lock. The door creaked slightly as it opened. Slowly she pulled the door towards her, whispering the cat's name.

What took place next happened so quickly that she didn't have time to shout for help. When the door was half-open, the cat brushed past her legs, desperate to get in. Just as she was about to push the door shut, a hand reached in and grabbed her. With a violent jerk, she was pulled outside, then slammed back against the wall so hard that all the breath was knocked out of her body. Another hand was clamped tightly over her mouth. Before she could think or even attempt to focus on her attacker, something struck the side of her head. She slid sideways against the rough plaster and fell to the ground. The night's darkness seemed to be seeping into her brain as Rachel lost consciousness.

The first thing that she was aware of, as she groped her way back into the world, was an excruciating headache. It felt as if her head had somehow come adrift from the rest of her. All sensation was concentrated within her skull; great dollops of pain threaded their way down behind her eyeballs and poured into her ears. Her body felt numb in comparison. She tried to open her eyes. The first pallid rays of daylight were filtering under a doorway. Although the light was still faint, it hurt her to look in that direction. Gingerly, she tried moving and found that her hands were tied in front of her with, what seemed to be, a piece of thick rope. Straw rustled as she shifted her position and turned her head slowly, attempting to take in her surroundings.

She appeared to be lying on her side in some sort of small barn or cattle shed. It was empty apart from bales of straw stacked near her. There was a stone drinking-trough on a wall to the right of where she lay. As her brain cleared, Rachel could see that wooden rafters stretched from one stone wall across to the other. The only apparent entrance was a stable door, divided into two. A narrow channel sloped down from somewhere behind her to underneath the door. She could feel its stone edges sticking into her through the thin covering of old straw. The sickly sweet smell of cow-dung hung in the air. Outside, the hoopoe called.

A church bell struck six o'clock. She recognised it

straight away. It was definitely the cracked, tinny sound the bell made in San Lorenzo. So, she must be somewhere quite close to Lennie and Douglas's house. She remembered that there was a cluster of ramshackle buildings further down the road. They belonged to one of the Digby-Whites' neighbours, who used it sometimes to house his animals.

As the minutes ticked by, Rachel experienced a range of emotions from fear to anger to misery. All of a sudden, she remembered Francesco. What had happened to him? She knew perfectly well that he would never have left the house without first telling her. What if, after knocking her unconscious, Frank had harmed or even killed him so that he could then get on with the task of dispatching her without being interrupted? All sorts of nightmare scenes flooded, uninvited, into her aching head. She realised that she felt sick.

Forcing herself to try and ignore her physical condition, Rachel turned her attention to thoughts of escape. Why wait to be murdered? She started to tear at the knot in the rope with her teeth. Concentrating as she had never done in her life, she chewed and spat and chewed again at the greasy rope. Several times she had to stop and retch dryly. A taste of bile, mixed with oil, filled her mouth. She dared not stop for more than a few minutes' respite. How much longer did she have before they came for her?

She could have cried with relief when the knot loosened enough for her to drag one hand free. Exhausted, she worked the rope over the other hand and slumped back onto the ground. Her lips were bleeding and she could feel wire-like fibres stuck between her teeth. After a few minutes, she dragged herself into a sitting position. Her first attempt at standing made her head swim. Shutting her eyes, she sank onto her knees before summoning up the strength to try again. Crawling over to the trough, she leaned against it as she hauled herself up its sides so that she was more or less standing erect. The stone felt smooth and cool to the touch. Leaning over, she scooped some of the cloudy water onto her sore wrists. Tempted as she was, she knew she must not drink from the trough, although a small voice inside her pointed out that if she didn't manage to escape soon, she would be murdered well before any ill-effects from contaminated water manifested themselves.

Tentatively, Rachel took a step in the direction of the stable door, then another. At any moment, she felt she would pass out from the combination of pain and nausea. Hanging onto the wall for support, she made her way, inch by inch towards where the morning light now flooded through the cracks in the wood.

She had just reached the corner nearest to the door when she heard the sound of someone moving around on the other side. A shadow blocked a portion of the light that fanned out from under the door. Shrinking back, Rachel desperately searched around her for somewhere to hide. It was obvious that there was nowhere. Neither was there any time left. She heard the rasping sound of a chain being pulled roughly through a metal loop. The next moment, a man stepped quickly into the shed, securing the door behind him with a wooden catch. He had narrow shoulders and a slight slouch. As Rachel had known it would be, it was Frank. She froze, waiting to see what he would do next.

He paused, letting his eyes adjust to the gloom. Then he started forward, giving an angry exclamation as he spotted the rope lying on the ground. Spinning round, he scanned the shed. Rachel knew she couldn't run. She knew that he would see her. As he turned towards her, she instinctively held her hands up in front of her to shield herself. His eyes seemed to glow as he came towards her. A step away, he stopped and gave a low, delighted chuckle.

"Well, now! Hasn't the feisty little lady nearly escaped! Good thing Frank came in time, don't you think?" The question was obviously a rhetorical one. He continued speaking, looking her up and down, rubbing his hands together in anticipation. "Di *will* be pleased, so she will!"

It looked as though he had picked the scab off the scratch on his face, making it look angrily wet and red, as if it were still bleeding. Almost gently, he took Rachel's arm and started to half pull, half push her across the barn, back to the place where she had lain a short time before.

"Sit down there," he instructed her. Peering at her as she sank down on the straw, he added, "Your face looks a terrible mess, so it does. I wonder what you've been up to. Was it chewing on the old rope did that to your lips, I wonder?"

"Where's Francesco?" Her voice sounded like a croak.

Frank hunkered down in front of her, staring at her with his pale eyes.

"Now, who would he be?"

For a moment Rachel was filled with anger. "You know perfectly well who he is, you bastard!" she spat.

The anger drained away as quickly as it had come. She

saw him clench his fists. Turning her head to one side, she shut her eyes as she waited for him to hit her. But instead, he gave a low laugh. There was no amusement in the sound, only menace.

"Hit the nail on the head! How did you guess, Rachel?"

She opened her eyes and stared back at him. "What do you mean?"

"Oh, didn't he tell you? Di and me – we're both bastards, so we are. Thanks to your husband's nice daddy."

She looked at him in astonishment. "I don't know what you mean. Are you talking about Simon's father?"

"Aye! I most certainly am. Who else would I be talking about? Oh, yes, we're bastards sure enough – not the sort of people that our big brother wanted to know about. He wasn't too friendly towards Di and me – your Simon. Hurt our feelings, so he did."

Her head was spinning badly. Rachel thought she would pass out. She tried to lick her cracked lips but she had no saliva and her tongue was like sandpaper.

"I don't know what you're on about. You didn't answer my question. Where's Francesco?"

Frank giggled. The sound was strangely unpleasant. "One down and one to go!" This phrase seemed to please him. He repeated it, getting to his feet. Twice more, in a singsong voice he said, "That's it! One down and one to go! One down and *one* to go!" He suddenly made a dive and pulled Rachel roughly to her feet. She let out a scream. He took hold of both her shoulders and shook her so that her head rocked wildly backwards and forwards like a limp doll's. "Now, put a sock in it and do as you're told." He dragged her over to a pile of straw bales and pushed her down so that she was spread-eagled on one. Then he looked up at the roof above them, then briefly back at Rachel. There was something in his glance that increased her fear. "Perfect! Now, Rachel. You are going to wait here like a good, wee woman while I go and get my sister." Without any warning, Frank's arm shot forward and his fist connected like a sledge-hammer with the side of her face. For the second time that day, she was knocked unconscious.

A little while later, she started to come round. Two voices came and went, mingling in her head: one she recognised as Frank's, the other was husky, lower-pitched but belonging to a woman. They appeared to be having an argument. She could hear the voices but couldn't understand their words. Their disagreement echoed in her mind, now loud, now soft as reality came and went. It seemed as though she were somehow above the two speakers. Drifting in and out of consciousness, Rachel gradually became aware that she was propped against the prickly bales of straw in a standing position. The bales seemed to be piled around her so that she wouldn't fall over. There was something around her neck that felt tight and uncomfortable and seemed to force her neck back and upwards. Slowly, the clouds in her brain cleared enough for her to hear what was being said. Her eyes flickered open for a moment but all she could see were the shadowy walls of straw.

"What are you waiting for?" asked the husky voice from the other side of the bales.

"I don't think it's right, that's all. There are other ways to pay them back," replied Frank.

"We've gone through all that. You know we agreed to do a thorough job, Frank. Have you forgotten what we promised Mammy on her deathbed?"

"I know, I know!" Frank sounded agitated. "But she's nice really. She doesn't know what happened." His voice took on a pleading quality. "We could keep her somewhere safe, so we could. Somewhere she wouldn't be found."

"No! Have you forgotten how that shit didn't even bother to come to Mammy's funeral? Have you forgotten that? Have you forgotten how he thought sending one miserable bunch of white flowers to the funeral would make everything all hunky-dory? Have you forgotten how long it took to track down the shit's son?"

There was a silence. When Frank spoke again, he sounded sad.

"You and me. We were the only ones at Mammy's funeral. No one else came, did they?"

"No, Frank, they did not." The other voice took on a caressing quality. "*We* were the ones to look after Mammy when she was ill. We held her hand when the pain got so bad she cried and the doctor didn't come. When she died, you only had me to keep you company when they locked you away. Do you remember how I talked to you at night when I came to visit? Remember I told you how it would all work out in the end? That we would get justice. Do you remember, Frank?"

"Aye. I remember," said the voice of Frank, so softly that Rachel could barely make out the words.

"Well then! You're not going to chicken out now when we can get what we want? You're not going to let your mammy and your sister down now, are you, Frank?"

"No. I won't let you down. There's only you in the world cares. I'll do what you say, Di. I'll do it."

Suddenly, Rachel was jolted into full wakefulness by the surrounding bales being pulled away. The wall of straw in front of her disappeared and she could see Frank's bony figure, standing below her. His pale face was level with her waist. He didn't look at her, but worked at removing the last of the bales, kicking and punching them out of the way in a kind of silent fury. When the bale behind her fell to the ground, Rachel realised the appalling fact that all that supported her now was the thing around her neck and that when the bale she stood on was removed; she would hang from the rafters above.

Somehow, she managed to force the words past her lips.

"Frank! Oh, God. Please don't! Don't do it!" she croaked.

He stopped and looked at her, his face inscrutable. His voice was strangely soft and calm.

"I have to, Rachel. There's no other way to finish this. Di said."

Rachel tried to focus her eyes in the half-light of the shed. Where was the sister? Had she gone and left him to kill her on his own so that the blame would seem to be all his? In a last attempt to save herself, she cried out.

"Diana? Please stop this! Diana?"

Frank put a dirty hand on her leg. It felt icy against her already cold skin.

"Don't fret! It'll be all over in two shakes of a lamb's tail. You won't feel a thing."

It was Frank standing at her feet, preparing to pull away the last bale – but the voice had been the husky one she'd heard earlier, the voice of Frank's manipulating sister, Diana. Rachel's mind spun. Was there really no sister at all?

She made one last desperate effort to get through to him.

"Please, Frank. We can work something out. I'll make up to you for everything. I promise! Please . . ."

Mercifully, Rachel succumbed to the black fog that yet again invaded her terrified brain.

Chapter Eighteen

"Jesus! What did he do to you?" The voice sounded shocked. "Rachel, it's Guy. Can you hear me?"

She didn't want to answer. It would be too much of an effort. Her head throbbed and her face and neck felt as though she'd done six rounds with Mike Tyson. But the voice persisted. It seemed to be coming from a long distance away.

"Rachel! Do open those lovely brown eyes of yours!"

With a tremendous effort, Rachel forced her eyes open and then quickly closed them again. From the brief glimpse she'd taken, she appeared to be in a hospital ward with a worried-looking Guy Haywood peering down at her. She felt so weak; she wished he'd just go away and leave her in peace.

Then she remembered the man with Frank's face, speaking with his sister's voice, telling her that hanging would not hurt. All the terror she had experienced poured back in to her. She let out a low moan, her eyes opening wide, her hands grasping the sheet convulsively.

"Where is he? Where's Frank?" Her voice was almost inaudible.

Seeing the look on her face, Guy took one of her hands in his, gently unhooking her fingers from the bedclothes.

"It's all right, Rachel. It's over. He's gone. I promise you. You're quite safe."

She stared at him, trying to make sense of it all. His face seemed to be dancing in space above her.

Rachel blinked. "Why are you here? What happened?"

She could barely push the words out through her sore lips. Guy had to lean closer to hear what she was saying.

"Lennie phoned and I got the first plane I could. Caro will be here next week when she's finished her wheeling and dealing. Apparently, ever since yesterday, you've done nothing but sleep. I don't know what they gave you but you've been away with the birds for the last twenty-four hours." He asked quietly, "Why didn't you let us know that things had got so bad?"

Wearily, Rachel shut her eyes. Why hadn't she told them? she wondered. Had it been pride, proving to herself that she could cope? Or just a feeling that what was happening would soon be sorted out with Lennie's help? But she found that with her eyes closed, she kept seeing the wild look on Frank's face as he kicked away the bales of straw in the stable. Hurriedly opening them, she forced herself to focus on Guy. She could see that he looked tired and anxious. His clothes seemed to have been slept in and his face shone with sweat. It was nice of him to have come all the way back from London but Rachel couldn't help wishing that he would let go of her hand.

"I had Lennie and Francesco to help me . . . I thought it would be silly to bother you . . . I . . ." Rachel let out a gasp. "Where *is* Francesco? What's happened to him? And is Douglas all right?" She made a weak attempt to pull herself up in the bed.

Just then, a nurse appeared, carrying a small dish with a syringe. She smiled at Guy and indicated that he should leave. He nodded, then turned back to Rachel.

"Listen, Rachel. I think it's time for your knock-out drops. We'll talk later. Just rest and get better." He smiled down at her. "Never knew anyone who could still look good with a black eye and a bruise the size of a soup plate on the side of her face. You're quite amazing! I'll be back tomorrow and we'll talk then."

He bent down and gave her a quick kiss on the unbruised cheek. In spite of her physical discomfort and feeling groggy, she had to stop herself from turning her head away from the smell of garlic and cologne, heavily laced with sweat.

The next time Rachel surfaced, it was getting dark. She realised she must have slept for several hours. Some of the lights in the ward had been switched on. An unseen woman beside her moaned and muttered. Tired flowers on the locker beside the woman's bed gave off a faint but stale smell. Two women in dressing-gowns chatted noisily by a window opposite. She caught a glimpse of a white-coated doctor hurrying down the ward, his footsteps brisk and percussive on the polished lino.

She felt a little less bruised and was able to keep her eyes
open without it being too painful. Her stomach felt better
too. They must have given her something for the nausea as
well as to send her to sleep. Carefully, she turned her head
on the pillow.

Lennie was sitting crookedly in a chair beside her, snoring
gently. Her face was crumpled with tiredness; purple circles
bloomed under her eyes. For the first time since she'd known
her, Rachel thought that her age showed. Most of her hair
had slipped out of its combs and it lay in fine grey swirls on
her shoulders. The long red dress looked the worse for wear.
It was badly creased and there was a dark stain on one of the
sleeves. A wave of affection swept over Rachel. How was
Douglas? She almost dreaded Lennie waking.

As if aware of Rachel's gaze, the woman's eyelids flickered
and opened. Immediately, Lennie heaved herself up in the
chair, her face full of concern.

"How are you, my dear?"

"I've felt better, I must admit."

Lennie smiled slightly. "You poor child! You came to
me for help and look what happened to you!"

"It had to come to a head, Lennie – at the Haywoods' or
with you." Rachel hesitated and then asked, "How is
Douglas?"

Lennie smiled a slow, sweet smile. When she spoke, her
voice sounded husky with fatigue. "He died, Rachel – two
hours ago. My lovely husband has gone and left me in the
lurch, I'm afraid."

Tears welled in Rachel's eyes, making Lennie's face
appear to drift and blur.

"Oh, God, Lennie! I'm so sorry. I dumped all my troubles on you when you needed to give your attention to Douglas. He was so kind and cheerful with me and I knew he wasn't feeling well . . ."

Lennie smiled again, taking Rachel's hand in her own.

"Don't cry, Rachel. He would have *hated* to have gone on the way he was. The stroke was a massive one. I know that he loved you being with us. We both did. He told me a few days ago that he would have liked to have had a daughter like you. Your being there over the past week cheered him up enormously. He loved having a pretty face around the place instead of just my worn-out old mug!"

"Oh, Lennie! It just seems so horribly final! I can't believe that he's not here any more." Rachel closed her eyes for a moment. Then she asked, "Do you think he still exists in some way? I mean, not in the sort of heaven we learned about in religion classes but that he's not gone completely?"

Lennie leaned closer to the bed and looked into her face. "I *know* he's not snuffed out like a candle. He'll always be there for me – in some way." She tilted her head slightly to one side, a glimmer of amusement in her tired eyes. "That's if he's not too busy chasing the best-looking angels in the joint!"

Rachel suddenly remembered the white flower in Douglas's hand.

"But what gave him the stroke, Lennie? It must have been Frank."

"I'm not sure," replied Lennie in a quiet voice.

"How can you be so calm about it?"

233

"We both knew, Douglas and I, that he'd not last much longer. Frank made it happen a little sooner, that's all."

"I'd like to kill him," Rachel said weakly.

"I'm afraid the police have already done that for you, my dear."

Rachel stared at her. "What happened?"

"Yesterday morning, it was just starting to get light and I was sitting beside Douglas, watching, waiting. Although I was concentrating on trying to get through to him, I suddenly had a feeling that something dreadful was happening at the house. I tried to ring you and there was no answer. So I rang the police and managed to convince them you were in great danger. When they heard that Francesco . . ."

"Francesco!" interrupted Rachel. "What happened to Francesco?"

"He's fine. He also had a little confrontation with Frank but he'll recover. When the police heard that Francesco was there at the house but hadn't come to the phone, they began to take things more seriously." She gave Rachel a dry look. "It's a good thing they did because if they'd arrived a few minutes later, you wouldn't be here now. They had no option but to shoot. They said he was like a madman. It was as though, one minute he believed he was his sister, then the next, himself. They killed him, Rachel, I'm afraid. There was no sign of the sister anywhere."

Rachel couldn't help it but just at that moment, she felt no sorrow at the news of the man's death – only intense relief.

Lennie continued quietly, "I know you hate him now for

what he did to you but perhaps, when you hear more about his life, I think you will feel only pity for him."

"How will I find out?"

"It seems that Guy knows a bit about it. We spoke briefly after he arrived back. He'll be coming to see you again tomorrow and you can ask him then."

It was no good. Rachel couldn't think straight. What had Guy got to do with it all? Had the Diana character been conjured up by Frank? Or did she really exist? Frank hadn't driven the car with the darkened windows. The car had been hired by Diana Forde. The messages left with the flowers on Simon's grave had been signed by her. Suddenly, it was as if a switch in Rachel's brain had been activated, shutting down all mental activity. Too exhausted to continue the conversation, she was vaguely aware of Lennie kissing her and promising to come and see her on the following day.

Propped up against her pillows, she watched as Guy walked towards her between the row of beds. Inquisitive eyes, on both sides of the ward, followed his progress. He looked a lot less tired – although his turquoise socks and bright pink shirt made Rachel wish she were wearing sunglasses. The pink clashed violently with the high colour of his face. He was carrying the largest bunch of flowers she'd ever seen. It too was a wild mix of shades as if he'd opted for a couple of stems of every kind of flower in the shop.

"Hi, there!" He gave her the unavoidable and unwanted kiss. "You look more like yourself, even with the multi-coloured designer make-up," he said, peering with interest at the bruise on her face. Straightening up, Guy waved the flowers vaguely in the direction of a passing nurse, who ignored him. With a look of resignation, he dumped them on the table at the end of her bed. "Are you very sore?"

"Not too bad. A lot better for a good sleep. Every time I surfaced, they stuck a needle into me." Rachel watched as he took off his straw hat and put it down on the bedside locker. It occurred to her that he looked a little like Van Gogh but plumper, more dissolute and with both ears intact. He pulled a chair over to the bed and sank into it thankfully. "I'm more worried about Francesco and finding out what you know about that man, Frank," she said. "Did I hear Lennie right? That you'd be able to tell me some thing about him?"

Guy shifted in his seat. Rachel thought he looked uncomfortable, hesitant. Aware that she was watching him, he gave her a broad smile.

"Well, Francesco first. Apparently, he fell asleep in the kitchen and was woken by Percy, yowling like a banshee. When he found the front door wide open, he got really worried and went outside. It seems that as soon as he stuck his head out of the door, Frank gave him an almighty belt with a spade. Knocked him out cold. When he came to, he found that he'd been dragged into the small loo off the hall and locked in. As you know, the window there is tiny and has a grill on the outside. He tried breaking the door down but it was too thick and anyway, he was in no fit state for physical gymnastics. The *carabinieri* found him there a couple of hours later when they came to your rescue. He's in the men's ward downstairs. They say he has concussion." Seeing the concerned look on her face he added, "Mild concussion – nothing to worry about. They're letting him out later on today, I think."

There was silence while Rachel digested this information.

Then she asked reluctantly, "And Frank? How in God's name do you come to know about him?" Again she noticed an expression of discomfort cross his face. "Did he have anything to do with Simon? . . . Guy?" she insisted.

Guy took out a red silk handkerchief from his trouser pocket and mopped his face. Then he cleared his throat.

"Well, yes and no."

Rachel stared at him. "What does that mean?"

"Are you sure you're ready for all this?"

Rachel nodded.

He stuffed the handkerchief back in his pocket with a resigned look on his face. "I'd better tell you what I know – which is not the whole picture but it's just what Simon chose to tell us."

"You mean, you and Caroline?"

"Yes."

So he *had* kept secrets from her after all. A pang of disappointment shot through her. He'd shared things with the Haywoods that he didn't want her to know about. She had so hoped that Simon wouldn't be implicated in any way in all this mess. Full of apprehension, she waited for Guy to continue.

"From what he told us, Rachel, it seems that when Simon was about eight, his father had a fling with a woman he met in some club or other. Apparently, he became infatuated with her – and it would appear, somewhat reckless. Eventually, Simon's mother found out about the affair and all hell broke loose. Simon didn't talk about it much but I think it had an enormous effect on him. He said once that he just couldn't forgive his father for what he'd put them through. From the age of eight, he never felt the security all children crave – that I presume is the sacred gift parents owe their offspring. Not that I'm in a position to make observations in that particular area." Rachel heard the slight harmonic of bitterness in his voice and wondered if Caroline had said no to them having children. "The crunch came when he got the woman pregnant. Then, surprise, surprise, she suddenly lost her attraction. When she came to him for help, he told her to go to hell. After several attempts to appeal to his better nature, she eventually went away, swearing that one day, she'd pay him back for his callousness. She took herself back to Donegal where she gave birth.

"And that baby was Frank?"

"There were twins. A girl and a boy. Frank and Diana."

Rachel frowned. "But, I thought that Diana was only someone he had made up, imagined so vividly that he'd come to believe that she was real. *I* certainly believed she was real, for God's sake. Until, at the end, when he spoke to me in her voice!" She shivered, involuntarily. "I don't understand. *Is* there a sister involved in all of this?"

"Oh, yes, I'm afraid she's real enough," Guy said, with a sigh. "Schizophrenia was only one of Frank's problems. She had the poor sod so frightened and confused, he didn't know who he was half the time. When he was under stress, that was the time when he started using her voice, slipping backwards and forwards between his own and hers. I suppose one should feel sorry for him. He was pathetic, really."

"But where is she? Did the police get her?"

Guy heard the panic in her voice. "No, there was no sign of her. They searched the area and, if she was around that night, I'm afraid she did a disappearing act. I spoke to one of the local plods this morning. They wanted to ask you some questions but it was obvious you weren't up to it. No doubt, they'll try and pester you later on." He smiled at her. "Don't worry, Rachel. They'll find her if she's anywhere around."

Rachel tried to relax back against the pillows. So Diana did exist! She wasn't just a figment of Frank's imagination. Of course, she reminded herself dizzily, there was the D on the card, the driver of the black car . . . She stared at him.

"So, what happened after they were born?"

"Well, they stayed up in Donegal for a few years. From what I gathered from Simon, Frank and Diana's mother really had it in for Simon's dad but she didn't have the ways or means to hurt him. But she made sure that Frank and Diana grew up blaming him for their circumstances. Frank suffered some brain damage at birth and, as he got older, the combination of that and his mother's all-consuming loathing for her ex-lover, tipped him over the edge. He spent quite a lot of his teenage and adult life in various psychiatric institutions. The girl was a different kettle of fish. She was tough, like her mother and under her influence, she grew to hate Simon's father too and began to try and work out how they could get their own back."

"How did Simon know about all this?"

"Well, apparently, the children's mother got cancer when they were about fifteen. Just before she died, she made some sort of pact with Diana that she would make sure that Mr Martin and his family would live to regret the day he treated her so badly. You can imagine the effect that sort of melodramatic deathbed scene had on the son. Diana came back to Dublin, bringing him with her, and tracked Simon's father down at work and confronted him. It just so happened that Simon was in the office at the time. His father was embarrassed and angry that they should have gone there and that his son should be there to witness what happened; there was an almighty row and he sent the two of them packing. Obviously, afterwards, Simon asked awkward questions; which his father dealt with rather badly, I gather. When the woman died soon after, he didn't go to the funeral and he refused to discuss it any further with Simon."

"But that's ghastly – so cold-blooded!" said Rachel.

No wonder Simon hardly ever talked about him. She'd always thought that was because he didn't want to be reminded about his parents' sudden death.

"Yes," said Guy, "Not a very compassionate bloke, Simon's dad. Anyway, all that just fuelled the hatred – in Diana especially. When Caro and I got to know Simon, he was twenty-four, twenty-five and his parents had just died in the boating accident. He was working as a junior in a solicitor's office on the opposite side of town to where his father's practice had been. He was pretty shaken up at the time, although I think he only really missed his mother.

Things had never been right between himself and his dad since he was eight. What really threw him though was the fact that Diana came to his parents' funeral and cornered him afterwards. She really laid it on with a trowel – described in detail how she'd had to look after their mother, with very little money, while her brother was having psychiatric treatment. She told him that Frank had had ECT and how he'd spent months in a padded cell because they thought he would kill himself, or somebody else. Diana even threatened him by hinting at the pact they'd made with their dying mother. Simon didn't say much about that but it upset him. The upshot was that he agreed to pay a lump sum over to her and Frank to recompense them a little for what they'd been through. Although I think he knew in his heart that handing out cash would never make any difference to their attitude towards him. He told me that it was as though all the loathing they'd felt for his father had been transferred to him. He also said that there was something about the pair of them that put the wind up him. He couldn't be specific but it made it impossible for him to treat them as his own brother and sister. Not that *they* wanted him to – their mother had made sure she'd instilled too much hatred into them for it to happen. Simon regretted that very much."

"So, that wasn't the end of it?" Rachel asked.

"No, I'm afraid it wasn't. Diana kept coming back for more. She seemed to have the ability to extract money out of Simon. He wasn't exactly what you'd call a soft touch but I think he did feel very guilty by association. So each time she appeared and threatened to make a fuss, he paid up."

"How long did all this go on for?" asked Rachel in a shocked voice. " He wasn't still giving her money when we were married, was he?"

"No, all that happened well before you two got together. She eventually pushed her luck too far and Simon lost his temper and told her that if she ever came anywhere near him again, he'd take her to court for blackmail, extortion, whatever. So, she stopped demanding money but not before making sure to tell him that he would live to regret his decision – filled him in a little about the deathbed promise they'd made to their mother. You remember that Simon worked abroad for a few years in the States?"

Rachel nodded. "Yes, he only came back a couple of years before we got married."

"Well, it got him away from Dublin and Diana. Caro and I thought it was a good idea for him to have a clean break. We hoped that when he wasn't around, she'd concentrate on getting on with her own life and eventually forget about carrying on with a ridiculous vendetta." He mopped his face. "It seems we were wrong. When poor old Simon was killed, it seemed to rekindle the whole thing and you became the target instead."

Rachel lay back against the pillows, puzzled. How strange that Simon had never told her anything about all this. She wondered if the outcome would have been different if he had. At least he hadn't been having an affair with Frank's sister. Rachel felt incredibly relieved and at the same time, guilty for doubting her husband's fidelity. But she still couldn't understand why he had kept it a secret from her.

"*Why* didn't he tell me, Guy?"

"He was deeply ashamed of his dad's behaviour and I think he just wanted to forget about the whole thing. Caro had a row with him just before your wedding day. She said that you were a grown woman and he shouldn't treat you like a poor little shrinking violet, or words to that effect. You know our Caro; nothing if not direct! Anyway, he lost his rag and told her to mind her own business. Actually, for once, I agreed with her. There was no reason, as far as I could see, why he shouldn't come clean. It wasn't as though *he'd* done anything awful, after all." Guy shrugged and smiled. "But you know how stubborn we men can be when we get a bee in our bonnet about something or other!"

Rachel smiled wanly. "I suppose so."

So was this one of the reasons why she'd always felt as though Caroline knew something, shared something, with Simon to which she was not privy. It could explain, she supposed, the other woman's sometimes slightly patronising and superior attitude toward her. Perhaps Caroline despised Rachel for being too cosseted and protected by Simon. At the back of Rachel's mind was the niggling observation of Guy's embarrassment. What did *he* have to look guilty about she wondered?

Just then, she became aware that a man was standing at the end of the bed. His head was bandaged and one of his arms was in a sling. For a moment she didn't recognise Francesco.

Guy glanced round and then got slowly to his feet, reaching for his crumpled hat.

"I'll come back and see you tomorrow, Rachel. I will leave you two in peace."

He gave Francesco a nod and bent over to kiss her. Rachel could feel the damp patch on her cheek where his lips had been. She noticed that, as he walked past the other man, he gave him a curious stare. His mind was obviously working overtime; adding two and two and coming up with five, she thought with a flash of irritation. Surely it was completely natural that Francesco, who had been dragged into this farce involuntarily, would visit her after what had happened? Why did something about Guy's attitude make her feel embarrassed?

But as Rachel looked over at Francesco, she was uncomfortably aware that there was nothing she could do to stop herself from blushing.

"Hello, Francesco!" she said timidly, noticing how pale and strained he looked. Carefully, as though to minimise any head movements, he lowered himself into the chair by her bed.

"You are well, *signora* Rachel?"

She smiled at him. "I'm well, thank you, Francesco. And you? I hope he didn't hurt you too badly."

"No! It was nothing."

He glanced away, uncomfortable at being watched by the other women, who made no pretence at hiding their fascination at the sight of a second male visiting Rachel. They recognised him from the picture in the local paper. The death of the mad Irish man was front-page news and everyone was talking about what had happened in San Lorenzo.

"I'm so sorry you got involved. I didn't know it would turn out like this."

He looked at her, his face serious. "I also did not want this to happen . . ." Rachel saw his hands clench and unclench nervously. "I did not want to start to love . . ."

Her heart stood still. Was he going to tell her that he loved her?

He suddenly stood up, swaying slightly. For a moment he looked as though he might topple over onto the bed.

"Francesco!" she exclaimed. "What are you doing? Please don't go. Please stay and talk."

With his good hand he made a movement as though dismissing both her and what he had just said.

"It is better I go," he said.

She watched as he walked slowly down the ward. All eyes were fixed on his retreating figure. Rachel realised that any conversation had stopped and, for a few moments, the only sound was of his footsteps.

Chapter Nineteen

After his hasty departure on the previous day, Rachel was surprised and pleased to see him back as soon as breakfast was over. She wasn't quite sure what had happened on the previous occasion – what had made him leave her in the way he had but, whatever the reason, she was determined to try and be as normal as possible and not make any reference to the unfinished sentence that had been responsible for her lying awake for hours during the night.

As soon as Francesco began to talk, it was obvious that he was full of remorse at having fallen asleep at the kitchen table the night Douglas was taken to hospital.

"I sit at the table in the kitchen. Many times I look from the windows to see if there is anybody in the garden. There is always nothing. It is very quiet – and I go to sleep." He sat on the edge of the chair by her bed, choosing to look down rather than catch Rachel's eye. "It was very foolish. I am so sorry, Rachel."

His normally quietly confident manner was gone. His face looked as strained as it had the last time they'd spoken. She guessed that he must have gone over and over what had happened and felt that he was entirely to blame.

"It's not your fault, Francesco. I shouldn't have opened the door to let Percy in." She smiled, willing him to look at her. "I know you think that cats are not a good idea unless they earn their keep."

He looked up, puzzled. "Earn their keep? What this means?"

"It means that cats should be useful – catch rats."

For the first time since he had sat down, he smiled slightly.

"But Percy *was* useful! He make so much noise by the door when the *carabinieri* come, they find me. If they not find me so quick, then it would take more long time to find you and . . ." His brown eyes were troubled.

Instinctively, Rachel stretched out her hand. He hesitated and then reached out to take it in his. Francesco couldn't stop himself from staring at the blue and yellow swelling on the side of her face and around her eye. Rachel laughed softly.

"Not a very pretty picture, I'm afraid at the moment."

He shook his head. "No, is not true. You are always most beautiful woman."

Suddenly, being covered in cuts and bruises with cracked lips and wearing a hospital nightgown was all worth it. Rachel wanted to hear Francesco repeat what he had just said – just to be sure all the drugs they'd given her hadn't made her hallucinate.

"Say that again, Francesco!" She smiled at him encouragingly.

He laughed. Then lifted her hand and brushed the back of it with his lips. It was more a caress than a kiss but it sent a shock-wave through her.

"I say you are beautiful. But I think you know this," he added, looking straight at her.

Suddenly unsure of herself, she hastily changed tack.

"What made you start to call me Rachel all of a sudden?"

Francesco shrugged slightly. "I do not know. Perhaps, because of that man who nearly kill you." He leaned back in the chair a little, forgetting his arm in the sling and catching his elbow on the arm-rest. He winced. "Sometimes, when dangerous things happen, it make people speak in . . . *un modo diverso* . . ."

Rachel nodded. "In a different way. I know what you mean. Perhaps because they have had a shock and that makes them wonder if . . ." She too didn't know how to put what she wanted to say into words. ". . . wonder if they had missed something before that was important. I don't know – but I'm glad you are calling me Rachel. *Signora* makes me feel too old and sensible!"

"And you are not sensible, *signora?*" he teased her.

She gazed into his face. "No, not in the least bit, *signore!*"

They both laughed, causing the women in the two beds opposite to stop talking and openly stare.

When Francesco left, promising to visit her again later in the day, Rachel lay back in her pillows. For a little while, all her recent fear, all her grief at Douglas's death, evaporated and she felt light-headed and strangely light-hearted. In fact, it seemed that, given the chance, it would be entirely possible to float up to the ceiling. Unaware that she was smiling to herself, she closed her eyes.

One of the women nearby leaned over the edge of her bed, pointing in Rachel's direction. She rolled her eyes and whispered to her neighbour, *"Ah, l'amore!"* The women smiled at each other knowingly.

It was agreed that Rachel would stay with Lennie for a while after coming out of hospital.

"You stay as long as you need or want," Lennie said. "It will be lovely to have you."

The younger woman felt relieved. Caroline was coming back in two days' time and, kind though Guy had been, she didn't want to go back to Podere Vecchio. The place was tainted for her and she certainly didn't feel up to facing Caroline's no-holes-barred style of questioning. Guy, however, had proved to be considerate in ways that surprised her.

"Look, I know you and Percy get on like a house on fire. Would you like him to stay on with you at Lennie's until you decide what you want to do?" he suggested on the day before she came out of hospital.

He had done everything possible to be useful, including driving Francesco home and making sure that Lennie didn't need any shopping or help of any kind.

The more she thought about it, the more convinced she became that he hadn't been entirely truthful when they had talked about Simon and his father's affair. There was something he had kept back; something that made him feel guilty. On that last afternoon in hospital, while most of the women dozed in the heavy heat of the after-lunch siesta, she tackled him.

"Guy, I think there's something you haven't told me."

He stopped flicking through the magazine he had brought her and looked instantly guilty, like a child caught with its hand in the chocolate box. For a moment, she could see that he was thinking of denying the charge. He closed the magazine and ran a hand through the sandy hair that rested damply on the crown of his head. Rachel noticed for the first time that he was starting to go bald. Perhaps that was why he insisted on wearing that ridiculous straw hat so much of the time.

"What makes you say that?" He sounded cagey.

"Oh, come on, Guy! After all that's happened, it wouldn't do any harm to come clean if there is something you haven't mentioned." She looked at him carefully. "It's not something to do with Simon, is it?"

She was relieved by his reaction.

"No, Rachel it's not. I swear," he said emphatically, dropping the magazine on to the bed. "No, it's something I did years ago and it's blighted my life ever since."

She had never seen him so consistently serious as he had been since his hasty return to Italy. He didn't parry everything she said with a flippant remark in the way that used to annoy her so much. Rachel found herself liking him the better for it.

"Well, you can confess your sins to me and I will give you absolution. Then you will be able to carry on – like a new man," she encouraged him with a smile. "It can't be that bad!"

"Well, yes, I'm afraid it is." The ubiquitous silk handkerchief was used to dab at his forehead while he tried to work out the best way of telling her. "You see, to put it bluntly, Rachel, I had an affair with Diana, and Caro found out."

She looked at him with incomprehension. "How could you have had an affair with her? When did you meet her?"

"You know I told you how she kept coming back to Simon for more money after her mother died? Well, it was really getting to him. Just before he went off to the States, I thought I'd warn her off. One day, Simon told me that she was meeting him after the office closed. So I waited and when I saw him drive off, I followed her."

"And what happened?"

"What happened was that she made a dead set for me." He looked at Rachel pleadingly. "You've no idea what she was like, Rachel. She was so beautiful and, my God, she could really turn on the charm! I know it sounds unbelievable that an eighteen-year old gold-digger could get anywhere with me but I was flattered. Look at me, my dear girl! I'm not exactly God's gift to womankind. In my heart, I knew perfectly well that she didn't care a fig about me. That girl didn't care and still doesn't care for anyone but herself. I realised later that she hoped that, by bedding me, it would bring her closer to Simon and make it easier for her to cause him harm."

Rachel digested this new information in silence. Then she asked, "But she can't have been all bad? She cared for

Frank, didn't she? You said that she looked after him when their mother died?"

"She didn't *care* for her brother, Rachel. She used him. When it suited her – she was kind and patient with him. The rest of the time . . ." He shook his head. "I saw her in action with him once when she didn't know I was watching. I think the appropriate word to use would be chilling. Most of the time, she behaved like the manipulative, scheming bitch she was – and no doubt still is."

"Is this why Caroline is sometimes rather short with you?" asked Rachel tentatively.

Guy snorted. "That's a kind way of putting it, darling. Yes, Caro was not best pleased that her man proved unfaithful. She's been getting her own back ever since. I can't say I blame her."

"But why do you stay together?"

"Come on, Rachel! Don't be naïve. You know how much Caro enjoys the lifestyle we have. She's not getting any younger either and she'll put up with a lot of things, including me, as long as the goodies keep on rolling in." Guy looked at her with a grim expression. "The trouble is that I love the damn woman – even if she's refused to have my children." He sighed suddenly. "Well, there you are! That's the truth, the whole truth and nothing but the truth, so help me God!"

He gave her a wry smile and continued his mopping.

Rachel wished she hadn't asked. The only relevance Guy's revelation had to Simon was that it was because of Guy's friendship with him that the affair with Diana had happened. She didn't know what to say.

"I'm sorry, Guy. I shouldn't have been so pushy and inquisitive. It's just that I thought you were hiding something from me about Simon. I was frightened that he'd had an affair with someone, that he was covering up a relationship with another woman after we got married – and that now, you were covering up for him."

"Don't be bloody ridiculous, Rachel! That man worshipped the ground you walked on. Because of what had happened with his father, Simon was determined that he would never hurt you in the same way. That's another reason why Caro's been less than pleasant with you sometimes. She was dead jealous of you and Simon. She thought you had everything and, when she saw the pair of you together, it just highlighted what she was missing out on. We're a sad pair really, she and I," he said, with a short laugh.

For a brief moment he had, inadvertently, allowed Rachel to glimpse beneath the loud, sweaty, red-faced exterior to the vulnerable man within. For the first time since she'd known him, she was suddenly aware of how he was determinedly ploughing his way through a life that was far from satisfactory, with no self-pity, meanwhile pretending to the outside world that all was as it should be. She thought it admirable and very sad.

Rachel found things remarkably unchanged at Villa Fiorita. Even the piano lid was still raised. Sheet music stood on its music desk, as if waiting to be played. Lennie appeared to be much the same as the Lennie she had known before Douglas's death. Perhaps she was silent for longer periods. Somehow it seemed that these quiet times were not sad but contemplative, as though she didn't want to make room or didn't have time for sadness.

"Are you all right, Lennie?" Rachel asked one day when she found her at the sink, staring out into the garden, a half-washed lettuce in her hand. "I mean, *really* all right?"

The woman turned around, as if surprised to see her there.

"Yes," she said slowly. "Forgive me if I'm not very good company at the moment, my dear. It's just that I'm so busy remembering Douglas, reliving our life together, savouring him as it were, before he starts to fade in my mind."

"But I thought you said that he would never completely leave you."

"Oh, *he* won't!" said Lennie, absent-mindedly waving a lettuce leaf under the tap. "He won't but I don't want to forget anything. So, what I'm doing is reminding myself of all the things we did and shared and enjoyed so much so that *I* won't start to fade – because I know my memory has never been one of my strong points. Does that sound daft to you?"

"Not in the least," said Rachel, putting an arm around her and giving her a hug.

On the evening after Douglas's quiet funeral, Rachel sat on the couch and stroked Percy, whose enthusiastic purr sounded like a volcano about to bubble up to the surface and erupt. At the same time, she watched Lennie as they listened to some Bach on the radio. The older woman's gaze kept straying over to where the piano stood, silent, in the corner of the room. She suddenly looked over at Rachel and caught her watchful stare.

"Can't you see him sitting there, playing his beloved Brahms, peering at the music through his specs?"

"Not really," said Rachel, wondering if the other's enthusiasm for the occult was leading her astray.

Lennie let out a shout of laughter. "No, you barmy creature! I didn't mean that Douglas was actually sitting there on the piano stool. I meant, can't you imagine him being there?"

When they had both stopped laughing, Rachel asked, "You won't be too lonely when I've gone, will you?"

"Yes, I probably will. But that's all right! It will take me a while to develop a routine for one rather than two and no doubt there will be moments when I will wish that I could have a handy heart attack and die. Don't forget though, I have Francesco and his family and one or two dotty old friends who are lingering on just like me. Mostly, I will be perfectly content to just potter on with the rest of my life." She gestured towards the bookshelves. "One of the really splendid things about growing old is that there are hundreds of marvellous books you once read and have forgotten. I'm going to read my way through them all again and remind myself why I liked them in the first place!" She looked around the untidy room. "Siena is only an hour and a half away and Florence not an awful lot further. And don't forget, there's always music and the garden to keep an eye on."

"And don't forget Italian politics and Italian politicians," added Rachel.

"Well, they're always good for a giggle," Lennie agreed.

Rachel had been at Villa Fiorita for three days before Francesco made an appearance. She had seen him at the funeral but with his family and friends around, he had seemed rather distant. They had exchanged greetings and some small-talk that had left her wondering if she had imagined their conversation in the hospital when she'd been sure he had been about to tell her that he loved her. She'd been careful not to snatch glances at him during the funeral tea afterwards, well aware that Caroline would be sure to latch on to the slightest nuance of anything being out of the ordinary. She had been pleasant to Rachel, even sympathetic, since she'd got back but Rachel knew that Caroline was always going to be, well, Caroline.

When she saw him again, she realised that her heart was fluttering inside her in a delightful and forgotten way. His arm was still in a sling but the bandage around his head had been reduced to a dressing over one ear. Francesco's hair was shaved on one side and some of it fell crookedly over the whiteness of the dressing, giving him a tousled, almost disreputable look.

Lennie suddenly remembered that she had 'things to do' and left them together in the garden. Rachel wondered why, all of a sudden, she felt shy, as they made their way towards the cherry-trees beyond the fishpond. She could feel it in him too. They walked slowly, side by side, unspeaking. When they reached the trees, they stopped in dappled golden light under a translucent canopy of leaves. Apart from the cicadas' scratchy music-making in the background, it was very quiet there. The branches curved slightly downwards with their weight of shiny, almost black fruit. There was a feeling of being apart from the rest of the world.

She reminded herself of their encounter under the trees in Podere Vecchio. No way was she going to make the first move now.

"Rachel, I have to say you something."

His voice and face were too serious. Her heart gave an unpleasant lurch. Was this going to be a brush-off? She waited. He was frowning now, concentrating on what he had to say.

"What do you want to tell me, Francesco?" she eventually asked.

His next move took her completely by surprise. Very gently he leaned towards her and kissed her on the mouth. It was a kiss of such sweetness that everything else faded. All Rachel was aware of was the light, lingering pressure of his lips on hers. Then, equally gently, he withdrew. Taking her by the hand, he led her over to an old wooden seat by an olive tree.

"Rachel, you know that I like you very much?"

"Yes," she managed to mumble. "I like you too."

God! she thought, we sound like a couple of moonstruck kids after their first kiss behind the bus shelter. What am I saying? I don't just *like* him. I think I love him.

"But we can never be more than friends."

"Why?" she demanded, taken off balance.

"You come from *Irlanda*. I am Italian."

"So?"

She was not going to make this easy for him. She could

257

see some small, cream flowers of the olive apparently making their own way across the grass in a jerky, disjointed manner. Rachel had noticed it before; how the ants carried the petals to their nest somewhere hidden in the base of the tree. She realised he was speaking again.

"We have many things that are not the same. Your life in *Irlanda* is very different from my life here in Italy, no?"

"Some things are different perhaps. But why should being different be a problem?"

He paused, frowning up at the surrounding trees.

"Lennie, she say I must tell to you the truth." Francesco stopped, willing her to look at him. Reluctantly she raised her eyes to his. "I did not want to tell you this but . . . my brother, Bernardo . . . is sometime not so kind with his wife." Rachel stared at him, unresponsive. He'd already told her that. "Sometime, he hit her."

She was startled out of her sulk. "Bernardo *hits* Clara?"

"Not very often. When he drinks, he is different man."

"So, what you're saying is, that because your brother hits his wife, there can be nothing between us?"

Francesco turned his face away from her before replying. He snatched a deep breath and said, "Is not just this. Clara is a good woman. My mother will not always be there to stop him from becoming angry. This is bad for the children also."

Rachel caught his shoulder, forcing him to look at her, her face suddenly flushed and angry.

"I thought you were going to tell the truth! What you mean is that you are in love with your brother's wife, isn't it?"

For a moment, he looked at her blankly. When he spoke again, his voice was controlled.

"Yes, I love Clara. But she is married to my brother. All I can do is to make sure that Rosa and Armando and their mother is OK – so that nothing bad happen to them. You understand, this I must do."

This simple statement was made with quiet finality. What could she say? Rachel looked at his strong, far from handsome face and she wanted to weep at the situation in which she found herself – the opportunity of loving and be loved back by this man. It was so unfair. Why couldn't he even consider the possibility of loving *her*? But she knew the answer. The thought that she was being selfish suddenly materialised, like an unwanted spectre, in her mind and she felt ashamed. When she next spoke, she knew that she must try and keep her voice even and reasonable. However, when she looked at him, she couldn't say the things she knew she should be saying. The words refused to come. All she felt was a great sense of loss. Loss of exactly what, she didn't know. She realised that she hardly knew Francesco but, deep inside, Rachel recognised that there was something about this man that made him especially unique. But the thought of never having the chance to really know him or love him filled her with bitter regret.

Refusing to allow the tears to escape, with her mouth twisted into a parody of a smile, she turned away from him and started to walk as fast and as straight as she was able in the direction of the house.

"Rachel, *un momento!*"

She stopped in her tracks and turned to face him, waiting to hear what else he had to say.

When he caught up with her he took hold of her hand. "Please listen! You do not understand what I say."

She gave him a small smile. "But I do understand, Francesco. I understand perfectly. You do not love me. What else is there to understand?"

He shook his head. "No, you do not understand. I think that I love you also, Rachel."

She stared at him. "But you just told me that you love Clara!"

"Yes!" The word was almost a shout. In desperation, he put a fist up to his forehead. "But is it not possible to love more than one person?" He looked at her pleadingly. "Please do not look at me in this way. I *do* love you, Rachel but I cannot leave Clara without – protection."

Rachel took a deep breath. "I'm trying hard to understand, Francesco. I really am." She chose her words with care. "Perhaps it is possible to love two women at the same time. I don't know because, until I met you, my husband was the only man I'd ever really loved." She placed her two hands around his and said softly, "All I know is, that if I find that I can accept that you love Clara – and if knowing that makes no difference to how I feel about you – I don't see that it should stop us from showing that we love each other." She released his hands and stepped back from him. "I have to have time to think. Do you understand what I am trying to say?"

Again he shook his head – but this time with an expression of amazement on his face. "You are a wonderful woman!" he said quietly. "Yes, you are right. We must both have time to think."

Chapter Twenty

Unexpectedly, it was Caroline who insisted that they drive Rachel to Pisa for her flight home.

"It's the very least we can do, Rachel. After all, we asked you to come and house-sit for us in the first place. None of this would have happened if we hadn't."

Secretly, Rachel was pretty sure that something like this would have happened wherever she was, possibly with an even more dire outcome. She would have much preferred to take the train from Grosseto to Pisa on her own. However, she knew that once Caroline had made up her mind about something, there was no point in arguing with her.

"Don't be daft, Rachel," said Guy. "Anyway, your bruises haven't gone yet. It makes you look sort of vulnerable – and we don't want anyone taking advantage of you on the journey, do we!"

"The only person likely to do that is you, dear Guy," Rachel retorted, annoyed.

"Ouch! Bad girl! You know perfectly well that I'm whiter than driven snow."

Caroline raised her eyebrows so high that they disappeared under her fringe. "Don't we just!" she commented, turning away from them abruptly.

It was a shame that he seemed to have slipped back into his old ways, Rachel thought. It seemed to her that he'd started to revert the moment his wife got back. The only serious conversation she'd managed to have with him in the past week had been on the subject of Diana. Rachel was understandably alarmed that the woman was still at large. The police had assured them that they were doing their best to find her and a watch was being kept at airports but she just seemed to have vanished into thin air.

"I know it's difficult for you, Rachel but I really think that Frank's death will have put the wind up her," Guy said. "If the police don't nab her, she'll not hang around. She's probably hightailed it to the Costa del Crime to lie low and lick her wounds. I wouldn't say you had anything to panic about."

Even though he seemed convinced that there was no cause for her to worry, it preyed on Rachel's mind. Would Diana just give up and disappear from the scene forever? She wasn't so sure.

During Rachel's last few days in San Lorenzo, Caroline and Guy called in to see her and Lennie a couple of times. Watching the way they continually sparred, she couldn't help feeling that they brought the worst out in each other. Why wouldn't they separate? But Guy had told her that he loved his wife; so that was that, apparently.

Francesco loved Clara. Angelica loved Francesco. Guy loved Caroline. Caroline loved Caroline. Lennie loved and was content with the memory of Douglas. Rachel tried to cheer herself up with the thought that Percy was obviously fond of her.

Her conversation with Francesco a week earlier had left her trying to keep her balance on an emotional seesaw. Initially full of hope, she'd been devastated that he hadn't come anywhere near her since then. Each day she'd woken, hoping that that was the day when he would come back and they would sit down together and talk. She could hardly believe it possible that, after all that had been said and their declarations of love for each other, he'd apparently decided that giving their relationship a chance was not possible. What made her feel especially miserable was the knowledge that she'd been planning to tell him that, in spite of his feelings for Clara, she wanted to try and see if they could work something out between them. His continued non-appearance seemed unbelievably callous and unfeeling.

When she told Lennie what had happened, the other woman was sympathetic but surprisingly pragmatic. "Well, I warned you that he was an honourable man, my dear, if a little misguided." She put her arm around Rachel. "It's no good crying over what you can't have, dear child. He's obviously decided that it wouldn't be right to ask you to have a relationship with him when it would be so very difficult and complicated. I don't think he will change his mind. You should know that. Once men have made their minds up about something they consider important, neither hell nor high water will get the blighters to budge."

263

"But he said he would go away and think about it. He didn't even bother to come back and see me and tell me that he couldn't do it. He obviously thinks that staying as a watchdog for Clara is more important. Does this mean he's denying himself the possibility of ever marrying? It's bloody ridiculous!"

Rachel couldn't stop the tears from running down her cheeks. Lennie gently wiped them away with her garden-roughened thumbs and peered into her face. "Not to Francesco it isn't," she said, gently. "Don't hate me for saying this but I'm a firm believer in doing what you can to make things happen and then, if they don't work out, accepting that it's most likely for the best. I know that's not what you want to hear just now, but if you could try and think like that, you will spare yourself a lot of tears, my dear."

No, it wasn't what Rachel wanted to hear but even in the middle of all the misery, she knew that Lennie was wise in the ways of love. Although thoroughly unhappy, she did her best to concentrate on thinking about going back to Dublin. She'd rung her parents to let them know the date of her arrival. Her mother had been surprised and delighted that their daughter was going home sooner than expected. Rachel didn't mention the reason for her early return. What was the point in alarming them both? It was better for her father to think that she'd come to her senses and was going back to job-hunt like a sensible young woman.

She had made one last visit to Podere Vecchio, to return Percy. Angelica was sweeping the terrace and saw her approaching across the grass, Percy following close behind.

Rachel was sure she saw the woman make a quick sign of the cross before dropping her sweeping brush and rushing indoors. When she reached the house, Angelica was nowhere to be seen. Caroline had observed what had happened from one of the windows. She seemed highly amused.

"Really! Angelica is better than a visit to the pantomime! Don't take any notice of her, Rachel. She's *quite* loopy!"

But Rachel would have liked to say goodbye to her. She regretted that they'd never managed to build any sort of relationship between them. Knowing a little about Angelica's background from Lennie, she felt sorry that she hadn't got to know her better and had the chance to offer her friendship to the woman.

Although Guy pressed her to stay and have a drink with them, she refused, saying that Lennie was expecting her back for an early lunch. She escaped as quickly as she could. Apart from Angelica's reaction to her, the only other regret Rachel had at leaving the Haywoods' house was that she could not take Percy home with her. When she left, he shadowed her as far as the bend in the drive. She stopped to give him a farewell stroke and, in characteristic fashion, he stood on her foot, gazing up at her with his inscrutable blue eyes. She left him there for a few minutes before gently pushing him away with a farewell caress.

Rachel walked on to where Lennie waited in her decrepit car parked in the shade of a tall chestnut tree. Head back, eyes closed, the elderly woman was smiling slightly to herself as if she had strayed deep into some happy memory.

The sunlit air beyond the trees seemed to pulsate with heat. The din of crickets was unbearably loud and persistent. An enormous black bee zoomed past, weaving a zigzag path through the chestnuts. All at once, Rachel felt out of place – an intruder. She really didn't belong at Podere Vecchio – it held too many unpleasant memories. Yes, it was a beautiful place, but that beauty seemed to have soured and faded. Suddenly, she wanted to be back in Ireland, away from all the strangeness and differentness of it all. Yes, the sun shone most of the time, the scenery was magnificent, Tuscany was stunning but her three-weeks' stay was so overshadowed by what had happened there, it had spoiled the place for her.

As she approached the sleeping woman in the car, she realised that the only reason to consider returning would be because Francesco wanted her to.

When she said goodbye to Lennie, Rachel didn't mention anything about future plans involving revisiting Italy but she guessed that the other woman didn't need telling.

"I will write, Lennie," she promised, hugging her.

"I hope you will be too busy living your life to have time to write to an old woman going happily to pot in her untidy house in the middle of nowhere!" replied Lennie, hugging her back. "But of course, if you can manage the odd line, that would be lovely." She gave Rachel a serious look. "I know you won't ever forget what happened here but try to avoid thinking about things that will upset you. You are still young and you have so much ahead of you that will be exciting. Go back to Ireland and live well and happily."

She planted a kiss on Rachel's forehead and stepped back. Rachel felt that it was as if she were saying, 'Our paths have crossed and now it's time to get on with our individual lives.' It was true that another chapter was closed in her life. And as for Francesco! Sadly, it appeared that there was no more to be written in that particular chapter.

She wished she could adopt Lennie's attitude and feel optimistic about the future. She also wished that the road ahead of her were a little easier to make out.

Once the cabin staff had done the rounds and Rachel had drunk a much-needed brandy and ginger ale, she tried to settle down for a nap. This was easier said than done. The woman in the window seat beside her seemed to suffer from a severe bladder problem, which resulted in her having to make frequent trips to the lavatory. The man in the aisle seat was large and overflowed in all directions, like a basking elephant seal. Rachel felt that she knew what it must be like to be a battery hen.

Her thoughts troubled her as much as her physical discomfort. The nearer her departure from Italy had come, the less sanguine Guy had seemed about Diana's whereabouts. In hospital, it had been Rachel who was frightened that the woman would materialise again and he had poo-pooed the idea.

But when he had said goodbye, his parting words had not been particularly comforting. "Promise you'll go and talk to the gardaì when you get back, Rachel." He added, "I'm sure there's absolutely no need, but just in case."

"Just in case, what?" she'd asked.

"I don't know. Perhaps I'm being paranoid. The Italian police really weren't exactly efficient and the gardaì do have a good reputation for tracking people down . . . all that sort of thing," he ended, lamely.

Rachel wondered if the reason for her having been increasingly less worried about the woman was because she so desperately wanted the whole ghastly episode forgotten; that if she behaved like an ostrich, the problem would just go away. She wished she didn't feel so alone. Francesco's face came into her thoughts constantly. What was he doing now? Would he miss her or even think of her much? At the end of two hours, she felt far more exhausted and confused than when she had first boarded the plane.

It was considerably cooler in Dublin when she landed, even though it was three-quarters of the way through June. Rachel wheeled her trolley past the sliding doors in the arrivals lounge and scanned the scrum of people in front and on either side. She saw her mother's tired face detach itself from the mass, followed by her father's.

She hugged them both, determined that, this time, she would try not to do or say anything that might upset them. It was a shame that the bruising on her face hadn't quite gone. Still, she'd prepared a not very original story that involved falling down a flight of stairs. She hoped that would satisfy them.

Sure enough, the first thing Jean Kerrigan asked was, "What on earth happened to your face, dear?"

As they waited for the lift in the carpark, her mother said,

"Such an odd thing happened yesterday, Rachel. There was a ring on the doorbell just after lunch and when I opened the door, you'll never guess what I found!" She looked unusually animated. For an instant, the pretty woman she'd once been showed in her face.

Her daughter smiled at her. "What did you find, Mother?"

"The most beautiful bunch of flowers. It was such a tasteful arrangement, not like the garish things you usually see being delivered by florists these days. All the flowers were white, every single one! But the funny thing is, they'd been left on the doorstep – no sign of the delivery person – and there was no card with them. It has us completely baffled! I've gone through a list of everyone we know, trying to think who would do such a nice thing. We can't understand it at all."

Rachel could hear her mother speaking, as if from a long way off. She suddenly felt as though her knees might give way. Something touched her arm. Dizzily, she turned to see her father looking at her strangely. He had his hand on her sleeve.

"Are you feeling all right, Rachel?"

She licked her lips and swallowed. "Yes," she said uncertainly. "I think I'm just tired that's all. You know how I loathe flying. It always makes me feel a bit strange."

Her mother had stopped enthusing over the flowers and was looking anxious again.

"I think the best thing for you, young lady, is to stay with us tonight." Rachel started to protest feebly. But her mother was having none of it. "Just for tonight. I'll bring you breakfast in bed in the morning. It will be lovely to have the chance to make a fuss of you again."

She sounded so pleased at the thought that Rachel hadn't the heart to tell her that all she really wanted to do was to curl up in her own bed in her own house and try to collect her thoughts. The idea crossed her mind that she might be putting her parents at risk if she did stay with them. In vain she tried to look at the situation objectively but there was no time. Her mother, in an untypically decisive manner, announced that the matter was settled and she wasn't to be silly. Trying hard to not let the alarm show in her face, Rachel agreed to stay for just the one night.

She wasn't sure how she managed to get through the next eighteen hours. Her parents wanted to know all about her Italian trip. Had she met anyone nice? What places of historic or architectural interest had she visited? Her father seemed disappointed that she had only got to Siena once (at Lennie's insistence: "You *can't* go home without seeing Siena at least.") and Florence not at all.

"What did you *do* with yourself for three weeks?" he asked.

Came in contact with a madman, nearly got myself killed, fell for a man who's a blind idiot. Where to begin?

Somehow, she kept up with the conversation, answering their questions as best she could. Rachel described Lennie to them. She told them how Douglas had had a stroke and died and that she had spent a large part of the last three weeks in the other woman's company.

270

"She's a lovely person. A one-off! Wacky and wise at the same time. I'm really glad I met her," she said with real enthusiasm.

She thought it might make Lennie more real to them if she described the way she was so haphazard in her choice of clothes. But they hadn't looked too impressed.

"She sounds a little odd to me," said her father.

Seeing the disappointed expression on her daughter's face, her mother said quickly, "I'm sure she's very nice, dear."

The next morning, her father drove Rachel home. They stopped at a small supermarket on the way so that she could buy milk and bread. As they continued their journey, he asked her what she planned to do next.

"Oh, I'll just enjoy being home again for a bit," she replied, trying to sound casual.

"Yes, but what are you going to *do* when you've done that?"

"You mean, am I going to look for a job?"

"That would be a good idea, wouldn't it?"

God! He could be so exasperating! Why didn't he leave her alone? Why did he always try and make her behave in the way *he* wanted? It had always been like this: her father, controlling, directing – her mother, in the background, placating, explaining, trying her best to defuse the tension rolling around the house and ricocheting off the walls.

Forgetting the promise she'd made to herself the day before, Rachel snapped, "I don't *know* what I want to do next. I'll tell you when I've made up my mind."

He didn't answer. The already compressed lips became more rigidly clamped together, his frown more noticeable.

When they arrived, Rachel got out of the car and collected her shopping from the back seat. Then she leaned in to kiss him.

"Thanks, Dad."

His eyes rested on her briefly. "Yes, well, I better be getting back. Don't forget to keep in touch. You know how your mother worries about you."

She wanted to say something more before he drove off, to soften his departure in some way but she couldn't think of anything. Her mind was too full of the bouquet of white flowers her parents had received two days earlier. They had stood in a cut-glass vase on the hall table, horribly luminous in the half-light from the strip of glass in the front door. She'd had to force herself to pretend to admire them while her mother repeated how lovely they were and asked her if she could think of who might have sent them.

As she turned the key in her own front door, Rachel hesitated. Guy's parting words of caution came back to her. What if Diana had managed to get into the house? Telling herself to stop being paranoid, she stepped into the hallway and over a small pile of letters. A larger pile sat on the table on the other side of the hall. The woman from next door must have been in recently. The red light on the answering machine blinked silently at her.

Rachel sniffed the air for signs of alien perfume or anything that might give her a clue as to whether the house were empty or not. She stood for a moment, listening. Her heart thumped in an unsteady syncopation with the hall clock. Clutching the plastic bags of shopping to her chest, she slowly pushed open the kitchen door with her foot.

She released her breath. There was no one there. Walking over to the counter, she put the shopping down. The morning sun streamed in the window and the room felt warm and stuffy. She leaned over the sink to open one side. She stopped, the handle half-turned. Perhaps it would be better not to, she thought. Suddenly, it all felt like a replay of an earlier theme. Sitting down on a kitchen stool, she held her head in her hands. Was she going to have to develop a siege mentality – checking rooms, not opening downstairs windows, terrified to go out? Was she going to allow herself to spend her time hiding from Frank's sister, a woman she'd never seen – a woman who was apparently hell-bent on destroying her?

Slowly, she became calmer. Like hell she was! Rachel told herself that she wasn't going to relive what had happened at the Haywoods' house. She was no victim. She was going to behave normally and sensibly. But she was going to watch her back very carefully and she would take up Guy's suggestion about going to the gardaí. In many ways, she reckoned, Ireland was a lot more civilised than Italy. At least here the police didn't tote guns and behave like something out of a bad cops-and-robbers film. Now she was home in Dublin again, if Diana was still intent on doing damage of some sort, her attention should switch from Rachel's parents back to Rachel herself. Surely she wished them no harm?

A soft thud outside made her freeze momentarily. Then, inching her way noiselessly towards the window, she stared out into the garden. Two inches away, at the other side of the glass, an eye glared into hers. She jumped violently as the large jackdaw suddenly took off from the windowsill in front of her with a noise like washing flapping on a windy day. He flew off with a loud caw. To her, it sounded almost as if he were laughing.

Slowly, she started to put away the shopping. She had to admit that this was not going to be easy.

By the time she had been back for a couple of days, Rachel found herself feeling less tense. She'd been round to the local garda station and spoken to a fatherly sergeant who, far from treating her like a hysterical female suffering from delusions, had patiently taken down everything she'd told him.

When she'd finished, he shook his head sympathetically, "That's terrible, so it is. And you just wanting a bit of peace and quiet in the sun! I'll make a few enquiries about this Diana Forde woman. We'll get in touch with the Italian police. You leave it with me. In the meantime, if you're worried about anything, just give us a bell," he said, with a reassuring smile.

Rachel noticed that when he mentioned the Italian police he had looked as though he didn't expect much light to be shed on the situation from that quarter. All the same, she had emerged from the station feeling that she had been worrying unnecessarily.

She had also rung her parents on the pretext of thanking them for collecting her from the airport.

"No more bunches of expensive flowers on the doorstep?" she joked.

Her mother laughed. "No, dear, I'm afraid not!"

"How's Dad?"

A slight pause, followed by her mother's soft voice, "Oh, well, you know dear. Much the same." She sounded tired.

"Are you all right, Mum?"

"Of course I am. Why ever not?"

"It's just that I thought you sounded . . . a bit weary, that's all."

"I'm as right as rain, dear. Now, when are we going to see you again?"

"Soon, Mum, soon," Rachel promised, dutifully.

A week later, she received a letter from Francesco. It was short and to the point. But, knowing how difficult it is to write in another's language, she realised that he must have spent some time over the composing of it.

Dear Rachel – I think that you may not wish to have a letter from me because I never come to you and explain. I thought that I could not offer you what you should have from a man and I thought that you would not understand why it is so difficult to explain how I am feeling. Please forgive me for being a coward.

Now you are in Ireland, I see how much I miss you. I think of you many times every day. Please will you write to me? Perhaps there will be something for us together here in Italy – if you wish it.

Carla send you greeting and also Lennie.

Your good friend, Francesco Desalvo.

She had taken it through to the kitchen and reread it several times, sitting at the kitchen table. She saw that Francesco had put his telephone number at the top of the page. The formal and slightly quaint expression, *Your good friend,* gave her especial pleasure. Simon had always insisted the reason their marriage worked so well was because they had become good friends first and lovers later in the relationship.

Her initial reaction had been one of shock. She had been trying so hard, if not to forget him, at least to push him to the back of her mind. And now this! She didn't know whether she felt hopeful or not at this new development. Lennie had warned her that, once a man's mind was made up, nothing would make him change it. It seemed that perhaps, in Francesco's case, she'd been mistaken. Or was it just that the Italian male was a more complex and confused being than she'd realised?

Fighting down the inclination to take the first available flight back to Italy, she decided to try and put the idea to one side. What she did next was too important to make any quick decisions. All the same, she couldn't help but be aware of a lightening of spirit. He was missing her – in spite of the beautiful Clara's gentle presence. Rachel guessed that the other woman, who had shown herself to be sweet-natured and who seemed completely unaware of Francesco's feelings for her, would be delighted to find out that he had found a woman to love. Rachel wasn't so sure of Francesco's mother's reaction. Or rather, she guessed that *La Mamma* would be far from thrilled if the truth were to come out about her eldest son's feelings for the young widow from Ireland.

A few days later, she found herself driving along the road near the turn-off to the cemetery. She really should have gone to see Simon's grave earlier. It would be covered in weeds, she thought guiltily. Deciding to pay a quick visit now, she turned off the main road. She'd bring some flowers and a trowel with her next time she came.

To her relief, there were no flowers of any description resting on his grave. For a little while, she knelt on the grass and tugged out handfuls of scutch. She gave up trying to pull out the dandelions, whose roots seemed to go down forever. It was a perfect day; with a clear sky, warm and with a gentle breeze – the sort of day that you treasured – especially when you were used to the vagaries of Irish weather. The place felt tranquil and she stayed for some time, the light breeze stirring her hair.

As Rachel knelt at the graveside, she thought of her husband. She was quietly grateful that he was absolved from all the wild accusations she had made against him in her mind. She thought of Lennie's advice to her: to go home and live well and happily. At the time, the future had seemed impossibly bleak. Now, a door had opened again. She fingered the letter in the pocket of her jacket. Simon would have expected her to get on with her life. He would have been scornful at the idea of her putting everything on hold because he was no longer there. She was sure that he would have heartily agreed with Lennie's attitude. What was more, Rachel felt that he would have liked and trusted Francesco. She felt strangely at peace with herself – almost dreamlike. Perhaps next week she would start looking for a job. Or perhaps she wouldn't. Perhaps she would speak to Francesco first.

A twig snapped. All of a sudden, the hairs on the back

of her neck prickled. She shivered. She was not alone in the graveyard. Someone was watching her. For a few seconds, she froze. Then, forcing herself to turn round, she quickly looked over to the entrance – just in time to see the small wooden gate swing silently shut. Without thinking, she stood up and broke into a run, jumping over the graves that stood between her and the gate. When she reached it, she saw a woman's figure moving swiftly along in front of some trees at the far side of the carpark. Just before disappearing into their shadow, the watcher seemed to turn for a brief moment and look over to where Rachel stood.

As fast as she could, she made her way to the spot where the woman had vanished into the trees. But when she burst out on the other side of the thicket, all she could see was an empty sweep of cornfield and the narrow road beyond it that snaked up from the main road to the church. For a moment she stood there, dazzled by the bright sunlight, shaking her head in disbelief. Then she turned back and searched the small cluster of birch and hazels, pushing her way through them so that the branches sprang violently back into place behind her.

Whoever it was had gone – completely disappeared. *Could* it have been Frank's sister? The woman who had stared back at her from the trees had been tall and slim with fair hair and an oval-shaped face. Just like Simon's. *But there was no one there!* she repeated to herself as she turned back towards her car, dazed. Her eyes seemed to swim, making her surroundings look strangely out of focus.

Forcing herself to breathe slowly, Rachel leaned against the side of the car. Her head throbbed and her mouth was dry. Was she going mad? Had her imagination been playing tricks? She'd been so jumpy for so long that she suspected that, on several occasions, she'd given quite ordinary situations a sinister interpretation.

She looked in the direction of her husband's grave. The headstone was stippled with sunlight that filtered through the trees. It looked peaceful. Nothing moved. There was no sound – not even of birdsong. Suddenly, the gate, flung open when she'd set off in pursuit of the vanishing woman, closed with a loud click of the metal latch. Funny that when she had watched it swing shut earlier it hadn't made a sound.

Rachel stared up at the blue sky. It suddenly struck her that, perhaps, she'd been wrong in coming back to Ireland. Her heart wasn't in it. So far, her life seemed to have been divided into sections: childhood, the school years, working in Dublin, life with Simon and then – Italy and Francesco. Perhaps it was time she stopped clinging on to the past. The time had come to stop waiting for things to happen. What she *should* be doing was making a clean break and moving on to the next part of her life. But would that life include Francesco?

She stopped gazing at the sky and looked at her watch. One o'clock. What was he doing at this moment, she wondered. Was he thinking of her? His letter said that he couldn't stop thinking of her, that he was missing her. Her heart skipped a beat as she thought of their last meeting and the troubled look in his dark eyes.

Suddenly energised, Rachel opened the car door and slid into the seat and started the engine.

THE END